"Watch what happens," Meriwether said, his voice an excited whisper. He shone his flashlight on one of the stones. When the beam hit the diamond-shaped object, the surface seemed to swirl and flash in an array of colors like mother-of-pearl. The glow that emanated from the stone grew in intensity, and as the light that it generated touched the lights on either side of it, they too shone more brightly. "It absorbs the light and amplifies it." Meriwether sounded entranced.

"What is this place?" Dane marveled. Before anyone could answer, footsteps sounded from the other side of the room.

Dane whirled and drew his pistol, hoping that the water hadn't treated it too roughly. He had allowed himself to be mesmerized by the magnificence of what he was seeing, and now their pursuers had caught up to them. Four men in dark clothing, armed with automatic rifles burst through the doorway on the far side of the room. They looked around in confusion for a moment, then caught sight of Dane's party.

"Get up the stairs!" Dane yelled. Bones shouted back, but his words were lost in a raging torrent of gunfire.

Praise for *Dourado*

"A gripping action thriller that leaves you wanting more."
Megalith Book Reviews

"Like an ocean wave, sweeping the reader into perilous adventure."
Sherry Thompson, author of *Seabird*

"A story of adventure and intrigue. Don't miss the excitment!"
Rebecca Shelley, *DKA Magazine*

"Fans of The DaVinci Code, Indiana Jones and Clive Cussler's *Dirk Pitt* novels will want to check out this book."
The Christian Advertiser

Works by David Wood
Dourado
Cibola *(forthcoming)*

DOURADO

DAVID WOOD

A Dane Maddock Adventure

GRYPHONWOOD
ADVENTURE

Gryphonwood Press

545 Rosewood Trail, Grayson, GA 30017-1261

ISBN: 0-9795738-4-X
ISBN 13:   978-0-9795738-4-2
Library of Congress Control Number: 200793751
Printed in the United States of America
First printing: May, 2004
Second printing: August, 2007

For my wife Cindy, my number one reader, critic and fan.

And David said, "There is none like that; give it to me"

1 Samuel 21.9

PROLOGUE

January 25, 1829-The Indian Ocean

The precious dream fled like the last mist of morning before the rising sun. Another wave broke against the side of the *Dourado*, the resounding crash booming like thunder in the tiny cabin. Monsieur le Chevalier Louis Domenic de Rienzi clutched the side of his bed to steady himself against the pitching and rolling. He had been dreaming of a triumphant return to France, where he would display the fruits of his years of hard work. He tugged the damp, musty blanket over his head, but it made a pitiful barrier against the shouts that penetrated from above. He squeezed his eyes closed and tried to force himself back to sleep, but to no avail. Muttering a curse, he pushed the sodden covers down to his chest and stared up at the aged wooden ceiling.

A man of his standing should have finer accommodations, he told himself. Of course, this was the best the captain had to offer. When he got back to France, when they saw what he had recovered, then he would be an important man. He would have only the finest lodging. He smiled. For a moment, the aged wooden cabin was transformed into a luxurious berth on the finest ship.

Another wave sent the ship tilting like a drunkard, and his imagined stateroom dissolved in a dizzying roll. Rienzi held on until the ship righted before rising to don his boots and coat. The shouts on deck grew strident, tinged with an urgency that had not been there before. The storm must be more serious than he had believed.

He spared a moment to glance in the tiny mirror nailed to the wall opposite the bed. He was no longer a young man, but age was blessing him with a touch of the dignity he lacked in his youth. He had left home a young man, but was returning as a seasoned adventurer with a fabulous story to tell.

His cabin door opened onto a narrow hallway. A petite woman in a dressing gown peered out of the door opposite his own. Her nightcap was askew, giving a comical bent to her pinched features. Their eyes met and she gave a little shriek before slamming the door. Rienzi chuckled and made for narrow stairwell leading up to the deck.

Tangy salt air filled his nostrils as he stepped out into the chill night. Fat raindrops struck his face, washing away the last vestiges of sleep. A crewman bustled past, jostling Rienzi in his haste. The sailor muttered something that might have been an apology, but Rienzi's Portuguese was very limited.

Angry black clouds proclaimed the ferocity of the storm that assailed the ship. The brig surged through waves that broke across the deck like hungry fingers clutching its prey. He drew his coat tighter around him to fight off the chill wind that sliced through him and thanked the Blessed Mother that it was summertime here on the bottom half of the world. What might this storm be like at home in the heart of a French winter?

With a fencer's grace, he stepped out onto the deck, keeping himself balanced on the tilting platform. Deckhands scurried about, obviously trying to put on a brave face in front of the knot of passengers who clung together near the mainmast. Strange that people felt safer on deck, where an errant wave might sweep them away, than down below where it was warm and dry.

He soon found the captain, Francisco Covilha, who was fighting with the wheel and simultaneously barking orders.

"Captain," he shouted, "may I be of assistance?" Rienzi had some knowledge of sailing, though certainly not as much as the veteran sailor. Yet, it seemed proper to at least make the offer.

The Portuguese sailor shook his head, and called back in heavily accented French. "I am sorry, Monsieur. I must keep us from the rocks." Maintaining his grip on the wheel, he nodded forward and to port.

Rienzi spun and saw with alarm a jagged line of rocks protruding from the sea, the faint glow of dawn illuminating their jagged features. Despite the crew's best efforts, the *Dourado* hurtled toward certain peril, borne on the crest of deadly wind and waves.

There was no helping the captain and crew, nor did he hold out much hope that the ship would avert her impending doom. But there *was*, in fact, something Rienzi could do. Reeling with each ebb and swell, he made his way to where the frightened passengers huddled in fearful disarray. Taking him for someone in authority, they all began calling out questions.

Most of them spoke English, but a few were French. Rienzi could speak the uncultured tongue of the oafs from the north side of the channel, but he would not do so unless it was absolutely necessary. He did have his reputation to consider.

"Do not speak," he shouted over their confused questions. "There is little time." Though his words were in French, everyone seemed to grasp his meaning and fell quiet. He stole another glance at the looming rocks. They looked like the teeth of some primordial beast, ready to crush their fragile vessel. There was no time to get the others below, and should the crash be a serious one, belowdeck would not be the safest alternative.

He found a length of rope lashed to a nearby rail. It was one used by crewmen to secure themselves to the ship in just such a situation. He sat the passengers down and showed them how to double the rope around each of their arms so they all could tie on to the same rope. One of the Englishwomen complained about the cold and the rain, but he ignored her. When everyone was secure, he wound the end of the rope around his wrist and dropped to the deck, waiting like a condemned prisoner for the guillotine.

My treasures! The sudden thought pierced the veil of apprehension and embedded in his heart. A cold sliver of fear soured his stomach and sent a tremor of fear through him. Priceless, irreplaceable artifacts representing a lifetime's work were stored below. How many years had he spent collecting them? Above all others, one item in particular could not be lost.

With that thought in mind, he rose up from the deck to look out at the ocean. The rocks still loomed perilously close ahead, the waves crashing over them sending up gouts of foam that put him to mind of a rabid beast. They now seemed farther to port. Was the captain gaining some control of the craft? They flew faster toward the far end of the line of rocks, the cold rain now stinging his face. He held his breath. Were they going to make it?

Unwinding the safety rope from his forearm, he belly crawled to the side, and clutched the rail, watching as the dangerous objects flashed by, the gap between the *Dourado* and these sentinels of doom ever narrowing. The last rock flew past with scarcely a foot to spare.

And then the world exploded.

A loud, ripping sound filled his ears, and everything somersaulted. He tumbled toward the bow, pain lancing through his cold, numb flesh as he half-rolled, half-bounced across the hard, slick deck. He crashed into the foremast with a breathless grunt and a sharp crack to the base of his skull. Dizzy, he struggled to stand. His feet and hands did not want to work, though, and his head seemed full of sand. Surrendering with an agonized groan, he closed his eyes.

"I have no choice, Monsieur Rienzi. I must give the order to abandon ship." A barrel of a man, Francisco Covilha stood a hand shorter than Rienzi, yet managed to appear as if he were looking down his nose at the explorer. The moonlight accentuated his crooked nose and lined face.

"Captain, you cannot be serious," Rienzi pleaded. "You have kept us afloat since morning. Surely we can hold out until help arrives." He rubbed his head, which still throbbed from the blow that had rendered him unconscious. He had tried drowning the pain with wine, but had managed only to dull his senses to the point of being an annoying distraction.

"No help is coming." Covilha shook his head. "We lost the rudder when we hit those rocks just beneath the surface. Most likely, we have drifted out of the shipping lanes. We cannot expect anyone to come to our aid, and this craft will not be above water much longer. The pumps have not kept pace with the inflow of water. Perhaps you have noticed, no?"

Rienzi stared at the shorter man for a moment. He had, in fact, watched the rising waterline with an equally rising sense of despair. He could not afford to lose this cargo. It was too precious. The *world* could not afford for him to lose this cargo. How could he make the man understand?

"Captain, if you do not know where we are," he argued, "then how can you possibly hope to get the passengers and crew safely to port?" Perhaps it was selfish of him to try to keep the sinking ship in the water, but he had no choice. It was imperative that he convince Covilha not to abandon the ship and cargo. There remained the remote possibility that someone might come to their rescue. Any amount of time he purchased, no matter how small, increased that chance.

"I do not know *precisely* where we are," Covilha said, holding up a scarred finger, "but we have drifted south and southeast all day. I have a general idea of our location, and I know that I can get us to Singapore. That is, if we get off this ship before we all drown." The Captain's face was a mask of determination, and in that moment Rienzi understood that he would never dissuade the man.

"Captain," called a voice from behind Rienzi. One of the crewmen, a short, swarthy man with a crooked scar running from his left ear to his upper lip, brushed past, a frightened look further marring his disfigured face. "The water is coming much faster than before. We may have only minutes!" He flashed a sympathetic glance at Rienzi. "I am sorry, Monsieur."

The moment of guilt he felt at having thought only of the sailor's ugliness dissolved with Covilha's subsequent words.

"Give the order to abandon ship," the captain instructed. Without further word, he turned away from Rienzi and began shouting hastened instructions.

Muttering a curse under his breath, Rienzi hurried to the foredeck and descended to the level where the crew bunked. He had made certain he knew exactly where his treasures were stored, the one in particular, and he quickly found the trapdoor that led down into the hold. The sounds of frightened passengers drifted down from above, as people who had believed the worst was over now found themselves abandoning ship. *Fitting this should happen at midnight*, he thought.

Yanking open the trapdoor, he mounted the ladder and began his descent. Only a few rungs down, he heard the sloshing of water inside. It must be filling rapidly. An icy sense of doom rising inside him, he strained his eyes to peer into the inky blackness, but it was too dark for him to see anything. He needed to find a lantern, though it would likely do little good. Why had he not stored it in his berth? He knew the answer; it was too large for him to hide it in the tiny room, and it would have proved too great a temptation for either captain or crew. It had seemed safer to leave it crated with the other artifacts. It was certainly safe from prying hands now. Or soon would be. He gave a mirthless laugh at the irony.

He clambered up the ladder and back onto the deck. The *Dourado* was listing to port, and he was hard-pressed to maintain his balance as he hurried back to his quarters. Inside, he gathered his small lantern, along with his journal, which he kept safe in an oilcloth bag. Hastily lighting the wick, he returned to the deck.

The ship now listed mightily, and he was forced to place his free hand on the deck and scurry along like a wounded crab. As he made his way toward the foredeck, a noise caught his attention. He raised his lantern and the light fell on two young women, their faces frozen in terror, clutching the mast.

"Get to the boats," he shouted. "Quickly!" The shorter woman, a blonde whose milky complexion was almost ghostly in the blended moon and lamp light, shook her head. The other did not respond at all. Fear held them rooted to the spot.

"Monsieur!" The Captain's voice boomed. "The second boat is leaving! You must come now!"

"Wait for us, Captain! There are yet passengers aboard!" Rienzi cried. If the man would not wait for Rienzi, perhaps he would wait for them.

"Hurry, I pray you!" Covilha's voice covered a remarkable distance. "The ship is sinking fast!"

"Mon dieu," Rienzi muttered as he scrambled over to where the frightened women sat. "Come with me," he ordered. "I will get you to the boats." The one who had sat in mute silence a moment before, a thin brunette with brown eyes, nodded. She released her grip on the mast with obvious reluctance, and crawled to his side.

"Come, Sophie," she called to the blonde. We must go quickly. There is no time." Still Sophie shook her head and refused to move.

This time not bothering to muffle his curse, Rienzi moved to the woman's side, his boots sliding on the damp decking. Gripping the oilcloth bag in his teeth, he used his free hand to pry Sophie's fingers loose from the mast. He grasped her around the waist, and heaved her onto his shoulder. He felt the other woman's arms encircle him, steadying him as they stumbled together across the sloping deck.

The captain was waiting at the rail. Together, they helped the women into the smaller boat. A short distance away, the longboat awaited. Each craft overflowed with anxious looking sailors and travelers.

"That is everyone?" Covilha asked.

Rienzi nodded and tossed his oilcloth bag down into the boat. "Cast off. I will join you shortly." He turned and left the captain gaping open-mouthed at the top of the rope ladder. He stumbled and skidded his way back down through the crewdeck to the opening that led into the hold. He dangled his lantern through the open trapdoor and felt his heart fall into his stomach. Everything was under water. All would be lost. *It* would be lost. *He should have taken it from the hold when the ship first struck the rocks. Burn it all, he had not believed that the ship would truly sink!*

A pitiful whimper snapped him out of his dark thoughts, particularly when he realized that it did not come from his own throat. He looked down to see a small dog furiously paddling through the icy salt water that sloshed through the flooded hold. How had it gotten there? The water level was so high that he was easily able to reach out and catch the pitiful creature by the scruff of the neck, and lift it to safety.

The *Dourado* lurched, and now he could actually feel the craft sinking. If he did not get clear before it went down, the suction could pull him under. He tossed away the lantern, ignoring the tinkle of shattering glass. Clutching the frightened dog to his chest, he stumbled to the ladder and clambered up onto the deck. Not even looking for the lifeboats, he dashed to the rail and leapt over. The *Dourado* was sitting so low that he scarcely had time to brace himself for the shock of the cold water.

When he felt his feet touch, he kicked furiously, trying not to go too far under. He raised the yelping, clawing dog above his head, and managed to keep the tiny creature above water. He broke the surface with a gasp and shook his head to get the stinging salt water out of his eyes. He was relieved to see the smaller boat close by, and heading in his direction. Ignoring his body's instinct to curl into the fetal position, he fought to stay afloat as his rescuers rowed to him. His legs felt like lead and his sodden clothes and heavy boots weighted him down. He kicked with desperate fury, but he was sinking. His shoulders sank beneath the surface of the water, then his chin, then his entire head. He was going to die.

Strong hands took hold of his shoulders and hauled him up. Covilha and the scarred sailor dragged him into the boat. He dropped to the bottom and slumped, exhausted, against someone's legs.

"All of that for a *dog*," a voice behind him whispered.

Rienzi was too tired and disconsolate to reply. Instead, he clutched the wet ball of fur to his chest, and watched with tear-filled eyes as the greatest discovery in the history of mankind sank into the depths of the sea.

CHAPTER 1

A dead ship makes better company than a live person, Dane thought as he propelled himself with two solid kicks through the gaping hole in the side of the sunken vessel. He drifted, careful not to upset the fine layer of silt that covered the boat's interior. It would be the underwater version of a whiteout if he did, and it would spoil his exploration. A school of bright blue sergeant majors, so called for their dark, vertical stripes that made them resemble a sergeant's insignia, swam past seemingly oblivious to this intruder into their watery domain. Dane greeted them with a mock salute and they scattered out into the sea. Another small flip of his swim fins and he slid deeper into the bowels of the wreck.

It was a tuna seiner, and not a very old one. The outside was white with broad bands of green striping down the side. He did not expect to find anything of interest inside, but he desperately needed a diversion after a long and fruitless day of searching for the remains of the sunken Spanish galleon.

He switched on the dive light strapped to his forehead and looked around. More than likely, this had been a drug runner's boat. It was stripped down to bare bones on the inside, all of the trappings of the fishing trade absent. A fire extinguisher was still strapped to the wall, one of the few remaining accoutrements in this sunken tin can. He floated over to it, and gently brushed away the silt over the inspection label to reveal the year 2002. He looked around a few moments more, his eyes taking in the crumbling upholstery on the seats and the bits of marine life that were beginning to homestead on the interior. There was nothing here to hold his interest. He took a quick glance at his dive watch and calculated that he had about ten minutes of air remaining. It was time to head back up.

He turned and swam out of the wreck. As he left the boat, a shadow passed above him and something large and dark appeared at the edge of his vision. He looked up to see the thick, gray form of a bull shark circling above him. Dane paused, watching the fierce creature swim back and forth. Aggressive and unpredictable, a bull shark was not to be trifled with. The best option was to wait until it went on is way.

The large creature swam a tight circle five meters above him. Dane held tight, not wishing to draw its attention. Faint shafts of sunlight filtered down through the crystalline waters, shining on its tough hide. The beast's angry eye seemed to fix on Dane, though he knew it was only his imagination.

Minutes passed, with no sign of the shark leaving. He could have sworn the thing was standing guard over him. Its jagged white teeth seemed to grin back at him, daring him to chance it. Again he checked his watch. Six minutes of air left. He couldn't wait much longer. He would have to chance it, but at least it was a shallow dive. The water was no more than thirty meters deep here, if that, but it was safest to make a slow ascent, making a couple of stops to avoid decompression problems. His heart beating a bit faster, he suppressed the urge to strike out hard for the surface, and began a slow, controlled rise.

He had read stories of men who had dived on bull sharks, and had even met a few of the guys. Most of them were crazed adrenaline junkies. It was, however, at least theoretically possible to share space without provoking the beast. Problem was, it depended quite a bit on what kind of day the shark was having.

Holding his arms close to his sides, he stretched out, propelling himself with controlled kicks. He slowly drifted upward toward his waiting boat, remaining as still as possible and trying to resemble nothing more than a piece of floating debris. *Don't rise faster than your bubbles,* he reminded himself.

The shark continued to patrol the area, showing no signs of agitation, or so Dane hoped. He now had a good view of the marine predator. It was at least ten feet long, probably a female. Viewed through aquarium glass or from within a dive cage she would be a real beauty. Sharks were fascinating creatures; all muscle, teeth and stomach, his Dad used to say. So far she gave no sign that she had noticed him. He flipped his fins, and he was now gliding upward at a steep angle. Just then, the shark veered to her left, heading directly at him.

Dane tensed. The dive knife strapped to his thigh would do him little good against her tough hide. Struggling against his instincts, he forced himself to remain still, feigning death, floating free. The wide, ugly snout and rows of glistening razor teeth filled his field of vision as the shark barreled toward him.

His natural survival response battered at his will, screaming for him to take out his knife and start hacking. Just as he was about to give in, the shark angled past him, brushing his shoulder with her rough hide as she swam past. As quickly as she had come, she was gone again.

Dane closed his eyes for a moment and said a brief prayer of thanks to the gods of the sea. Without looking around to locate the shark, he hastily pinched his nose closed and blew, forcing his ears to pop, before resuming his gradual ascent. He looked down at his wrist. Five minutes. Glancing up, he was surprised to see two boats floating above him. His attention had been so focused on the shark that he had not heard the second craft's arrival. He continued on with suspicious thoughts rising in his mind. The newly arrived craft floated directly above him. Warily, he surfaced just behind the stern.

The bright Caribbean sun danced on the cerulean water, and he squinted against the glare. The boat was an old Coast Guard cutter. Someone had repainted it an ugly shade of green with the Cuban flag emblazoned sloppily on the back. Four men stood with their backs to him, three of them holding rifles at the ready. One of them was talking to the crew of Dane's boat, the *Sea Foam.* The newcomers were armed with old AK-47's and garbed in a motley mix of military uniform bits, as green and ugly as their vessel.

Aboard the *Sea Foam*, Dane's partner, Uriah Bonebrake, known to friends simply as "Bones", stood facing the unwelcome intruders. A false smile painted his face, and his body was deceptively relaxed. The Carolina-born Cherokee, and Dane's friend since their days together as Navy SEALS, carried a nine-millimeter Glock on his right hip, out of sight beneath his loose-fitting Hawaiian print shirt. Bones was outgunned, but Dane could tell that his friend was looking for an opening. Matt Barnaby and Corey Dean, the other two members of Dane's crew, stood behind Bones. Matt's lean, tan face was drawn in concern, while Corey looked frightened.

"You are in Cuban waters, Señor," the man without a rifle said. "We must inspect your boat for drugs." One of his comrades snickered, and he shut him up with a wave of his hand.

"These here ain't Cuban waters, Chief," Bones said, his deep voice relaxed, almost friendly. "Like I told you, we're marine archaeologists. This is a research vessel. If you're looking for drugs, there's this dude who hangs out on the corner near the Wal Mart by my house who can probably hook you up."

Bones knew as well as Dane that these clowns might be Cubans, but there was no way they were government agents. They were self-styled pirates, thugs who preyed mostly on private pleasure craft. He needed to help his crew, but how?

"You, my tall friend, are not so amusing as you seem to think. I suggest you cooperate. Do not force us to harm you." The fellow's voice was as oily as his skin.

"No need for any of that now," Bones said in a friendly tone. "We've got a cooler in the cabin. Maybe you fellas would like a Diet Mountain Dew or something?"

Bones was stalling for time, waiting for Dane to do something to help them out. Hoping he would not be heard over the sound of the cutter's idling engine, Dane quickly submerged and dove back down to the tuna boat. He had an idea.

He re-entered the submerged vessel, scraping his shoulder on a jagged piece of metal. The salt water burned, but he had no time to think about it. He checked his watch again. Less than three minutes now. He had to hurry.

A quick swim through the dimly lit vessel, and he soon found what he was looking for. He hefted it and turned to find himself blind. In his haste, he had disturbed the silt on the bottom of the craft, and the interior of the submerged craft was now filled with a thick, opaque cloud of sediment.

More angry than concerned, he took a moment to orient himself. It was a small boat, and he should not have any problem getting out, but precious seconds were ticking away. He blew out a few bubbles just to make sure he knew which direction was up, and reached up to put a hand on the ceiling. He swam his way to the opposite side of the boat, the side in which the hole was rent, and hugged the wall as he worked his way back.

The way out appeared like a sliver of sky through gray clouds. Exiting the sunken craft, he made ready to return to the *Sea Foam* and his crew. Something moved in his peripheral vision. *The shark again!* This time he had no choice but to make a bolt for the surface and hope that the primordial creature would continue to ignore him. He set his jaw and swam to the surface as fast as he could. The shark ignored him, and he surfaced without drawing notice.

Tensions were at a peak. The leader of the intruders was waving his arms and shouting in Spanish. Dane caught a few of the words; enough to know that they contained threats of bodily harm. Bones' eyes flitted in Dane's direction for the briefest of instants. It was enough to let him know that Bones had seen him, and was ready. Dane kicked free of his flippers just as the bull shark resurfaced on the other side of the boats and made straight toward him, its fin slicing through the calm gulf waters. The cut on his shoulder! It had scented him. First things first, though.

This had better work, Dane thought. He hefted the fire extinguisher he had retrieved from the drug runner's boat, and opened it up full blast on the pirates.

Surprised shouts rang out from the men on the cutter, and gunshots erupted as Bones used the diversion to draw his Glock and open fire. The two intruders farthest from Dane went down immediately. The man in the stern opened up wildly with his AK, spraying the *Sea Foam* with a deadly torrent of hot lead.

The shark was ten meters away and closing fast. Flinging the fire extinguisher in its direction, Dane grasped the side of the boat and heaved himself out of the water. He tumbled over the stern and rolled to his feet, freeing his dive knife as he went. Only a few paces away, the confused attacker, still struggling to keep his burning eyes open, spotted Dane and turned, bringing his weapon to bear.

Bullets buzzed past Dane's ear as he closed the gap between himself and the Cuban. He lashed out with his left hand, smacking the barrel of the weapon to the side. Simultaneously he thrust hard with his right. Still gripping his rifle, the Cuban could not protect himself. Dane drove his knife into the man's chest. Giving it a quick jerk to the left, then back to the right, he yanked the weapon free, and shoved the dying, self-styled pirate away.

The last attacker was down on one knee, exchanging gunfire with Bones. He was armed with a .38-caliber revolver, of all things. Holding his breath, Dane dashed toward him. The brigand must have espied him in the corner of his vision. He turned and leveled his pistol at Dane, and pulled the trigger. The hollow sound of a hammer striking repeatedly an empty cylinder seemed deafening to Dane as he charged in. Cursing in Spanish, the man threw the useless weapon at Dane's head, and then jumped up to meet his attacker.

Dane thrust low and hard at the man's midsection, but his opponent was a skilled fighter. The Cuban spun to the right, grasping Dane's left wrist in both hands and tried a shoulder throw. Dane saw the move coming, and managed to grab hold of the man by the loose fabric of his uniform pants behind his left thigh. He yanked up hard, throwing them both off balance. As they tumbled to the deck, the Cuban struck Dane's wrist, sending his dive knife sliding across the deck. He rolled away, sprang to his feet, and leapt at Dane again.

Years of combat training kicked in. Dane dropped into a long stance, bending at the knees. He wrapped one arm around the man's waist and the other between his legs. Allowing the attackers momentum to carry him, he heaved the man onto his shoulder like a log. Ignoring the pain from his wound, he turned and dropped his opponent over the side of the boat and into the water.

The Cuban broke the surface, shouting angrily, but his cries quickly turned to frightened shrieks as the water around him began to churn and froth. The bull shark ripped into him in an eerie, silent assault. The man shrieked and beat at the shark with his fists, but to no avail. Dane saw Bones, who had held his fire during the fight for fear of hitting the wrong man, raise his pistol and take aim at the shark. Just then, the Cuban ceased his struggles. Great gouts of blood erupted from his mouth as the ferocious predator carried him under, leaving a crimson pool spreading between the two boats. It was surely his imagination, but Dane thought he could smell the coppery scent of carnage.

The strength left his legs and he leaned heavily against the rail

"Thanks for coming to my rescue," he called across the intervening waters to his friends.

"Hey man, just because he didn't see the shark doesn't mean we all missed it," Bones yelled back. "The guy was a moron, anyway." The big, ponytailed native leaned his muscled, six-foot frame over the rail, cupped his hands, and shouted down at the water, "How many shots in a revolver, pal?"

"That's cold," Dane said, feeling a touch guilty at his enjoyment of the dark humor Bones had adopted as a means of coping with the realities of combat they had experienced in the service.

"Yeah, but I'm right." Bones' mirthless grin reminded Dane too strongly of the action they had seen in the SEALS.

"I put a call in to the Coast Guard when we first saw these guys coming," Matt said, leaning against the rail of the *Sea Foam*. He ran his long, tan, fingers through his spiky brown hair, and scanned the horizon. The condition of his hair was always of paramount importance to him. "They should be here any minute." Matt was a former army grunt, but the skinny mate and engineer had proven himself an able seaman.

"You know what that means," Corey, the fair-skinned, redheaded computer specialist interjected. He sat on the deck behind Bones with his elbows propped on his knees and his chin cupped in his hands, looking despondent.

"I know," Dane groaned, "back to the docks." They could not afford a delay. Business had been slow, and he had been counting on the Spanish galleon to change their fortunes. He had done his homework, researched it thoroughly, and was certain he had a line on it. But nothing remained secret for long in this business. His competitors would hear about the shootout and wonder what he was looking for out here.

"It should only be for a day," Bones said hopefully. "It's pretty obvious what these guys are. Or should I say *were*?" He twisted his mouth in a wry smile."

"It had better not be for long," Dane said. "We've got to get back to work." He did not add, *or we're going to go under*. Everyone knew that fact already. "If somebody finds that wreck before us…" His words trailed away as a Coast Guard cutter appeared on the horizon.

CHAPTER 2

D
ane and Bones were surveying the damage to the *Sea Foam* when the sound of approaching footsteps drew their attention. Though they had returned to port, they remained on their guard after the attack. Even Corey, who abhorred violence of any sort, had armed himself with Matt's spare .9 millimeter and was keeping an eye out for danger.

A young woman, perhaps in her mid-twenties, stood at the end of the dock. She was tall, with long, deeply tanned legs, which her khaki shorts displayed to good effect. A tight, white, sleeveless shirt clung to her trim, athletic body in all the right places. The intense Key West sun glistened on her long, white-blonde hair, which she wore pulled back, displaying a strong, yet attractive face that appeared untouched by the humidity. Her chin was a bit too small and her nose just a touch too big for her face, but that only added character to her appearance. She regarded Dane with an intense, green-eyed stare that took his breath for an instant. She was a beauty.

"Good afternoon," she said, smiling broadly. "Permission to come aboard?" She asked the question as if it was a mere formality, which Dane supposed it was. Beautiful women on the *Sea Foam* were few and far-between.

"Granted," Bones replied quickly, shouldering Dane aside. He offered his hand to help the young woman onto the deck. She did not need his assistance, though, vaulting the rail and landing on the balls of her feet with catlike agility. Bones stepped back and grinned in approval. "Not bad. What are you, anyway, one of those Romanian gymnast women or something?."

"Hardly." She brushed some invisible dirt from her shorts. "Well then. I assume you would be Bonebrake and Maddock," she said, nodding to each of them in turn.

"As if we had a choice," Dane replied, and immediately wondered if that sounded as dumb to her as it did to him. Bones was the clever one. "And you would be?"

"I am Kaylin Maxwell." She looked at him as if he ought to know her.

Dane was certain that he'd remember that pair of legs, if not the name. "I'm sorry Miss Maxwell, have we met before?"

"Sure we have," Bones interrupted, his smile shining brighter than white against his deeply tanned features. "You know, at that thing, at the place…" His voice trailed off under Kaylin's bemused stare.

Kaylin folded her arms and looked down at the bullet holes riddling the side of the boat. "Termites?" she deadpanned.

"Cubans," Dane said. "It's a long story."

"But it's a *great* story," Bones interrupted. "We were heroes. How about I buy you a drink and tell you all about it?"

"I'll take a beer if you have one handy," she said. "But I know enough of your reputation to not let you buy me anything."

Dane waited for the woman to explain herself, but no explanation was forthcoming. "You never told us where we know you from."

"You don't know *me*," the blonde replied, "but you both knew my father quite well."

Dane paused for a moment, and then took a step back. "Hold on! You're Maxie's daughter?" Commander Hartford Maxwell had led his and Bones' unit during their service in the SEALS. Dane had held the rank of Lieutenant Commander under Maxie. "I haven't heard from him in years. How is he?"

Kaylin looked away, her bright eyes cloudy and her face crestfallen.

Dane's heart sank. He already knew what she was going to say.

"I'm sorry to have to tell you," she said, her voice husky with emotion, "that my father is dead." She paused, taking a deep breath. "He died a week ago. That's why I'm here."

"Oh," Dane said, caught off guard by the surprise announcement. He did not know what to say, so he grimaced and looked down for a moment. He had seen his share of death, but he knew all too well that loved ones were different. Matt and Corey had joined them, and they offered their condolences to Kaylin, who nodded her thanks.

"You're in the will, Maddock," Bones joked, clapping him on the shoulder. "Lord knows Maxie wouldn't have left me anything." The commander had appreciated Bones as a soldier. Problem was, Bones held his liquor about as well as any other Indian: not well at all. Maxie was constantly busting his subordinate for some shenanigan or another. Every time it had been when Bonebrake was drinking. After retiring from the service, Maddock's friend had curtailed his drinking to the occasional social drink, but his offbeat personality remained intact.

"I'm sorry, but I fear there's no inheritance," Kaylin said, smiling sadly.

"Yeah, I guess that wasn't very sympathetic of me," Bones said, looking a bit abashed. "I gotta' tell you, I'm not very good with the whole serious thing."

"No problem," Kaylin said. "As I said before, I've already heard a little bit about you, so I was prepared." She offered a sad smile to show there were no hard feelings, but then her face grew serious. She frowned and looked around uncomfortably. "Is there somewhere the three of us can talk?"

"Oh, sorry. Of course." Matt and Corey excused themselves, and Dane and Bones ushered her into the main cabin of the *Sea Foam*. They sat down around a small table that was covered in charts and various books and papers. Dane hurried to clean up the clutter while Bones took three Samuel Adams from the small refrigerator and passed them out. Kaylin took a long, slow drink and sat in quiet contemplation for a moment before launching into her explanation.

"My father was murdered," she began. "The police say he interrupted a burglary in progress."

Dane took a drink of his beer. It was dark and rich, just the way he liked it, and so cold that it stung his throat on the way down. He was listening to what Kaylin had *not* said, and that was what he responded to.

"But you think differently."

"I *know* it wasn't a burglary," she replied, meeting his gaze with a level stare. "Not long before he died, my father gave me a package and told me to keep it safe. He said it was something he was working on, and that people were after it. He planned to get it back from me when he felt that things had 'cooled off', whatever that meant."

"I don't get it," Bones interrupted, his beer forgotten as he concentrated on the issue at hand. "Maxie was good. If he knew somebody was after him, he should have been on his guard. How did they get to him?"

"That's another reason that I know it wasn't a burglary," Kaylin replied. "As you said, Dad was good. Whoever got him must have been better." She paused and cleared her throat, her eyes beginning to mist. She accepted the napkin Dane offered with a nod of thanks and dabbed at her eyes.

"What was the condition of the house when the police got there?" He felt strange continuing the discussion when she was obviously upset, but he sensed that it would be better to give her something to talk about, rather than sitting in gloomy silence.

"It *looked* like a burglary," she said, her voice thick with emotion. This was obviously difficult for her to talk about. "Drawers had been rummaged through or dumped on the floor. His DVD player was missing, and what little bit of jewelry he owned. Things like that."

"Let me play the devil's advocate here," said Bones, raising a long finger. "How can you be certain that it wasn't a burglary? You know, Occam's Razor and all that."

"For one, it was too clean," Kaylin said. If she minded the question, she did not show it. "They left no fingerprints. Zero. No signs of forced entry, no alarm from the security system, and I know for a fact that Dad never went anywhere without locking up and arming the system."

"He never missed a detail," Dane agreed. Maxie was the most professional officer he had ever known. "I can't imagine Maxie forgetting anything."

"Also, the hard drive on his computer was erased, save a few mundane files. All of his research was wiped clean. That isn't the sort of thing a burglar would do. The biggest reason, though, is what they didn't mess with." She paused. "Dad's study looked untouched: his desk, his filing cabinet, his books."

"Why would burglars mess with his books?" Bones asked. "Is there a big black market for old James Micheners?"

"People will sometimes hide money in their books," Dane explained. "Or they'll get those fake books that are hollow on the inside and put their valuables in there."

Bones raised his eyebrows in surprise. "Dude, I would make a lousy burglar," he said. "The desk, I get. They'd be looking for checks, credit card numbers, money, stuff like that."

"You said the study *looked* untouched." Dane had caught the inflection in Kaylin's voice. "What makes you believe someone had been in there?"

"The work Dad was doing," Kaylin looked up at the ceiling, seeming uncertain how to answer, "was sort of a research project. He told me that along with his real work, he kept a fake journal. Some of it was accurate, but with key information altered or missing. He kept it in the safe in his study. If someone got hold if it, they'd think it was real, because he'd gone to the trouble of locking it up."

"The sneaky son of a..." Bones whispered. "Oh. Sorry. No disrespect or anything." He stared out the window with a faint smile and a distant look in his eyes. "I don't know if you remember him the way we do. It's all good, though."

"That's all right, he *was* sneaky." Kaylin laughed and reached out to pat Bones' shoulder. "He figured that if whoever was after him ever got hold of it, it would protect us, and also keep them from finding what he was looking for." She shook her head in admiration.

"I assume the false journal was missing," Dane said, finding himself drawn into the puzzle despite his surprise at the news of Maxie's death.

Kaylin nodded. "The safe was locked. All his other papers appeared to be undisturbed, but the journal was gone."

Dane folded his hands behind his head and looked up at the ceiling. He just could not believe Maxie was gone. The man had always seemed indestructible. Dane's parents had died in an auto accident while he was in the service, and Maxie had stepped in to fill the void left by their loss, serving as a guide and role model. The two stayed in touch for a short while after Dane left the military, but life had gotten in the way. Now, he regretted not having put more effort into the friendship.

"I truly am sorry to surprise the two off you with all this," Kaylin said. "Someone comes out of the blue and drops a bomb on you. It isn't the best way to deliver news. In any case, Mr. Maddock…"

"Please, call me Dane." It jarred him to realize that, after their conversation, they still were not technically on a first-name basis.

"All right, Dane." The way she said it reminded him of how Melissa used to try a new flavor of lipstick: pursed lips and sort of a withholding judgment expression on her face. "I know this is all comes as a surprise, and not a pleasant one at that, but I need your help." She reached across the table and laid her hand on his arm.

"Hold on. Why me?" Dane was momentarily taken aback. What could he do to help with a murder investigation? He fixed the woman with a questioning gaze, but let her hand remain where it was. "I mean, you didn't come all this way just to deliver bad news. Why are you here?"

"Dad told me how to find the two of you." Her eyes darted to Bones and back to Dane. "He said that if anything happened to him, I should come to you." She let that statement hand in the ensuing moment of stunned silence.

"Wait a minute," Bones finally said. "Maxie wanted you to come to *me?*" His look of exaggerated shock would have been comical had Dane not been so completely caught off-guard by Kaylin's revelation.

"He knew the two of you were working together. He told me that *you* ," she gestured at Bones with her beer bottle, "were a character, but as trustworthy as they come. He's definitely right about the first part. As to the second part, that remains to be seen."

"But we're marine archaeologists, not policemen," Dane protested. What had Maxie been thinking? "We dive on wrecks and look for treasure. How can we help you?"

"Marine archaeologists are precisely what I need," Kaylin said. She bit her lip and looked from Dane to Bones and Back to Dane. It seemed as if she was uncertain whether to say any more. Finally she continued. "I need you two to help me find a shipwreck."

CHAPTER 3

*I*n my lifetime, I have had many joys and few regrets. The greatest of those things I regret, however, is the loss of my beloved treasures that January night. I was the first to rediscover the wonders and riches of those historic cities. I should have been the one to bring their secrets to light. But without that most precious of artifacts, no one would listen to me. I was scoffed at by my peers, ridiculed in scholarly circles, condemned from on high. I had no choice but to hold the truth close to my breast.

It is strange to think that I boarded the Dourado with the belief that I would return home a hero. The truths I had to share would have shaken the foundations of mankind. But alas, the fates have denied me the renown that I so richly deserve. Because I do not wish to hold myself up to the mockery of future generations, I will not record my findings in this journal. I will say only that truly, there is none like it.

Dane closed the translated copy of Rienzi's journal. He ran his fingers across the smooth cover. Maxie had bound his translation in a simple, three-ring binder, and had printed "Journal" in his precise hand.

"So Maxie was looking for whatever this guy Rienzi lost. Do we have any idea what it was?"

Kaylin stood with her back to him, not answering, staring over the balcony and down at the Ashley River's slow moving waters where the river flowed into Charleston Harbor. Content to wait until she was ready to talk, Dane left his seat at the bar that separated the kitchen from the living area of her small apartment, and joined her outside. Propping his forearms on the rail, he took in the peaceful view. A few sailing vessels plied the calm, gray harbor waters, their white sails glistening against the blue sky. He had always had an affinity for the water. If he could not be on the water, he wanted to at least be near it. He wondered if perhaps he had found a kindred spirit in Kaylin.

He and Bones had arrived late the night before, three days after their initial meeting. Despite their reservations, it had not taken much coaxing from Kaylin to convince them to sign on for her project. Their latest expedition was a complete bust, and even though the Coast Guard investigation had cleared them of all wrongdoing, it would be a while before the *Sea Foam* was ready to ply the seas again. The compensation Kaylin was offering was more than enough to repair the damage to their craft. More, in fact, than he thought an art teacher should be able to afford. When he had pressed her on the point, she explained that her father had provided well for her. That, Dane did believe. Maxie was the kind of man who took care of his own. He and Bones admired the man greatly. But more than that, they wanted to see his last wish carried out.

"I'm sorry," Kaylin finally said. "It's difficult to talk about Dad's work." She turned to look at Dane, her green eyes downcast. "Rienzi never names this treasure that was so precious to him. I've only had a few days to look over everything, but it seems that Dad was thorough in combing through everything the man ever wrote. He says all sorts of grandiose things about how important his discoveries were, but never reveals what, exactly he found."

"I picked up on the grandiose part," Dane said. "He sounds like a character. Makes you wonder if it's all just bluster, or if he really did accomplish anything of note."

"He lived quite a life," Kaylin said. "He took part in the battle of Waterloo. He also fought for Simon Bolivar in Colombia, then came back to Europe where he was wounded at Marathon. He traveled most of the known world and became a self-styled discoverer. Not exactly a colonial times Indiana Jones, but something close." She grinned, and some of the strain melted away. She looked younger, more energetic. "He claimed to have been the first person to rediscover the ruins of Syre and

Assab in Abyssinia. He also claimed that he was the first to excavate them, as well as Petra in Arabia."

"Wasn't Petra a crappy Christian band back in the eighties?" Bones called from the kitchen. He dropped a bag on the table and joined them on the balcony.

"It's also a famous city in the Middle East," Kaylin said. "It's literally carved into the sides of cliffs."

"You know, like in the third Indiana Jones movie," Dane said, recalling Kaylin's analogy. He nudged his friend with an elbow to the ribs.

"Oh yeah!" Bones said, as if this were all a startling revelation. "You guys are so smart."

The blonde rolled her eyes and continued. "Anyway, Rienzi was returning to France on the *Dourado* with all the treasures he had accumulated during his world travels. He lost everything when the ship sank."

"Bummer," Bones said. "Reminds me of the time I hooked up with this really cute sorority girl. We made it about halfway back to my dorm and then she hurled all over..." He took one look at Kaylin's disapproving stare and cut the story short. "Nevermind. Rewind to where I said 'bummer' and just leave it there."

"Good idea." Kaylin folded her arms across his chest and frowned, but there was a twinkle in her eye that had been absent moments before. "Rienzi certainly thought it was a 'bummer' as you put it. He went back to France and made a bit of a name for himself writing. He never did get over losing his life's work, though."

"What happened to him?" Dane asked.

Kaylin hesitated. "He killed himself eighteen years later."

"Ouch. Sounds like the guy had a flair for the dramatic," Bones observed, shaking his head. "So, what do we know about the last voyage of the *Dourado*?"

"It's a strange story," she said. "Besides Rienzi's belongings, the captain claimed to have been carrying more than half-a million dollars on board when the ship went down. That was a great deal of money back then. When the survivors reached Singapore with word of the sinking, the British sent out a detachment of troops in three ships to guard the wreck from the local pirates while divers tried to salvage the ship."

"I can't imagine trying to dive using nineteenth century technology," Dane observed. He shuddered at the thought of braving the depths with only the aid of primitive dive equipment. Modern diving was hazardous enough.

"They didn't have to. The ships returned very quickly. They were unable to find the *Dourado*, and assumed that it had gone down in deep water. Less than a week later, though, the wreckage was found off the coast of the island of Bintan. Salvage efforts only turned up a few items: a silver statue, a box with some papers, and a couple of personal items. They found no sign of the money, nor of Rienzi's treasure. After three months, Rienzi gave up on ever recovering his property, and returned to France."

The doorbell rang, bringing their conversation to an abrupt halt. Kaylin answered the door, and returned a moment later with a tall, lean, ginger-haired man of middle years in a black suit and priest's collar. His thin-lipped smile was the only sign of emotion in an otherwise bland face. His eyes, narrowed in either curiosity or suspicion, flitted from Dane to Bones, then back to Dane.

"Father Wright," Kaylin said, "I would like to introduce two friends of my father. This is Dane Maddock." She gestured to Dane with a wave of her hand. "And this is Uriah Bonebrake. They were in the Navy together with Dad."

The priest shook Dane's hand first, then turned to Bones. "Uriah," he said, clasping Bone's hand. "A strong, biblical name."

"Let's hope I don't share his fate," Bones said with a mischievous smile. "Getting killed over a woman hits way too close to home." Dane's surprise must have registered on his face, because his Bones frowned at him. "Think I don't know my Bible? I was raised on the reservation. Pentecostal preachers everywhere you look."

"I suppose we can forgive you for that," Father Wright said. He actually cracked a smile, but only a small one. "Kaylin," he continued, turning to their hostess, "I won't stay but a moment. I just came by to check in on you."

"Thank you, Father. I'm doing fine, all things considered."

"Glad to hear it." Father Wright paused, rubbing a pale, slender hand absently across his chest. He seemed nervous or uncertain. "I hope you'll forgive me, but I have a bit of an unusual question. Your father had in his collection a very old French bible. I must not have hidden my admiration for it very well, because he offered to donate it to the rectory library."

"Oh," Kaylin said, a frown creasing her brow. "I haven't gone through his things yet. I'll keep an eye out for it, though, and let you know if I come across it."

"Perhaps it is in his library?" the Priest asked. Dane thought it a trifle rude for the man to persist, but he held his tongue. "I could drop by his house sometime when you are going to be there."

"Actually, that's the one place I *have* inventoried," Kaylin said. "After the burglary and the police investigation it seemed like it needed doing. As I said, I *will* look for it." Her voice had taken on a tone of impatience, and she stood with hands on hips.

"Thank you," Father Wright replied, touching her shoulder gently. "I just wanted to mention it. Please let me know if there is anything I can do for you."

"I will, Father. Thank you for dropping by." Kaylin showed the priest out and returned to the living room where Dane and Bones had wandered in from the balcony. She had a puzzled look on her face.

"That was an odd conversation," Dane said, dropping down onto Kaylin's black leather sofa.

"It was very odd," she said, taking a seat next to him. "Father Wright is a good man. It just feels so inappropriate for him to be asking for something of Dad's so soon after…" Her voice trailed away. "You know what I mean."

"You'd think a priest would have better bedside manner," Bones observed. He fished beer and a package of beef jerky out of the bag he had laid on the kitchen table. "Anybody else?" He held up his drink and snack.

"It's a little early for that much gas," Dane said. "Thanks anyway, though."

"Breakfast of champions," Bones said. He joined them in the living room, dropping down into a papasan beneath one of Kaylin's seascapes.

The rattan chair creaked under his weight, and he overflowed it like a gorilla in an inner tube. Dane chuckled at the mental image. Bones raised an eyebrow but did not ask what was funny.

"Cool artwork, Kaylin," Bones said, looking around at the paintings that adorned the living room walls. "You painted them all, huh? Anyway, I want to talk about this wreck we're supposed to find," he said. "If it was salvaged back when it first went down, and they didn't find much, it either means that Rienzi was full of it, or this alleged incredible discovery was lost somewhere between the point where the ship sank, and the point where the wreck was finally discovered. At best, we'll have to scour the ocean bed looking for some item which, by the way, we don't know what it is. I'd say it's impossible."

"It can't be impossible," Dane argued. "Maxie wouldn't have wasted his time if it couldn't be done." Dane had the utmost confidence in their former commander. He had no doubt that Maxie had been on to something. "There's something he knew that we don't. When we figure it out, we'll know how to proceed."

"Do you have anything other that the papers you showed us?" Bones asked Kaylin.

The girl shook her head. "We're missing something. I've been through Dad's journal and Rienzi's and I can't find anything." She folded her arms and set her jaw. Her eyes were fixed on some invisible spot in the distance as she thought. "It has to be there. It just has to."

Dane thought he knew someone who could help them. He excused himself for a minute and stepped outside to make the call. When he returned to the living room, Bones and Kaylin looked at him with curious expressions.

"I've got a friend on the case," he explained cryptically. He would leave them in suspense until he heard something back.

"So that's how you're going to play it?" Bones asked, grinning suspiciously.

"Yep," Dane said. He did not want to get their hopes up until he found out what kind of results his contact could get. That, and he enjoyed keeping them in suspense. At any rate, there was more that they could do in the meantime.

"Kaylin," he said, turning to the blonde, "What do you say we check out your dad's library?"

CHAPTER 4

The books in Maxwell's library were arranged in meticulous fashion by subject, author and date of publication. The precise rows were totally in keeping with the commander's personality. Everything in the room, from the painting of the shipwreck on the wall above the computer, to the single, framed family portrait, reminded Dane of his mentor and friend. A pang of sadness welled up inside, but was immediately overwhelmed by a wave of bitterness. He wanted to find whoever it was who had done Maxie in. He wanted them bad. He clenched his fist, imagining the murderer's throat.

"I wonder what bible Father Wright was talking about?" Kaylin asked. She stood next to him, looking over the books. "I know what Dad had in his library, and I never saw an old bible."

"I didn't know Catholics even read the bible," Bones said, "at least not in English."

"He didn't read it, genius. It was in French," Dane shot back. "You don't see it anywhere? Maybe whoever broke in took it." He didn't know why someone would steal a bible. He scanned the shelves but saw no obvious empty spaces where a book might be missing.

He set about the task of examining the library, pulling books off the shelves at random and thumbing through, looking for notations, papers, anything that might give a clue as to what they were looking for. Kaylin searched through the file cabinets, while Bones sat popping Maxie's CD-ROMs into his laptop one at a time, scanning their contents.

His cell phone vibrated against his chest. Dane withdrew it from his jacket pocket and flipped it open. It was the call he had been waiting for.

"Hey Jimmy, what you got for me?" Jimmy Letson was a writer for the Washington Post. He had access, legally, to a myriad of internet databases. He was also a hacker who had access, illegally, to resources Dane didn't even want to know about. The two had been friends in the service, remaining in contact even after Jimmy had rung out of SEAL training, and left the service when his tour ended.

"What's that? No, 'Wow Jimmy, that was fast!' or 'Hey Jimmy, thanks for dropping everything to check on this for me,' or 'Gee Jimmy, thanks for risking your job…' "

"I get the point," Dane said, laughing. "Fine, I declare you the Pope of Cyberspace. Now what did you find out?"

"Funny you should mention the Pontiff. This guy Rienzi, he came back from his world travels sounding off to anyone who would listen about all the great treasures he had lost."

"We knew that much already. Did he ever say what, exactly, he had lost?"

"He must have, because within several months, he had managed to tick off all of the scholars in his field, or at least the ones we have any writings from. Unfortunately for you, they all talk about his 'ridiculous' claims, but they never say what specifically those claims were. A year after his return, he pretty much shuts up, and goes back to being a run-of-the-mill writer."

"Do you think the ridicule got to him?" Dane asked.

"I think it was bigger than that. Jimmy paused. He loved drama. *NAILS turned up a letter from the bishop in Paris to a cardinal back at the Vatican, written nine months after Rienzi's return to France."*

NAILS was an acronym for "National Archive and Informational Linkage System", an amazing connection of informational resources used by the CIA. Jimmy had somehow found a way to clandestinely link up to the system. Dane had told his friend on more that one occasion that he did not want to be around when Jimmy was finally busted. Jimmy just laughed and boasted that he was much too smart to be caught by those bozos. His cockiness made even Bones appear humble.

"I'm waiting for you to tell me why I should care," Dane said, feigning disinterest.

"The Cardinal wanted Rienzi excommunicated. That interest you?"

Dane reflected on this new bit of information. Could they be connected in some way? The timing was certainly right.

"Thanks, Jim, that's great. Anything else?"

"Probably nothing you don't already know. I'll shoot a summary over to you. Anything else you need?

"Actually, would you see what you can find out about the *Dourado*?"

"I suppose you're in a big hurry on this one too," Jimmy groaned.

"No, last night will be soon enough." Dane ignored Jimmy's profane reply. "Thanks again. I'll stand you to a bottle of Wild Turkey next time I'm in DC." Maxie had taught him long ago how helpful it could be to know a man's weakness.

"You've got a deal," Jimmy replied, and broke the connection.

Dane hung up the phone and shared this new information with Bones and Kaylin.

"So Rienzi comes back from his trip and starts ruffling feathers," Bones said. He stood with his chin cupped in his hand. His brown eyes stared vacantly out the window. "Whatever claims he's making, they're enough to get somebody in the church all riled up. They threaten him with excommunication, and he clams up."

"With the kind of clout the church carried, it wouldn't be out of the question for the Vatican to find a way to get rid of any written record of Rienzi's claims, whatever they were," Kaylin added. "What could he have found that would upset the church that much?"

A flicker of movement at the corner of his eye caught Dane's attention. "Did you see something out there?" he asked Bones, pointing toward the window.

His friend shook his head. "Sorry, man. Lost in space." He tapped his temple with a deeply tanned finger.

"Thought I saw something." Dane drew his pistol, a German-made Walther P-99, and moved to the windowsill, carefully peering out over the narrow backyard that ran down to the shore of the Cooper River. It was a calm, sunny afternoon. Nothing seemed amiss in the quiet neighborhood. Bones appeared at his side, Glock drawn.

A knock at the front door broke the silence, causing the two of them to jump. Kaylin looked at him questioningly. Dane nodded, and walked with her to the door. She opened it to reveal an elderly black woman in a neatly pressed dress.

"Bernie!" Kaylin cried, crushing the woman in a tight embrace. The old woman smiled and hugged her back.

"Gently, child," she said in a tender voice, "I'm not as young as I used to be." She smiled a warm smile and patted Kaylin.

Kaylin pulled back and held the woman at arm's length. "It's so good to see you."

"It's good to see you too. Can I come in?" The woman gave Kaylin a motherly pat on the shoulder and stepped through the doorway. After Kaylin introduced Dane and Bones, the four of them made their way to the kitchen, where they sat down around a stout oaken table in front of a wide bay window.

"Bernice took care of me when I was little, after Mom died," Kaylin explained. "I call her Bernie."

"I'm so sorry about your father," Bernice said. "I've been in Mississippi visiting family for a few weeks. I went to your apartment as soon as I heard, but you weren't there."

"I'm glad you found me," Kaylin said. Her smile underlined the sincerity in her words.

"So am I. There's something I have to give you." The woman fished into her bag and produced a large, manila envelope with something thick and rectangular inside. Dane could see that it was one of the packing envelopes used for mailing delicate items. "Your father gave me this a few months ago. He made me promise to keep it a secret. He said that I should give it to you if anything should ever happen to him." She shook her head. "I never thought it would be so soon, if ever. Your father always seemed indestructible."

Dane turned his head toward the window, giving the two a modicum of privacy to share this painful moment. Outside, a solitary boat drifted lazily down the Cooper River.

Kaylin nodded to Bernie, her eyes misty, and carefully undid the clasp on the envelope. Reaching in, she carefully withdrew a battered, old bible, the leather cover worn with age.

Dane leaned forward, his heart beating faster. This had to be it.

After a moment's pause, Kaylin opened the old book, and gingerly flipped through the pages. The writing was French! In various places, someone had written notes in the margins in a bold, ornate hand. The ink had faded with time, and was, in parts, nearly invisible. Beside her, Bones whistled, and leaned closer. She turned back to the inside cover. There, on the front page, in the same flowing script, was the name: *Louis Domenic de Rienzi.*

"Rienzi's personal Bible," Bones marveled, his tone near reverential. "This is what the priest was after."

As Dane sat staring at the ancient volume, something drew his attention. The boat had stopped drifting. A solitary man stood on the deck, and appeared to be pointing in their direction. Immediately, Dane realized what was happening, and he sprang to his feet.

"Down!" he shouted, grasping the edge of the table and upending it toward the bay window. The others fell to the floor as bullets shattered the glass and ripped into the heavy tabletop. An instant later, the sound of rifle fire drifted across the water, echoing hollowly through the house. Dane drew his Walther with the futile knowledge that boat was too far away for him to have any hope of hitting the shooter.

"Out the front," he ordered. He did not have a clue who was shooting at them, but he had an idea why. In any case, they had to get Kaylin and the bible out of there right away. He reached up over the table and fired blindly, the report of the Walther loud in the small space.

"Come on Granny!" Bones yelled to Bernie. His pistol in his right hand, he wrapped his left arm around the woman's waist and pulled her toward the door. Her eyes were wide with fright, but did not argue.

Dane followed behind, snapping off two more hasty shots at the boat in hopes of slowing the sniper's fire. He turned to see Kaylin rummaging through a drawer. "What are you doing?" he shouted. What could she possibly need from the kitchen that could not wait?

She turned back toward him, a .380 automatic and two reloads in her hand. "Dad kept guns everywhere. Let's go." She nodded toward the door.

He was impressed by her lack of panic, but there was no time to remark on it. He rushed to the front door where Bones and Bernie waited. He nudged the door open and looked up and down the deserted street. Behind them, the sniper continued to rain bullets on the house. From the sounds of shattering glass, Dane determined that the shooter was methodically firing into each room, working his way across the back of the structure. They needed to get away immediately.

"Bones, you take Bernie in her car. Kaylin and I will go in mine."

They hurried to the vehicles, weapons at the ready. Dane threw open the door of his rented green Tahoe and fired it up. He glanced at the rear view mirror and saw a silver Taurus whip around the corner and come barreling down the street toward them. The passenger side window was down, and the man opposite the driver reached out the window and opened fire. Kaylin, Bible clutched in one hand, returned fire with her .380 before joining Dane in the SUV. Dane floored it, hoping to stay ahead of the attacker's vehicle.

He looked in the rear view mirror in time to see Bones make a u-turn in Bernie's cream-colored Lincoln and tear down the street, headed on a collision course with the Taurus. Bones thrust his pistol out the driver's window, blazing away left-handed with his nine as he charged their assailants.

"He's crazy," Kaylin whispered in awe. She climbed into the back seat, .380 still at the ready, and watched out the back window.

"You have no idea," Dane said. In his rear-view, he saw the windshield of the Taurus shatter. The driver yanked the car hard to the right as Bones flashed by, still shooting. The silver car fishtailed as it drifted into Maxwell's front yard, but the driver recovered quickly and continued the pursuit. Dane groaned. "Are you all right using that thing?" he asked, tilting his head toward Kaylin's pistol.

"Please," she said. "You knew my father." She turned back toward the rear of the vehicle, her .380 trained on the pursuing car.

He took a hard right, nearly bringing the Tahoe up on two wheels. He stepped on the accelerator and weaved through the sparse afternoon traffic heading into downtown Charleston. Behind them, the Taurus whipped around the corner, tires screeching. Dane cursed as he watched the other drivers move out of the way of the speeding silver vehicle. How were they going to get away?

"Maybe they won't shoot at us with witnesses around," Kaylin said. Her hope proved in vain as shots rang out, and spiderwebbed cracks spread around a bullet hole in the bottom corner of the rear window. "Okay, forget I said that."

"Gotcha," Dane said as he whipped the wheel back-and-forth, zigzagging as he sped along, but trying not to slip into a pattern that would make them easy targets. He heard the rear driver's side window roll down, then the report of Kaylin's pistol as she squeezed off rounds, maintaining a slow, steady fire at their attackers.

"Where are the cops when you need them?" he growled. The light ahead turned red. He pressed the pedal to the floor and veered into the oncoming lane to pass the traffic that had stopped for the light, narrowly avoiding a collision with a cab that was crossing the intersection. The cab screeched to a halt, and he hear the cabbie shout a physically impossible suggestion as they shot past. Once through the light, he yanked the Tahoe back onto his side of the road and continued on.

"They're through," Kaylin called to him, snapping off another shot. Unfortunately, the light traffic worked in both drivers' favor.

A quick glance in the rear view mirror showed the Taurus again narrowing the gap between the two vehicles.

"How can they possibly keep up with us when they're driving with a broken windshield?" Kaylin grumbled.

Dane did not answer. It was further confirmation that whomever Maxie had run afoul of, they were good. He turned a hard right onto Market Street, the Taurus now in close pursuit. Kaylin exchanged a few more shots with the passenger in the pursuing car.

"Something has got to give, here," she said, popping a reload into her pistol. "They're way too close."

"That's an understatement," Dane replied, glancing in his mirror. The traffic ahead of them was at a standstill. The oncoming lanes were almost gridlocked, and tourists packed the narrow sidewalks. The last thing they needed was an old west-style shootout, but it might come down to that. He looked around for a side street, anything that would afford an escape. Ahead of him, the stalled traffic loomed ever closer. And then, to his left, he saw what he was looking for. It could work, but they would have to be fast.

He tapped the brake, and then yanked the wheel hard to the left, nearly rolling the top-heavy vehicle. Horns blared as a he cut across the street directly in front of oncoming traffic. Hitting the brakes hard, he maneuvered the Tahoe into a controlled skid, then released the pedal and whipped the vehicle into an empty parking space.

"Out," he barked. He hopped out of the car and looked across the street, where the sheer volume of vehicles had managed to hold up the Taurus. The driver was trying to force his way across through the heavy oncoming traffic. Through the driver's window, Dane was finally able to get a look at their pursuers.

The two could have been twins. Each had short, dark hair, and wore wrap-around sunglasses and dark colored polo-style shirts. *Dressed to blend in with the crowd*, Dane thought. *That's what I intend to do.* He took Kaylin's hand, and led her away from the car. They hurried across the parking lot and into the Charleston Slave Market.

CHAPTER 5

The Charleston Slave Market was a long, narrow building that spanned the length of two city blocks. Contrary to common wisdom, the market was not a place where slaves had once been sold, but a place where slaves from the surrounding area had gathered to sell their wares. Now it had been converted to a sort of giant flea market, which drew thousands of visitors each day. Dane hoped that the milling throngs would provide him and Kaylin with a way to disappear.

His cell phone vibrated. He opened it up and checked the display. It was Bones.

"Maddock, where are you?"

"We're in the slave market. You know how to get here?" Dane squeezed through the throng of shoppers milling about the displays. He turned to see the Taurus pulling in to the parking lot.

"I'll find it. What's the deal?"

Dane explained their situation and gave his friend a general description of their pursuers. Bones assured him that he would be there soon. He flipped the phone shut and turned to Kaylin, who was turning off her own phone.

"I called the police, but I don't think the dispatcher believed me. She kept going on about the penalty for phony 911 calls."

"Two cars flying down the street, guns blazing have to have gotten someone's attention," he said. "Let's stay alive until they get here."

"Should we try and slip out of the market farther on down?" She stood on her tiptoes trying to see over the milling throng. The market offered exits at the end of each segment, but was woefully lacking in side doors.

"I think we're safer in the crowd," he replied, as they moved deeper into the throng. He was walking sideways, pretending to look at the merchandise, all the while keeping an eye on the front entrance. So far, there was no sign of their pursuers.

A bit farther down, he saw what he had been hoping to find. He nodded toward the display of Hawaiian print shirts. Kaylin smiled, understanding his thoughts immediately. At the display, Dane purchased two shirts, a straw hat for himself and sunglasses for Kaylin. They donned their new clothing quickly, throwing the shirts over what they were already wearing.

"You look totally lame," Kaylin said as she twisted her long, blonde hair up into a bun.

"That's the idea," he replied with a grin. "Tourist camo." He was fairly certain she was rolling her eyes behind her sunglasses. He offered her his elbow, which she took in a tight grip that conveyed her tension. Arm-in-arm the two continued to browse, looking, he hoped, like nothing more than a happy couple on vacation. All the while, they kept a lookout for the men who were after them.

Moments later, Dane spotted one of their pursuers, the driver, he thought, enter the market. Trying to look inconspicuous, the man made a show of checking out the displays on either side of the aisle as he worked his way into the marketplace.

"Only one of them," Dane whispered. "The other guy must be coming in from the back. That's what I would have done."

Kaylin examined a fat, silver bracelet inlaid with turquoise. "Buy this for me, honey?" she said in a syrupy voice.

"Not this close to our anniversary, sweetheart," he kidded. She screwed up her face in an exaggerated pout.

"Keep sticking that lip out there and a bird's going to poop on it," he said, arching an eyebrow.

She frowned and smacked him on the shoulder. In response, he pulled her close and gave her a squeeze, giving him a chance to look over her shoulder at the man who was coming toward them.

"He hasn't seen us yet, but he's getting closer," he whispered in her ear. Who were these guys?

"I still don't see anyone coming from the other direction," she whispered back.

They broke from the embrace and continued moving. Dane guessed that they were about halfway through the first section of the market. He wanted to look back, but he could not afford to draw attention to them. A bit further, then they paused at a book vendor's display. Dane picked up a large picture book and held it up close to his face. He stole a glance back in the direction from which they had come. The man was no more than thirty yards away, moving slowly, but coming steadily closer. At least they had not yet been spotted.

"Dane, here he comes," Kaylin whispered, her voice strident with urgency.

Dane turned his head and caught a glimpse of the second man, much farther away, but also headed toward them.

"What do we do?" Kaylin bit her lower lip. Worry was evident in her green eyes.

"They're probably expecting us to bolt out the back door. Our best chance is to try and slip past the first guy."

"What if that doesn't work?" she asked.

"Got your gun ready?"

She nodded and patted the large handbag she carried slung over her shoulder.

"Good. Now we just need a way to get past him without him seeing us." He racked his brain. There was only the wide center aisle running the length of the market. Were their disguises good enough that they could just walk past the man? Not likely. He did not know what kind of look the men had gotten at him and Kaylin, but they would be searching for a man and woman fitting their general descriptions.

"What about this?" Kaylin took his face in her hands, and forcefully pulled him toward her. Their lips met in a long, deep kiss. After an instant of surprise, he cupped her face in his hands as well.

He cracked his eyelid just enough to see the first man move past them on the far side of the aisle. He waited two seconds, then drew away from her. She looked at him with disappointment in her eyes. Whether it was disappointment over the quality or the duration of the kiss, he did not know.

"He's past us," Dane whispered. They set off at a fast walk in the direction of the front entrance, with Kaylin walking just ahead of him. They wove in and out of the shoppers. After a few moments, Dane stole a glance over his shoulder. He could not see their pursuers. Had they lost the two men?

Dane and Kaylin continued at their hurried pace. The front entrance loomed ahead of them. Dane cursed inwardly. No matter how fast they moved, the entrance seemed to get no closer. They dodged and sidestepped as they tried to make their way out of the market. Dane looked back again, painfully aware that too much weaving through the crowd would draw attention.

As he turned around, someone grabbed him from behind by the shoulder. An arm clamped around his neck. He managed to shove Kaylin forward as he was dragged backward.

"Run," he grunted. One of the men shoved past him, going after Kaylin, who was pushing people out of her way as she ran toward the door. Dane kicked out with his right foot, tripping him up. He could do no more for Kaylin until he got rid of the guy who held him in a chokehold.

Palms facing out, he grabbed his assailant by the wrist and inner forearm. He tilted his head forward, and yanked it back up, catching his attacker across the bridge of the nose. As he bashed the man in the nose with the back of his head, he simultaneously pushed up and out with his hands, forcing that attacker's arm up off his throat. Dane drove a solid left elbow into his opponent's stomach, stomped down hard on his right instep, then spun to his left with all of his strength, breaking the man's python grip.

Now facing his opponent, Dane ducked under a right cross and punched the man in the throat, scarcely noticing the cartilage give beneath his knuckles. His attacker, already bleeding from a broken nose, stumbled backward, fighting to suck in breath.

Dane leapt forward, pistoning a right cross to the temple and following with a sweeping kick that took the man's feet out from under him. He fell hard to the ground, arms splayed. Dane turned and sprinted after Kaylin.

The crowd had drawn away from the fight, giving him a clear path to the front door. Up ahead, the second attacker dove at Kaylin's feet, tripping her up. He scrambled up onto all fours and grabbed at her handbag. She shouted and kicked him hard in the face. She continued to impress Dane with her toughness.

Closing the gap, he leaped into the air and delivered a flying kick to the man's chest, knocking him onto his back across a nearby table, sending the display crashing to the ground. From outside, sirens wailed over the din inside the marketplace.

Kaylin's assailant climbed to his feet and drew his gun. Screams erupted from the crowd. For a moment, Dane thought the man was going to open fire inside the crowded marketplace. Instead, he held it threateningly in front of him and dashed out the door. The man with whom Dane had fought rushed by an instant later. Dane drew his own weapon and gave chase, Kaylin following close behind.

Just as he ran outside, a sheriff's department patrol car screeched to a halt directly in front of him. Dane raised his hands above his head, not wanting any misunderstandings. A deputy hopped out of the driver's side door, weapon drawn. Ignoring Dane and Kaylin, he sprinted around the corner of the slave market in the direction the attackers had run. A moment later, Bones clambered out of the passenger side door and followed the deputy.

"Had trouble with the locks," he shouted as he ran by. "Glad you're all right."

Dane could now hear sirens coming from both directions, and soon, three City of Charleston police cars pulled up to the front of the market. Bones and the deputy reappeared together a short while later.

"Lost 'em," Bones said. He holstered his pistol, cursing their still-unidentified assailants.

"Where's Bernie?" Kaylin asked, a note of concern in her voice. The encounter in the slave market did not seem to have fazed her a great deal.

"She's fine," Bones said. "We flagged down the deputy here." He nodded to the man in the tan uniform. "She's in the back of the car." He turned and waved. Through the tinted glass, they saw Bernie waving back.

"The call came over the radio about a running gun battle in the street just as your friend was telling his story," the deputy explained.

"Thanks for bailing us out," Dane replied. He was confused and frustrated. Who were these guys, and what did Maxie have that they wanted so badly?

CHAPTER 6

ey, babe. Thought you'd be home by now."
"*Sorry, I had to make a stop. I've got a surprise for you!"*
"*I hate surprises. What is it?"*
"*Dane! You are no fun at all."*
"*I know. Now, what's my surprise?"*
"*I'm not..."*

Dane bolted up, gasping. Sweat trickled down his cheek, or was it a tear? He didn't care. Wiping it away, he shook his head, as if that could clear the memory from his mind. He hated the dream, and now he hated the sun that had made him drowsy enough to doze off. Rising, he snapped his notebook shut and went back into the condo. He hurried past Bones and Kaylin, who were working at the small kitchen table.

Inside the bathroom, he closed and locked the door, doused his face with cool water, and appraised his reflection in the mirror. He looked a bit older than his thirty-five years. Sun and salt water had weathered his skin and bleached his ash blond hair almost white. The empty look in his green eyes matched the hollowness in his heart: both remnants of the dream. He breathed deep and puffed out his cheeks as he exhaled. Pronouncing himself ready to face the world, he returned to the kitchen.

"Have a nice nap?" Kaylin asked. She looked up from Rienzi's bible and smiled. "Nice digs you and Bones found, by the way. I forgot to tell you earlier."

Fearing for Kaylin's safety, and assuming that their assailants had the resources to discover Dane's identity through the car rental agency, they had packed up and headed for North Carolina, where Bones' cousin, Crazy Charlie, who dealt in used Cadillacs and brand new casinos, owned this vacation condo. They had brought with them everything that might be pertinent to the *Dourado* investigation. At Kaylin's insistence, Bernie had returned to Mississippi to stay with relatives.

"How's the translation coming?" He sat down across from her, forcing his focus onto the case. He was getting good at walling away those memories.

"Challenging. Many of these notes he's written in the margins are so cryptic that I don't know if we'll be able to get any meaning from them out of context. A few of them are pretty interesting, though.

"Here in the book of Genesis, he's underlined a passage which describes a time when *'there were giants on the earth'* who married the *'daughters of men.'*

"Sounds like simple folklore to me," Dane said. Religion and the Bible did not mean much to him anymore. God, if He existed, wasn't paying any attention to what was going on down here.

"That's what Bones said. But here," Kaylin pointed to a phrase jotted in the margin, "Rienzi has written *'could it be?'* in big letters. He's at least considering the possibility that it's more than folklore."

The story of David and Goliath had strange markings around it as well. Dane had not been much of a churchgoer since childhood, but, like most people, he supposed, he was familiar with the tale. A Philistine giant named Goliath had challenged any soldier of Israel to single combat. Only a teenage shepherd named David was up to the challenge. The story went that Goliath, nearly ten feet tall, was armed to the teeth, while David brought with him only a sling, some rocks, and his faith in God. David nailed Goliath in the head, knocking him out. While the giant was down, David cut the off Philistine's head with his own sword. It was actually a gruesome story if you stopped to think about it.

This, like most of the familiar children's bible stories, was one Dane assumed to be less history than fable. It was, in his mind, a story to teach a lesson about not giving up in the face of overwhelming odds, and, of course, to believe in God. Dane was not interested in any of that. God had given up on him a long time ago.

Rienzi had apparently seen something of great value in this story. Goliath's name was underlined in bold strokes. Oddest of all was a strange drawing in the upper right corner of the page. It was a stick figure of some sort. A series of dots of various sizes were linked by straight lines, creating an oddly familiar image.

Kaylin returned to translating Rienzi's notes, while Dane reviewed Maxie's work, and Bones looked over the research Jimmy had done on Rienzi.

"I don't get it," Bones said. "Whatever Rienzi found, he obviously lost it when the *Dourado* sank. That's not exactly a secret. Neither is the location of its sinking."

"What do you not get?" Dane asked.

"Maxie was after the *Dourado*. Why don't the guys who are following us just try to beat us to the ship? What do we have that they need?" He tossed the stack of papers onto the table, and sat back. Hands folded behind his head, he looked up at the ceiling and sighed loudly. "It's enough to make a guy crave a bottle of Jose."

"Not a chance, pal." Dane didn't like Bones when he was drunk. In fact, Bones didn't like Bones when he was drunk. The big man did not reply.

"It's a good question, though," Dane mused. "Maybe they don't know what they're looking for."

"Why would that matter?" Bones asked.

"Think about what we know of the *Dourado*," Dane said, turning the details over in his mind as he spoke. "The wreck turned up some distance from where it sank, with very little of the cargo remaining. Obviously, everything inside the ship spilled out over the course of several miles. There must have been something unique about this one object that made Maxie believe he could find it."

Bones sat in silent contemplation for a minute.

Kaylin looked up from her work, a thoughtful expression on her face. She seemed about to say something, but then shook her head and returned her attention to her task.

"All right," Bones said. "We almost have to assume you're right. Nothing else has made sense so far. If that's the case, then what is it about this object that would make him, or us for that matter, believe that we could find it?" He folded his arms across his chest and fixed Dane with a challenging stare.

Dane had wrestled with this question since reading Rienzi's journal two days earlier. It was crazy to believe they could find a single object that had lain on the seabed for almost two hundred years. But he knew, without a doubt, that Hartford Maxwell was anything but crazy. If Maxie thought something could be done, it most likely was quite possible, if not probable.

"It could be a very large object," Dane said. "Something he could have hoped to find with sonar."

"Like what? A statue?" Bones shook his head. "It could be buried in silt, maybe pitted and misshapen, grown over with all kinds of organisms. It's possible, but I don't like the odds."

"It's not totally out of the question that the cargo could be found, is it?" Kaylin asked, looking up again from her reading. "I remember reading about the discovery of some Roman artifacts. When the ship started taking on water, the crew threw things overboard in an effort to stay afloat. Underwater archaeologists were able to trace the ship's path by the trail of relics scattered across the seabed."

"That was in deep water," Bones protested. "The water between Singapore and Bintan is relatively shallow in most places. Storms and currents have more effect on shallow water wrecks than they do in deep water." He paused for a moment, stroking his chin, his brown eyes narrowed. "Still, you're right. It's not out of the question."

"Okay," Dane said. "Let's explore a completely different line of thinking. What if whoever is after us only knows that Maxie was on to something big, but they don't know what? The fake journal he planted probably wouldn't have mentioned anything about Rienzi or the *Dourado*. They might have discovered right away that the information was no good, and come after Kaylin to get the real story."

"That could be." Bone's frown indicated that he was not satisfied with Dane's idea. "But they're coming at us awfully hard for something they know very little about."

"The information from Jimmy said that the church was ready to excommunicate Rienzi over the ramifications of whatever it was he claimed to have found. We also know from the journal that even the scholars of the day rejected his claims, whatever they were." Dane chose his words carefully. "What if the implications of this discovery would be just as controversial today as they were back then?"

"Too many "what-ifs" for me," Bones groaned, rubbing his temples. "I just don't see…"

"Look at this!" Kaylin's soft voice trembled with excitement. She had returned to her examination of Rienzi's Bible. Dane and Bones leaned toward her. Her slender finger was pointing to a single word, *"vraiment"*, written in the margin next to an underlined passage.

"What does that mean?" Bones asked. "Sounds like some kind of stinky cheese."

"It means 'truly', or 'truthfully'," Dane answered, drawing a raised eyebrow from Kaylin. "I took high school French. Good way to meet hot girls."

Kaylin narrowed her eyes and fixed him with a withering stare. When she was annoyed, she reminded Dane a little bit of Melissa. Melissa… he was definitely not going to travel down that road right now. It was almost sad how easily he could push those thoughts away these days.

"Listen to the passage Rienzi underlined. Kaylin's knuckles whitened as she tightened her grip on the book. *"And the priest said, 'The sword of Goliath the Philistine, whom you killed in the valley of Elah, behold, it is here wrapped in a cloth behind the ephod, if you will take that, take it, for there is none but that here.' And David said, 'There is none like it; give it to me.'"* She slammed the bible closed, dropped it hard on the table and smiled triumphantly.

"So he likes Goliath's sword," Bones said.

"Wait a minute!" Dane snatched Rienzi's journal off the table and flipped to the last page. He read aloud, *"I will say only that truly, there is none like it."*

Bones whistled between his front teeth. "Son of a… Do you think he might have…"

"He found Goliath's sword," Kaylin said. She held the aged bible in trembling hands. "That's what Dad was after. It would stand to reason. Rienzi was the first to rediscover those ancient cities in the Holy Land. Why wouldn't he find biblical artifacts?"

"The sword of Goliath." Bones said the words slowly, as if trying them on for size. "I don't know anything about it."

"Jimmy can run it through NAILS," Dane said. "Right now, we need to get ready for a dive."

CHAPTER 7

D ane sat in the cabin of the *Queen's Ransom*, the ship they had chartered out of Darwin, Australia. They were cruising the northern coast of the island of Bintan in search of the wreck of the *Dourado*.

It had been no mean feat to arrange the needed ship and equipment, as well as a crew, without drawing the attention of the people who were looking for Kaylin. Perhaps Dane was being paranoid, but he had insisted on playing it safe. They had made the arrangements through a friend of a friend: one who asked few questions. An old Navy buddy had arranged transportation for the group on a cargo plane. No tickets were required, and thus no record of their flight. Dane, Bones, and Kaylin had been careful not to use their credit cards, or do anything that might give away their whereabouts or their destination.

He and Bones leaned over a chart, comparing it to the information Jimmy had put together for them. Jimmy had accessed an amazing computer program belonging to the Navy. The program factored in such details as currents, water levels, the terrain of the seabed, and historical weather data. Utilizing this information, along with the ship's last known location, the computer then made a projection, based on the size, shape, and composition of the *Dourado*, of where the wreck could now be found. The program had shown itself to be highly reliable in helping the

Navy locate sunken ships, though to Jimmy's knowledge, the program had only been used to locate vessels of the World War I vintage, or newer. Nevertheless, he and Dane held high hopes that they could locate the missing vessel. Whether or not they would find the sword, however, was another question.

"We're approaching ground zero," Corey Dean called from his seat in front of a computerized display behind them. Corey, a slightly overweight, balding thirty-something was a computer geek with a love of the sea and a nose for treasure. To Dane's knowledge, Corey had never dived, but he was a vital part of the crew.

Dane and Bones moved over to stand on either side of Corey. Staring at the GPS display, Dane felt the same thrill that he always felt when he began a hunt. He never grew weary of it. It was not the treasure that kept him coming back; it was the challenge. He loved putting together clues to solve the mystery. He relished pitting himself and his crew against the sea, daring it to surrender its secrets. He even enjoyed the time consuming sonar sweeps, waiting patiently for that anomaly on the sea floor that would tell him that he had nailed his target.

A few minutes later, they were circling the spot that Jimmy had pinpointed as the probable location of the *Dourado*.

"Slow it down, Matt," Corey called to the helm. "You want to take it a little to port."

"Thanks Corey," Matt deadpanned, "I could never have read the coordinates myself." Matt and Corey enjoyed needling each other almost as much as they enjoyed working together.

"The game is afoot," Bones said, clasping Dane's shoulder. Dane smiled and nodded. Bones tended to enjoy the hunt for about forty-five minutes, after which time he was ready to dive.

"Get the sonar going, and let's start our grid," Dane instructed.

"How big?" Matt asked.

"Let's go a quarter-mile square to start off." Matt nodded, and Dane left the cabin. In the bow of the ship, Kaylin lay stretched out on a deck chair. Her red bikini left little to the imagination. She was chatting with Willis Sanders, a former SEAL comrade whom Dane had brought along as added security.

"Are we there yet?" Willis' shaved head and deep voice reminded Dane of Dennis Haysbert's character Cerrano in the "Major League" movies.

"Yeah, get out," Dane shot back.

"Sorry, Dad." Willis got up, and stretched. Dane noticed with a slight pang of jealousy that Kaylin was admiring his friend's thickly muscled back. "You need to make this quick, man," Willis said. "Black skin don't handle the sun too well."

"I told you, you should've let me pay you by the hour."

"Don't you dare pay that man by the hour," Bones called out as he exited the cabin behind Dane. "He'll ride the clock for all he's worth."

"Go back to the reservation, Tonto," Willis taunted.

Dane laughed at the surprised expression on Kaylin's face. Bones and Willis had always had an odd relationship. Their years spent together in the SEALS had helped them build a bond of trust that allowed them to say anything at all to one another without ever questioning the other's friendship. People who were unaccustomed to their banter sometimes found it disconcerting.

"Gotta' make this dive first," Bones said in a gravelly voice. "Find gold, buy heap much fire water."

"I really don't understand you two." Kaylin peered over her sunglasses as she spoke.

"Don't worry, you're not alone," Dane assured her.

Willis and Bones wandered off, heading for the ship's stern, still insulting one another.

"What happens now?" Kaylin asked.

"To put it simply, Matt draws a square on his map, with our target location in the center. He takes the boat out to one corner of the square, and takes us back and forth, moving a little farther across the square with each pass until we've covered the entire thing. Corey keeps an eye on the sonar, looking for anything that looks like a ship. "

"What if we don't find anything?"

"We cover the same square, but we change directions. If we went east-west the first time, we go north-south the second. If that doesn't work, we expand our grid until we find what we're looking for."

"Sounds time-consuming," she observed, turning over onto her stomach. "Will you get my back?"

"Sure," Dane replied, picking up the sunblock and kneeling beside her, "since we've got such a 'time consuming' job ahead of us."

"You know what I mean." Kaylin gave him a half-hearted slap on the shoulder. "When you hear about hunting for sunken treasure, you imagine it being a lot more exciting than making grids and looking at sonar readouts."

"Fair enough." Dane slathered the lotion across her back, and methodically worked it into her skin.

"Do you do everything that way?"

"Do what?" The question caught him off-guard.

"Systematically. Like the grids, or the way you put lotion on me." She turned over and sat up, looking him in the eye. "Don't you ever just, I don't know, wing it?"

"The Navy pretty much took that out of me," he answered truthfully. It was not the whole truth, but it was all he was willing to reveal.

"You sound like my Dad," Kaylin said, looking away. "He never lightened up."

"I know perfectly well what your father was like. He was a great man."

"Yes, he was." Kaylin turned and looked him directly in the eye. "And he was impossible to please. Everything had to be his way, and it had to be perfect."

"Is that why you're an artist? So you can be in control of what you create?"

"I'm an artist because I appreciate beauty. What do you find beautiful, Dane?" She leaned close to him, her face inches from his, their gaze still locked.

She had hung him a big, fat curveball that he couldn't miss. Bones would have knocked that sucker out of the park. Somehow, he couldn't bring himself to take a swing. A part of him wondered why he didn't feel something for this girl more than physical attraction. He doubted he would ever feel that way for someone again. He sat up straight and looked out across the ocean.

"The sea is beautiful. The way the sunlight dances across the waves. The way the colors play over the surface. I love it."

Kaylin was silent for a moment, then reached out and put a hand on his shoulder. "Is there room in your life for any other love?"

Dane was spared the uncomfortable necessity of answering that question when Corey called from the cabin.

"Hey Maddock, get in here!"

He hopped to his feet and hurried into the cabin. He was relieved that Kaylin did not follow him. He moved to Corey's side. Bones and Willis hurried in and stood behind him.

"What have you got?" Dane asked.

"Sonar picked up something promising. Matt's taking us back for another look."

Dane held his breath, staring at the sonar display, and waited for the ship to pass over the anomaly again.

"We're coming up on it again," Matt said. "Slowing down."

The image coalesced on the sonar.

"Print it," Dane instructed. Corey had already captured the image and sent it to the printer. Dane picked it up and examined it carefully. "It's a ship. Got dimensions for me?"

Corey clicked the mouse a few times.

"Too much of it's submerged, but it could be the *Dourado*."

"All right. We'll send Uma down." Uma was the nickname of their unmanned miniature submersible camera. Bones was a fan of the movie "Pulp Fiction", and felt that Uma was a "sexier" name than the acronym UMSC. That, and UMSC was too reminiscent of the Marine corps acronym.

Bones went back out onto the deck where the little submersible was prepped and ready to go. Just over a meter in length, Uma resembled, if anything, a half-flattened egg with three "eyes" set in the front edge. A camera lens was set in the center, with a headlight on either side. A propeller in a circular frame was attached to either side of the device. The entire frame could rotate forward and back, and each propeller could oscillate inside the frame, controlling the direction of the small craft. Another propeller set in the back provided thrust. Uma could also take on and discharge water for ballast and for diving. He carefully placed the instrument in the water and gave Corey the thumbs-up.

Controlling Uma from his console, Corey instructed the device to take on water in order to accelerate her dive. He flipped on the lights and the camera. The wreck was in relatively shallow water, and soon the sea floor came into view on the monitor. Fish scattered as Uma careened at them, piloted remotely by a maniacally cackling Corey.

"You're enjoying this way too much," Dane told his colleague, placing a hand on his shoulder.

"Don't you want me to enjoy my work?" Corey said, still laughing.

"I want you to find the ship."

"Done," Corey replied. The faint outline of a sunken ship appeared in the distance. Corey picked up the pace, and the bulk of the ship gradually filled the screen.

"It's an old one," Bones whispered.

The wreck had gone down bow-first. The stern stuck out of the silt at a gentle angle, and the outline of much of the ship was discernible beneath the silt. A heavy mast lay half-buried. Everything was encrusted with sea life, but its old age was obvious.

"Take her around the stern," Dane instructed.

Kaylin entered the cabin, and stood next to Bones, as far as she could stand from Dane and still be able to see the monitor. Dane took little notice of her. His eyes were on the prize. As Uma rounded the far side of the wreck, his heart sagged.

"It's not her," he said flatly.

"How can you be sure?" Willis asked.

"See the rudder?"

Willis nodded. Beside him, Bones cursed loudly, and Kaylin hung her head.

"The *Dourado* lost her rudder when she hit the rocks. This ship has her rudder, and her stern appears intact."

Everyone was silent for a moment. Dane took a deep breath and tried to lighten the mood.

"Hey, we didn't really think we were going to find her in five minutes, did we?"

"Hell yes," said Bones. "You know I don't like to wait." He turned and stalked out of the cabin. Willis followed behind, chuckling.

"Bring Uma back up," Dane instructed.

"Gotcha," Corey replied. Under his control, Uma discharged the water she had taken on, and began a steady climb to the surface, where Bones was waiting to fish her out. "Maybe the next one," he sighed.

CHAPTER 8

"Maybe this one is it." Corey's voice was void of all conviction. They had struck out so far: three wrecks that had looked promising, three misses. Such results were not unusual, but it dampened their enthusiasm in any case.

Dane stared at the screen, watching as the submerged ship came into view. This one lay on its side, a gaping hole where the center of the deck had been. The masts were long gone, but it was obviously a wooden sailing ship.

"Can you see the rudder?" Dane asked, as Uma approached the stern.

"Negative," Corey replied. He leaned closer to the screen, narrowing his eyes. "Let me get a little closer."

Uma banked sharply, and dove down toward the ship's rear. Dane leaned closer to the screen. It was difficult to tell beneath the crust of barnacles that coated the wreck, but the ship appeared to be absent its rudder. As the image clarified, Dane's suspicions were confirmed. The rudder was missing.

"Looks good," Dane said. "How close are we to where Jimmy predicted we'd find her?"

Corey consulted a chart, tracing his finger across the lines and moving his lips as he read. Satisfied, he looked back at Dane with a broad grin on his face.

"Spitting distance."

That was all Dane needed to hear. "Let's get wet!" he shouted.

Bones whooped and clapped his hands.

They hastily donned their dive gear. Willis leaned against the rail, a rifle held loosely in one hand, looking at them with undisguised envy.

"Man, I know y'all are gonna' let me dive sometime, right?" He grinned. "No fair letting y'all two have all the fun."

"Let's see how it goes," Dane said, strapping on his dive knife. "For now, we need your eyes up here." He hoped Willis would not, in fact, be needed on the surface, but he was playing it safe.

"I know," Willis replied. "At least I can chill with the lovely lady." He gave Kaylin a playful wink.

Kaylin smiled but did not answer. She took Dane's hand and drew him closer to her. "I know this sounds cheesy, but I hope you can do it, you know, for Dad."

Dane nodded. This one was for Maxie. He hoped they would not let him down. He turned to Bones.

"Ready?"

Bones raised his right hand, palm outward, in a sarcastic imitation of an Indian salute. Dane returned the salute with an upraised middle finger. The two divers sat down on the rail, turned and nodded at one another, and flipped backward into the water.

The water was cool, but not unpleasant and the initial shock wore off quickly. Dane got his bearings. A few strong kicks, and he was shooting down toward the wreck that lay beneath their boat. Bones swam alongside. The faint shafts of sunlight dissolved as they penetrated the depths of the ocean. As the darkness swelled around them, Dane flipped on the dive light strapped to his forehead.

The sunken ship was just barely visible in the distance. Once again, he welcomed the shiver of excitement that ran through his body whenever he dived on a new wreck. They approached it cautiously, careful not to stir up any more silt than necessary. The closer they swam to the ship, the more certain he became that this was the *Dourado*. It was the right size, the right apparent age, and in the right location.

They swam to the stern and made a careful inspection. The rudder had definitely been broken off. Dane ran his hand along the back of the ship, moving it down toward the ocean floor. There it was! He took out his dive knife and gently scraped at the barnacles that coated the ship's exterior. Where the ship disappeared in the silt, a jagged hole gaped like the mouth of an angry leviathan. It was just as Rienzi had described in his journal. He looked at Bones, who nodded his understanding.

Together, they swam toward the gaping hole in the deck. Bones, ever vigilant, peered into the hole, letting his light play around the hold in search of unwelcoming hosts. He gave Dane the "all clear" signal, and let his body drift down into the boat. Dane followed behind.

This was the most dangerous part of a dive. The fine layer of silt that collected on the inside of a sunken vessel could easily be turned into a swirling maelstrom by an incautious flip of a swim fin. A diver could get lost inside an unfamiliar ship, blinded by the blizzard of dirt particles suspended in the water. Dane was not worried, though. He and Bones knew how to take care of themselves.

He looked around at the interior of the ancient ship, but there was little to be seen. Random bumps and bulges beneath the surface of the silt indicated that a few items might remain inside the hold. If this was the *Dourado*, he did not expect to find much inside the ship, given that items had apparently been salvaged from it at the time of its sinking. Still, he wished he could find something, anything to confirm the ship's identity.

Bones waved to him. Dane looked over, and saw his friend gesturing for him to exit the wreck. He trusted his partner enough not to question his judgment. Dane carefully turned and swam out through the hole in the deck. When he reached the outside, he turned about and peered back into the hold.

Bones was looking at something covered in silt. Occasionally he would look up toward Dane, as if fixing his location, then look back down at the spot on the ocean floor. Finally, he began digging in the fine dirt. A massive cloud of silt erupted, spreading as if in slow motion to fill the hold. Dane caught a glimpse of Bones scooping something up before the other diver vanished from sight. He held his position, keeping an eye out for his friend. Moments later, he made his appearance, bursting forth from the cloud that poured out of the ship, his fine mesh dive bag clutched in his hand. He held up the bag for Dane to see. *Coins!* Dane gave his friend the thumbs up, and they headed for the surface.

Breaking the surface, Dane swam to the side of the *Queen's Ransom*, where Willis offered him a helping hand. The muscular, ebony-skinned man lifted him from the water with ease. Bones clambered aboard with help from Kaylin, who wore the expression of an expectant parent.

"Well?" she asked.

"Let's clean those up first," Dane nodded toward Bones' bag of coins. "They ought to tell us a great deal." He tried to suppress his excitement. He had learned a long time ago not to get his hopes up, but right now he had a good feeling.

Retiring to the cabin, Dane and Bones set to cleaning the coins. Patiently they scoured away two hundred years of tarnish and grime. Glints of gold began to peek out from the black circles. Soon, thereafter, details appeared: writing, numbers and images. Forty minutes later, a small pile of gold coins lay gleaming dully in a bowl of preservative solution. Dane fished one out gingerly, held it up to the light and inspected it carefully, turning it around in his fingers.

"Portuguese," he announced. He could feel the grin spreading across his face.

"And the date?" Bones asked, leaning forward, his pearl-white teeth glowing in the sun.

"Hmm…" Dane stalled, letting the tension build. "It's hard to say, but I'm pretty sure…"

"Oh, just tell us, Maddock!" Kaylin scolded.

"Fine," he said, chuckling. "The year of our Lord, 1824."

The room erupted in shouts of joy. Kaylin threw her arms around Dane's neck and gave him a squeeze. Willis, still standing guard on the deck, pumped his fist and smiled.

Bones scooped another coin out of the bowl and examined it. His smile widened. "Portugal, 1821." He raised his clenched fist in triumph.

They repeated the ritual, taking turns examining the coins, until they had inspected every one. The final tally was eleven coins: seven

Portuguese, three Spanish and one French. All were dated four years or more prior to the sinking of the *Dourado*.

"Gentlemen," Dane began, "and lady," he added, "I believe we have found our ship."

CHAPTER 9

The *Dourado* had definitely been salvaged, though they went through the motions of excavating the wreck. By the end of the day, they had found only a few more coins, a statuette, and a few pieces of china. The statuette, in Kaylin's opinion, was further proof that this was the *Dourado*.

"It's definitely Middle-Eastern," she said. "It's very likely something that would have been found in Rienzi's collection."

The following morning, they mapped out their plan to search for the remaining artifacts. Utilizing the same program with which he had predicted the location of the *Dourado*, Jimmy had provided them with a chart that plotted the probable location of the remaining artifacts from the *Dourado's* cargo. The search area was a crescent-shaped swath that swept down in an east-southeast arc from the initial wreck site to the spot where the ship had come to rest.

Dane inspected the chart and shook his head. It was a large area to cover, with artifacts possibly spread thin across the sea floor. He was beginning to feel discouraged, but knew that a negative attitude would kill morale.

"We'll make our way to the wreck site keeping to the center of the target zone." His finger traced a path through the middle of the shaded area, up to Pedra Branca. "We'll run both the side scan sonar and the wave spectrometer, which ought to give us a unique signature for the different objects on the bottom. Once we get to Pedra Branca, we'll take stock of the readings we took along the way, and start our grid in the most promising place."

"Let's do it," Corey said enthusiastically. He was still excited over their success the previous day in locating the wreck.

The others nodded their heads, but Dane could read the skepticism in their faces: skepticism that he shared.

Dane looked out at the rocks of Pedra Branca, so named because of the massive quantities of seagull guano that had colored them permanently white. These very same rocks had claimed the *Dourado*. Somewhere between this spot and the ship's watery grave, he hoped, lay the sword of Goliath.

The readouts they had taken along the way had not painted a hopeful picture. Admittedly, it was only a narrow strip in a wide swath of search area, but the lack of positive hits was worrisome. His cell phone buzzed against his thigh, and he answered it with an annoyed voice.

"Yeah?" he snapped.

"Dane, how's the fishing?" Jimmy asked.

"Haven't caught a thing."

"Want to know why?" the hacker's voice had an odd ring to it, almost as if Jimmy were taunting.

Dane closed his eyes, took a deep breath, exhaled and forced himself to relax. Jimmy could be annoying. A byproduct, Dane supposed, of spending too much time at a computer terminal. "Jim, I'm tired and more than a bit hacked off right now."

"Fine, I'll start making sense. When you asked me to do some checking on the Dourado, I spread out the parameters of the search a bit. You remember how the captain claimed that there was half a million dollars on board?"

"Yes," Dane said.

"Well, I checked on the colonial governor who reported the finding of the Dourado off the shore of Bintan. Seems that not long after the salvage efforts came up short, he found himself one quarter of a million dollars richer, and living high on the hog back in England."

Dane perked up. This was starting to get interesting.

"Next, I followed up on the captain, a Francisco Covilha. He retired to America, a rich man. Settled in New York, and became a benefactor to several museums. Guess what he donated?"

"Artifacts from the Holy Land," Dane groaned. "The son of a gun was in on it with the governor. They hoodwinked Rienzi and made off with everything."

"That's the bad news. The good news is, I can't find any record of a Middle-Eastern sword turning up on the collections of any of the museums he supported."

"So either he held on to it," Dane mused, "or it's still somewhere on the bottom of the ocean."

"Want to hear the weirdest part of all?"

"Not really." Dane didn't think he could take any more of Jimmy's weird news.

"Just for a lark, I ran his name through Nexus, and I got a hit."

Dane felt as if he had been plunged into an icy bath. He sat down clumsily on the deck. His legs were suddenly too weak to support him. "But, Nexus searches *current* periodicals. For Covilha's name to show up in Nexus means…" He paused, trying to get a handle on his thoughts. "Where did his name turn up?"

"In a small item buried in the New York Post. Someone robbed his grave."

CHAPTER 10

Dane gritted his teeth as he weaved the rental car through the snarl of traffic coming out of LaGuardia. He and Kaylin had made the difficult decision the previous day to leave Bones and the crew behind to finish the search, while the two of them pursued Jimmy's lead.

"It says that the police apprehended the man who dug up the grave just as he was opening the coffin," Kaylin read from the article Jimmy had forwarded to them. "He was a local drug addict and trouble maker. He said that a guy he had never met before had paid him a hundred bucks, and promised him a thousand more if he would bring him whatever he found in the coffin." She turned and looked directly at Dane. "Obviously, he didn't have a chance to take anything out of the coffin. That's good news, Maddock." Since their uncomfortable exchange on board the Queen's Ransom, she had taken to calling him only by his last name.

"I know," he muttered. "I just..."

"You're just a cynic," she completed the sentence for him. "How did you get that way, anyhow?"

Dane was not about to tell her the truth. He shrugged and went on with his previous train of thought. "I just worry that this is a sign that whoever has been after you is ahead of us. They knew about the captain before we did."

"Look at it this way. The grave was robbed last week. That means that, as of that time, the sword had not yet been located. Given that they were already working on the captain angle, we can safely eliminate the museum collections, or anything from his estate that might have been on record anywhere. That eliminates a lot of dead-end investigating on our part."

"And leaves us where? What new lead do we have to follow up on? If you're correct, the bad guys have already checked them all out."

"Have faith, my friend." She patted him on the shoulder, a gesture of condescension more than companionship. "My dad used to tell me there's always a stone unturned if you'll only look in the right place."

The problem they faced, Dane thought, though he kept it to himself, was finding the right place.

The basement of the Stoney Falls Public Library was damp and musty, a terrible place to keep books, particularly old ones. The walls were ancient brick, discolored by years of leaks and a light dusting of mold. The shelves looked as if they had been donated by a local warehouse or automotive repair shop. The dull gray metal was pitted by rust and most of the shelves sagged in the middle. Dane scanned the spines of the aged volumes, withdrawing them one by one, flipping them open to the inside cover to look for Francisco Covilha's name.

Jimmy had learned that one of the captain's descendants, a great, great granddaughter, had died without heirs, and had left her estate to her church. The estate included a number of very old books, which the church had in turn donated to the local library.

Given that the woman was the granddaughter of the Covilha's granddaughter, his surname was in no way associated with her in any public records. This, Dane and Kaylin hoped, was a new angle of investigation.

The librarian, Mrs. Meyers, was of little help, expressing first surprise, then suspicion at their interest in the aged volumes. She was reluctant to let the two of them see the books, citing the need to "protect them from damage." Kaylin concocted a story about searching for her ancestors. It was a plot replete with lost loves and parents she had never known. Dane thought it sounded like a pile of crap, but it won over the aging woman who looked to him like she spent her free time with her nose buried in a gothic romance. She took them down into the dark basement and guided them to the area in which the books "should" be kept.

"Found them,' Kaylin called. She held open an old book. Written on the inside cover was the name "Francisco Covilha".

Dane knelt down next to her. A number of very old books were grouped together on the bottom shelf. He pulled out a thick tome that was obviously written in a foreign language. He was not familiar with Portuguese. He opened it at random, and held it out for Kaylin to inspect.

"Portuguese," she said, and returned to paging through her book.

Dane leafed through his own volume, crinkling his nose at the musty smell. Page after page passed across his vision with nothing catching his attention. "What do you hope to find?"

"I don't know," she said. "Truthfully, I had hoped to discover his personal journal. Short of that, maybe we could find some personal correspondence that belonged to him. If the sword was passed down to his descendants, maybe we could find some hints from one of them. I know I'm clutching at straws here, but there has to be a clue somewhere. The sword is too important to have just disappeared."

"Do you think he knew it was important?" Dane asked. "I mean, what if, to him, it was just a sword?

"I can't believe that. Rienzi considered it his greatest discovery. Given how much he liked to boast, I wouldn't be surprised if he bragged to someone on the ship, if not several someones. There would be few secrets from the captain on such a small ship."

Dane could tell by the tone of her voice and the expression on her face that she was picking up steam now.

"Also, Rienzi lost nearly all of his personal papers in the wreck. Allegedly, `some' of them were recovered. I'll bet a lot, if not all of them, were found. Just not by Rienzi."

"So you think the captain knew something about the sword's significance," Dane said.

"I believe he hid it away somewhere. I think the clues are there if we can just find them."

Dane waited for a moment. "Kay, how much of this is about your Dad?"
Kaylin's eyes widened. "Who are you to ask me that?"
"It's just a question." Dane was already wondering why he had gone down this road.
"Have you ever let me in? Have you told me what makes you tick? Shared your pain?" Kaylin stood up, hands on hips. She looked down at him like a vulture circling over dead meat.
He looked her in the eye, staring for several heartbeats. Perhaps he should tell her. "You're right, I..."
"I'm not finished." Tears welled in her eyes. "Yes, it's about my Dad, but the why of it is none of your business. Furthermore, that does not mean I don't believe in what we're doing. I know we can find the sword!"
"Fine, I'm sorry." He did not truly feel like baring his soul, and she seemed to be in no mood to make nice. He returned to the book he had been looking at, letting an uneasy silence fall over them. Something caught his attention, and he chuckled. Kaylin flashed him a resentful look, so he explained quickly. "Somebody was a doodler."
On one page, on the bottom inside corner, was a rough sketch of a large tree, perhaps an oak. He held up the book for her to inspect. She nodded and returned to her work. Dane shrugged and flipped through the remaining pages. He saw nothing else of interest, so he set the book aside, and selected another. This one was in English, but the date, if he remembered his Roman numerals correctly, marked it as old enough to possibly have been part of Francisco Covilha's collection. Again, nothing but a small drawing on a random page in the book's center. This one was drawn on the same spot on the page, the bottom left corner next to the spine. Instead of a tree, this one was a rough illustration of what appeared to be a wrought-iron fence. He inspected it for a moment, and then scanned the remainder of the pages before placing this book atop the other.
"Here's another," Kaylin said. "It looks like some sort of weird hat, or something."

"It's a sinking ship," Dane corrected. He pointed to the wavy line that she had apparently taken to be the brim of the hat. "This is the water."

"Now I see it," she said, gazing at it a bit longer. "I wonder if the *Dourado* weighed on his mind." She suddenly cocked her head to the side, like a dog hearing a strange noise. "Wait a minute. Isn't the captain supposed to go down with his ship?"

"Not this captain," Dane said. "It's kind of strange. Usually, the captain would make certain that everyone else is safe before he abandoned ship. Sometimes, if the ship went down too fast, he really did go down with the ship."

"If you believe Rienzi's story, he was the last one off the ship, and Covilha would have left more people aboard if Rienzi hadn't saved them." Kaylin looked thoughtfully up at the ceiling.

Dane caught himself admiring the slender blonde's profile, and had to shake his head to clear the haze.

"Covilha didn't exactly act ethically in stealing Rienzi's loot, either. If he had any sort of conscience, I wouldn't be surprised if the memory of the *Dourado* shadowed him all the way to the grave." Dane understood how one day could darken the rest of one's life. "Guilt is a terrible thing."

Kaylin nodded but did not answer. She seemed lost in her own thoughts. Obviously, she was haunted by her own demons, apparently relating to her father.

Dane pulled three more books off the shelf, and sat cross-legged on the floor. He was not optimistic about finding anything meaningful in these volumes, though some of them had obviously belonged to the captain. The first book on the stack he flipped over and went through it backward, just for a change of pace. His optimism, which had not been high to begin with, continued to wane as he looked at every page, and again found only a doodle.

"This is getting weird," Kaylin said. She held a slim book in her hands. The front cover, old and worn, simply read '*Poems*'.

Dane looked up at her, waiting for her to elaborate.

"Do all of your books have a drawing in them?" she asked, frowning and pursing her lips.

"So far," he replied, uncertain of her train of thought.

"Do all of them only have a single drawing on the bottom left hand of the page?" She held up her book to illustrate.

He nodded, thinking. It was a little odd. If the man were a doodler, one would think he would draw in various places in each book. Another thought occurred to him.

"Come to think of it, books were usually treated with respect back then, weren't they?" He did not wait for her to reply. "It's strange that a grown man, even one who absent-mindedly draws pictures, would sketch childish cartoons in his books."

Kaylin stared at him, and odd expression on her face.

"Now what?"

"Isn't it even stranger," she said slowly, as if thinking her way through the problem as she spoke, "that he always drew on page one hundred twenty-five?"

Dane picked up the stack of books he had already gone through, and added them to the pile in his lap. He checked them. Each of them had a small sketch drawn in the bottom left corner of page one hundred twenty-five. Obviously there was some significance, but it escaped him at the moment.

"I think we should copy these down," Kaylin said. She checked her watch. "I'll do it. You go through the rest of these books and see what you can find."

"I love it when you boss me around," Dane teased, hoping to melt the icy wall that had risen between them. She responded with a smile that, though tired, seemed sincere enough.

Dane searched through the remainder of the books on the shelf while Kaylin set herself to the task of copying the sketches onto a notepad she had brought along. As he flipped through the last book, this one with no drawing in it, a piece of paper, folded in half and yellowed with age, fell onto the floor. He picked it up and opened it, being careful not to tear it.

The ink was badly faded. The words, barely discernable, were written in a tight, choppy script. The letter was in Portuguese; he had now looked at enough books written in that language to recognize it easily. He could not translate the writing, but one word instantly leapt out at him: *Dourado*.

He was about to share his discovery with Kaylin when the sound of footsteps rang hollow from the nearby stairwell. The librarian appeared in the doorway, a look of apprehension on her pallid face. Dane hastily turned his back to the woman and slipped the paper inside his jacket pocket as he re-shelved the book.

"I'm sorry to interrupt you," the librarian said, sounding anything but sorry, "but the library will be closing soon."

"We were just finishing," Kaylin said, her voice syrupy. "Thank you so much for your help today, Mrs. Meyers."

She was really laying it on thick, Dane mused. He would have to ask her why she was never that sweet to him. Then again, he had upset her enough for one day.

"I also thought you might like to know that a man is upstairs looking for you," Mrs. Meyers added. Her voice carried a tone of suspicion, bordering on judgment.

Dane and Kaylin exchanged glances. This was an unexpected and unpleasant surprise..

"What does he look like?" Dane asked, trying to keep his tone conversational.

"Short brown hair, average height, expensive sunglasses that he is too rude to take off." As the woman rattled off the details, Dane could see why she made a good librarian. "Blue oxford cloth shirt, navy pants, fair skin, sort of thin."

He souded to Dane like one of the guys that had pursued them in Charleston.

"Thank you," Kaylin interrupted. "So, you didn't tell him we were down here?"

"No," the woman replied, blushing a bit. "To tell you the truth, I didn't care for his manner. He was rather abrupt. I told him that I was certain you had left. He asked where I had seen you last. I told him you had been checking the census records up on the second floor. He went up there looking for you up there. Did not even thank me." She folded her hands across her chest and frowned at Dane, as if the man's behavior were somehow Dane's fault.

"I'm sorry about that, Ma'am," Dane said. He racked his brain for a good story, but he couldn't think of anything.

"It's my ex-boyfriend." Kaylin entered the conversation smoothly. "It's embarrassing, but he's been stalking me. I can't seem to go anywhere without him finding me. I have a restraining order against him."

That was all the librarian needed to hear. Her eyes flared and she stood up ramrod-straight.

"That is just terrible. One of our regular patrons was stalking me just last summer," she shook her head and tapped her foot on the concrete floor. "I thought I was going to have to turn him over to the proper authorities."

Dane struggled not to smile at the thought of anyone stalking this dowdy old woman.

"Is that so?" he asked, keeping his facial muscles in firm check.

"I shall go back to my desk and call the police," the woman said firmly. "There is a utility entrance in the back. I will let the two of you out there."

They thanked her profusely, and began picking up the books they had been looking through.

"Don't you mind those. I will reshelve them later." The librarian shooed them out of the room, down a narrow hallway, and up a small flight of stairs to a metal door. She unlocked it and ushered them out.

"Are you going to be all right?" Kaylin asked the woman. They certainly did not want the woman's kind aid to cause trouble for her later. She was a bystander in all this.

"I'll be right as rain," the woman replied firmly. From the look on her face and the tone of her voice, Dane did not doubt her for one moment.

As they hurried to their car, Dane's cell phone beeped once, indicating he'd received a voice mail message. As he entered the car and turned the ignition, he retrieved his message. Apparently, he had not been able to get reception in the basement. There was static on the other end, then shouting, and a sound like a gunshot. *"Maddock!"* a strained voice shouted, then a loud thump. The message ended.

"You look like you're going to be sick," Kaylin said. "What's the matter?"

Dane swallowed hard. For a moment he thought he might actually prove her right, and lose his lunch right there. "That was a voice mail from Corey. Something's wrong."

CHAPTER 11

Bones looked up at the man who was holding him hostage in the cabin of the *Queen's Ransom*. Thin nylon rope held his wrists together tight behind his back, cutting into his skin, and was knotted around his ankles. Next to him, Matt was similarly bound. Corey was lay unconscious on the floor, blood trickling from a wound he had suffered when one of the attackers had hit him in the head with the butt of a rifle.

"You have found the *Dourado*, no?" his captor asked in heavily accented English.

Bones did not reply. He looked up at the man with what he hoped was a defiant glare.

His captor merely smiled and shook his head.

"My friend, we can play games all day. But I promise you, sooner or later, you will answer my questions." He knelt down in front of Bones, and smiled. "Oh yes, you will tell me everything I want to know."

"And then what? You'll kill me." Bones had no illusions about the situation, and would not believe any false promises the man or any of his cohorts might make.

"Yes," the man said, taking a long drag off his cigarette.

Bones was taken aback by the man's candor.

"The question is, do you want your last hours to be painful, or pleasant? If you cooperate, I promise you will die of a bullet to the back of the skull. Quick. Painless."

Bones stared at him. The man seemed to be waiting for him to ask what would happen if he did not cooperate. He wasn't about to give the jerk the pleasure.

"What if we don't cooperate?" Corey asked. He was trying to sound tough, but Bones could hear the strain in his voice.

"You will be made to suffer. And then you will die in the most painful way imaginable." The man stubbed out his cigarette on the bottom of his shoe, and flicked the butt out of the cabin door and onto the deck.

Bones eyed him. The man was tanned, with black hair and a slightly oily complexion. His face was wide, with eyes set a bit too far apart. He paced back and forth in front of his captives, his hands folded behind his back.

"I believe what I shall do is to begin with you," he nodded toward Corey. "Your friend shall watch what we do to you. Perhaps that will convince him to talk to us. Once we have finished with you, we will revive your colleague and deal with him."

"Take me first," Bones said. "Neither of them knows anything. Leave them out of it."

"Oh no, my friend." The man leaned down close to Bones' face. "I know the reputation of the American Indian. You can remove your spirit from your body, and watch your own torture, even death, dispassionately. I am wagering that your weakness is that you cannot watch the suffering of your friends with the same lack of concern." He smiled, confident in his theory.

"You don't really believe that fairy tale crap, do you? That's just something we made up to scare white people," Bones said. "Besides, what can we tell you, anyway? We're a research..." A loud pop burst in his ear as the man kicked him in the side of the head.

"We will not make satisfactory progress if you insist on playing games." He looked at Bones, with empty, dispassionate eyes. After a moment, he casually removed the pack of cigarettes from his breast pocked and shook out another of the cancer sticks into his palm. The pack was white with a black sailing ship set in front of a blue wheel. They were Esportazione's, an Italian brand. The armed peon rushed from the cabin door he had been guarding, and lit the man's cigarette with a hastily produced Zippo. The oily man took a deep draw, held the smoke in for a moment, and slowly exhaled.

"I will give you one last chance," the man said, walking over to where Corey sat. He held the cigarette near Corey's cheek. The computer wiz winced and turned his head away from the glowing ash.

"First," the man said in a calm, conversational tone, "did you find the wreck of the *Dourado*?"

"Yes," Bones replied. He saw no point in denying it since the man obviously already knew. Now, he needed to buy time until Willis could do something to help them. The two of them had been underwater when the attack came. Bones had surfaced only to find guns drawn on him. They hauled him aboard, relieved him of his dive knife, and tied him up. He cursed his own laxness. Things had proceeded so uneventfully up to this point that he had not insisted that Willis stand guard, convinced there was no danger.

"We found it two days ago. You can see the spot on the chart over there," he nodded toward Corey's instrument panel, above which a chart of the area between Bintan and Singapore was mapped. Straight pins were pressed into the map, marking the location of the *Dourado*, the probable site of the sinking, and places in between where they had successfully recovered artifacts from the ship. These had been few and far between.

The man glanced toward the chart, then back at Bones. He seemed satisfied with the answer.

"What did you find?"

"Gold coins, a few statues, stuff that you'd expect to find on a ship." Where was Willis? "The *Dourado* was salvaged years ago. There's almost nothing left."

The man thought about this for a minute as he took another long drag off his cigarette. He turned and blew the smoke in Corey's face, then held the ash close to Corey's neck. "You are certain?"

Bones nodded, his heart racing. If these people knew about the *Dourado*, then they had to know that the ship had been salvaged. That was part of the historical record. It was the other information, about the sword and the captain that he needed to protect.

"Can I at least know your name?" Bones asked. He had to stall as much as possible.

"I do not see the harm in revealing my name to a dead man. My name is Angelo."

"Thanks, Angelo," he said, feigning friendliness. "Good to know you. My name is.."

"Your name is Uriah Bonebrake. You work with Dane Maddock on the *Sea Foam*, along with Matthew Barnaby and Corey Dean. At present, you are working for Kaylin Maxwell."

"Nice job," Bones said. "I was never much for homework, myself. I just copied off of the cute girls."

"Enough of this." Angelo made a slashing motion with his hand. "After you finished your excavation of the wreck of the *Dourado*, what did you do next?"

Bones took a deep breath and exhaled slowly, trying to appear as if he were debating whether or not to answer the question. Anything to stall.

"We went to the spot you see marked on that chart. It's the pin farthest to the northwest. That's where we think the *Dourado* went down."

"And then?" Angelo fixed him with an impatient glare, the cigarette dangling between his fingers burning down slowly.

"We started scanning and making short dives at places in between the site of the sinking and her present location." Behind his back, he worked at the ropes. He had tensed his arms as much as he could while they were tying his hands together, but the bonds were on tight. He didn't have much wiggle room.

"What have you found on these dives?" Angelo leaned toward him, an intense look in his eyes.

"Again, almost nothing. We figure the cargo gradually spilled out onto the seabed between the place the ship went down and the place it turned up off of Bintan several days later. Over time, the currents will have scattered it pretty wide.

Angelo, without changing expression, buried the cigarette into the exposed flesh of Corey's upper arm. Corey screamed, as much in surprise, Bones supposed, as from pain.

"What the hell did you do that for?" Bones snarled, jerking in his bonds.

"I did not ask you what you think happened to the cargo. I asked what you found. You will answer me specifically and explicitly." Angelo's eyes now held a slightly demented look.

"Fine." Bones pretended to rack his brain, though their take had been so small that he could probably rattle off the list without a second thought. "Two statues, both in poor condition. Each of Middle Eastern origin."

"What country?" Angelo snapped.

"Not my specialty." Bones shrugged, using the motion to mask his struggling with his bonds. "We'll have them checked out when we get back."

"No. *We* will have them checked out when *we* return. You will not be returning."

"Whatever," Bones pretended to dismiss Angelo's words with a shrug, using the motion to twist against the ropes around his wrist. He felt them give just a bit. "We also found a small, ornated wooden box that had probably contained someone's personal papers once upon a time."

"There were no papers?" Angelo leaned toward him again, frowning as he spoke. Suspicion dripped from his words. "You are absolutely certain of this? I caution you. No attempt to deceive me will work. You will succeed only in making your friend suffer."

"It was a wooden box, genius," Bones said. "It filled with water. Whatever was in there has pretty much dissolved into some mush in one of the corners. You're welcome to scrape it off and try to read it if you like."

For a moment, Bones thought that Angelo was going to punch him, or burn Corey again, but the dark-haired man relaxed visibly and nodded for him to continue.

"Seven coins... no, eight...no, it was seven." He was running out of stalling tactics.

"Seven or eight. I do not care! Get on with it."

"Sorry, you said to be explicit." Bones had worked his wrists looser. He had to be careful to keep Angelo from noticing any movement. "Beyond that, we've found some dishes, a pistol, and a small cannon that might have been kept aboard the *Dourado* for defense, but we aren't sure about that. We couldn't have raised it, anyway. That's everything." Having finished his list, he stared at Angelo defiantly. "What else do you want to know."

"What else?" The man seemed agitated now. He stamped his foot and crossed his arms in front of his chest.

"I told you, that's everything," Bones said. "Of course, we're not finished with our search. Who knows what else we'll find if you let us keep working?"

Angelo did not seem satisfied with the answer. He began pacing again. After a moment, he stopped and scrutinized the map on the wall. He dropped what was left of his cigarette on the floor, and put his finger on the site of the wreck. Silently he traced the path they had marked out on the map.

"Where is the rest of your crew?" He asked, almost nonchalantly. Bones did not know how to respond. Angelo didn't wait long before he continued. "Come now. I know that you are missing both Mr. Maddock and Ms. Maxwell."

Bones relaxed a bit. So they didn't know about Willis. That was a point for their side.

"They went back to the states." He wouldn't be surprised if the guy had the resources to know where they had gone.

"Why did they go back?" His voice took on an impatient tone.

"There was a death. Someone in Kaylin's family. I think it was maybe her cousin or somebody. Dane went with her, since she's been attacked before." He stared intensely at Angelo. "But I guess I don't have to tell you that."

"You are not being completely truthful with me, Mr. Bonebrake," Angelo said. "Mr. Maddock and Ms. Maxwell left because you found what you were looking for, didn't they?"

"What?" Bones didn't know what else to say.

"You were left behind as a ruse, continuing the search so it would seem to outsiders that you had not found that for which you were searching."

"We're not looking for any one thing." Bones' searched for a way to stall Angelo further. "We're just excavating the wreck. Kaylin's father had researched it all of his life. It was his pet project, and she wanted to finish what he started."

Angelo produces his own lighter, lit another cigarette and moved back to Corey's side. He knelt down and held the burning end next to Corey's left eye. He gripped Corey's hair in the other hand.

"My patience is at an end. I will know what you found, or I will blind this man"

"We didn't find anything," Corey grunted, trying to jerk his head away. "He's telling you the truth. Everything we've found is on board the ship."

Angelo thought this over. He did not, however, move the cigarette away from Corey's head or loosen his grip. "For argument's sake, let us say that I believe you. Answer this, Mr. Bonebrake; what is it you expected to find on this wreck? And no more lies about not looking for one specific thing. There was something special aboard the *Dourado*. Tell me what it was."

Bones could tell that the time for stalling was at an end. As he watched Angelo push the hot ash of the cigarette ever closer to his friend's eye, he hoped Willis had come up with a plan.

CHAPTER 12

I can't get any of them." Dane snapped his phone closed and slammed it down on the table. "I don't know what's going on!"

"We've notified the authorities in Singapore. There's nothing else we can do," Kaylin said. "Besides, if you smash your cell, they definitely won't be calling you anytime soon."

"I shouldn't have left them," he muttered, the feeling of helplessness was driving him crazy. Her assurances didn't make him feel any better. He stood up and walked across the room they had rented under a false name in a rundown roadside inn. Reaching the far wall, he turned and stalked back to the window. "I need to do something. I can't stand waiting around like this."

"You're not accomplishing anything by walking around the room. Sit down and help me with this letter." She sat at a small table, rickety and badly stained, comparing the letter Dane had found against a Portuguese-English dictionary they had picked up at a local bookstore.

"I don't know any of that stuff," he grumbled. He slumped down in the cheap, fake leather chair across from her, feeling every bump against his back. He folded his arms across his chest, and stared. He knew he was acting childish, but the frustration he felt at being unable to help his friends, or even know what was wrong with them, was almost more than he could bear. But he also realized it was pointless to sit and complain about something over which he had no control.

"What do you want me to do?"

"Here. See what you can make of these." Kaylin slid her notebook across the table to him.

He flipped it open to her copies of the sketches they had found in Covilha's books. His eyes took them in with only moderate interest. He exhaled long and loud, sighing impatiently.

"I don't know what we're going to learn from these," he complained. They were just doodles, after all.

"And you never will if you don't shut up and get to work," Kaylin snapped, not looking up at him.

"Fine." She was right, but he did not like to be reminded of it. He looked them over again, this time more slowly. The sinking ship was probably the *Dourado*. But what to make of the others? A wrought iron fence, an old house, a river, an oak tree, a tombstone... He turned the page. There were more on this sheet, but nothing caught his eye as being of particular significance. What could they mean, if anything? And why were they all written on page one hundred twenty-five? After mulling it over for a few long, boring minutes, he flipped the notebook closed and pushed it back toward Kaylin.

"How's your translation coming?" he asked, more to fill the silence than because he expected her to have discovered anything of significance so soon.

"Slowly," she replied. "If I've got this right, it's an unfinished letter to his mistress. He mentions someone named Domenic, and talks about his regrets."

"Maybe they had a son together?" Dane asked.

"Could be. The mention of the *Dourado* isn't of much significance. He just talks about how his life changed when the *Dourado* went down 'on that January night.' " She bit her lip and looked up another word.

Something in her statement seemed to trip a switch in Dane's subconscious.

"Say that again."

"What?" She looked at him with a blank expression.

"That last part about the *Dourado*," he said, closing his eyes and pressing his hands to his temples. "Read it back to me."

"All right. *I tell you, darling, my life was forever changed when the Dourado went down that dark January night.' '*"

"What date, exactly, did the *Dourado* go down?" His heart beat faster as a wave of adrenalin surged through him.

Kaylin picked up another notebook and turned to one of the first pages. "January twenty-fifth. Why do you ask?"

"That's it!" He pounded his fist on the table. "January twenty-fifth! One-twenty-five."

"Page one twenty-five!" she cried with delight. "You're right. That's got to be it!" She pushed the letter away, grabbed the notebook, and scooted her chair around the table so that she could look at the sketches along with him.

"Now that we're fairly certain these symbols are tied in with the *Dourado*, we need to figure out what he was trying to tell us." Dane said, feeling confident for the first time since getting Corey's cry for help.

"Could it be a cipher of some sort?" Kaylin asked.

"I don't think so. There aren't enough icons to cover much of the alphabet, and nothing repeats."

"Perhaps it's more complicated than that. Maybe we take the words for these different things, combine all the letters, and rearrange them to spell out a message?"

Dane turned and stared at her, his eyes wrinkled in a frown. "How in the world do you think of these things?"

She shrugged. "Ciphers were common back then, and some of them were pretty complicated."

"I hope that isn't the deal," Dane said. "It would be hard enough to unscramble in English, but if he did the cipher in Portuguese…" He left the rest unsaid, as understanding dawned on her face.

"Does your friend have access to a computer program that could decrypt a message like this?"

"First of all, we aren't sure that there is a message to decode." He was growing frustrated again, and with the feeling came renewed concerns about Bones and the crew. He pushed away from the table. "I want to get out of here. Let's get a drink."

"I'm really not in the mood for a drink," she said.

"Fine, you can watch me." He grabbed his jacket and keys, and left the room without waiting to see if she was following.

"Maddock, wait a minute!" she called.

Something in her voice, some underlying tone of revelation, made him turn around.

"What if we're making this too complicated? What if it's just a simple map?"

Maps he understood. Curious, he returned to the table and stood looking down over her shoulder.

"The sinking ship is probably the *Dourado*, so that's most likely the first symbol in the sequence. Maybe these other images represent real places. Put the clues in the right order, they lead us to the sword!" Her eyes were bright, her face positively aglow. Dane stared at her for a moment, admiring her fresh, youthful beauty.

"Are you still with me?" she said, waving her hand in front of his face.

"Oh, sorry, just thinking." Dane shook his head, trying to get his thoughts back on to the subject. Guilt soured in his stomach as he thought of Melissa. "If they're real places, what is this thing?" He pointed to a drawing of four arrows emerging at right angles to each other from a central point, pointing up, down, left, and right. Another smaller arrow pointed down and to the right at an odd angle.

"What's the matter, sailor boy? Never seen a compass before?" She smiled up at him, and he grinned in spite of himself.

"Fine, you got me on that one." He settled back in to the chair he had vacated moments before. "The problem I see is that so many of these drawings are too generic. How many streams are around here? Or wrought iron fences? Where do we even start?"

"How about the house? It's a little more detailed than the other images."

Dane looked at the sketch. It was certainly distinctive, with a large porch running across the front and wrapping around the right side. An odd, tower-like architectural feature graced the front left corner. Chimneys peeked up from either side of the steeply pitched roof. Two second- floor windows extruded Cape Cod-style from the front of the roof. Ornamentation had been sketched in to the porch rails and posts. It might be possible to locate the house. It was as good a way as any to pass the time until he could find out what happened to Bones and the crew.

CHAPTER 13

Antonio stepped away from the door of the cabin. Angelo had everything under control inside, while Louis and Vincent patrolled the deck. He pulled a brand new pack of cigarettes out of his pocket and slapped the bottom of the box a few times before removing the wrapper. It was a personal tradition of his; bring a new pack on the job, and do not open it until the work is done.

This one had been too easy. The people on board had not been expecting anything out of the ordinary, and the diver who had been down at the time had not heard them coming. He was supposed to have been a SEAL, but their reputations must have been exaggerated; they had subdued him quickly. According to Angelo, two of the crew members were missing.

It would not have mattered if the entire crew had been there, Antonio thought, smiling. They had taken their victims completely by surprise.

"And to think they wanted to send Stefan," he said to no one in particular. Stefan was good, there was no doubt, but Angelo's team, of which Antonio was a member, was good as well. If only their superiors would let go of their foolish attachment to Stefan. Antonio hated being underestimated.

He leaned against the rail and admired their speedboat. It was a sleek model with a low profile and a powerful but nearly silent engine. The hull was painted a swirl of blues and greens, allowing it to blend in with the sea. A bulletproof, green-tinted windshield swept back in a tight curve. It was a beautiful piece of workmanship.

A loud splash from the stern drew his attention. He looked back, but saw nothing. A porpoise, perhaps? He scanned the horizon. The blue-green waters were choppy today, and devoid of any crafts other than their own and the one they now controlled. There had not been any since they had taken control of the boat. He shrugged and dug out his lighter.

Antonio thumbed the lighter and raised it only to freeze. It suddenly occurred to him that when he had looked to the stern it had been empty. Had not Vincent been sitting there just a minute ago? Surely, he would not fall in. It seemed a bit strange. Perhaps his comrade was in the bow with Louie.

Antonio lit his cigarette, inhaled deeply and blew a cloud of smoke into the air. He made the short walk around the ship's bow, skirting the exterior of the cabin and stopped short. The bow was empty as well. His jaw fell and the burning cigarette dropped to the deck.

He looked around. Where had they gone? He needed to tell Angelo. He hurried to the cabin door but the sound of Angelo's voice, raised in anger, gave him pause. He needed to at least check the situation out before reporting to his boss that half of their team was missing. He did not want to think about delivering such a message. Angelo's was a prodigious temper.

Perhaps they were in the cabin. He wanted to check, but that would risk incurring his leader's wrath. He thought for a minute. No, they could not be in the cabin. He would have seen or heard at least one of them pass by. Something was very strange here. He turned a complete circle, reassuring himself that there was nothing on the horizon. There had to be an explanation. Rifle firmly in his grip, he walked quickly to the stern where he had last seen Vincent. He peered over the rail and saw nothing. He turned back toward the bow of the ship and scanned the entire deck. Where were they?

A cold, wet hand clamped down hard across his mouth, and he felt himself yanked backward. Frantically he dropped his weapon and grabbed for the railing, trying to prevent himself from tumbling into the sea. A hot, searing pain shot across his throat, and consciousness fled as he fell into the cold, dead arms of the sea.

Bones worked furiously to free his wrists. On the other side of the cabin, Angelo had duct taped Corey into a chair, and had begun his questioning. Corey was holding out, denying that they were after anything other than whatever could be salvaged from the *Dourado*. Angelo stood, cursing loudly and shouting.

"You are lying to me!" he cried, shaking his fist in the crewman's face. "You know it, I know it, and your soon-to-be-dead Indian friend knows it as well." He drew an automatic pistol from an ankle holster and aimed it at one of Corey's fleshy white thighs. "I warned you. Perhaps I can impress upon you just how serious I am."

"No!" Bones shouted, scooting across the floor toward their captor and his intended victim. "Leave him alone!"

Angelo turned toward him, smirked, then returned his attention to Corey. As he turned, something caught his eye, and he looked to the deck with an expression of disbelief on his face. He grunted in surprise, then seemed to regain his composure, and leveled his pistol toward some unseen target.

Willis! Bones had almost reached Angelo's side. Rolling onto his back, he raised his feet, still bound together, and struck with both heels, driving them into the side of Angelo's knee.

There was a loud pop, and Angelo cried out in pain as his knee buckled under the force of Bone's kick. His arm flew up, and his shot went through the ceiling as a blue and black blur hurtled through the cabin door, bowling him over.

Willis, clad in his wetsuit, rode Angelo to the floor. He held the man's right wrist with his left hand. He clutched a dive knife in his right. A faint smear of blood, apparently not his own, stained the chest of his blue neoprene suit.

Angelo frantically fired off a shot that flew harmlessly through the cabin roof. He held Willis' thick ebony wrist, struggling to keep the stronger man from bringing the knife down on him. He shifted under the black man's weight, and brought his left knee up hard between Willis' legs.

The former SEAL grunted. Bones saw his friend's face contort in pain. His grip slipped ever so slightly on Angelo's gun hand, and his knife ceased its steady downward descent. Bones twisted and contorted, and finally succeeded in freeing one wrist. There was no time to loose the bonds that held his ankles. He pushed himself up to his feet, and jumped.

Javelin had been his sport in high school, but his standing long jump hadn't been too bad. He came down feet-first with his full weight on Angelo's face, hearing the satisfying crunch of cheekbones snapping, and the squeal of pain that leaked from the man's ruined face. The squeal turned to a shriek as Willis buried his knife in Angelo's chest.

Their former captor's struggles ceased as life drained from his body along with his blood, bright red on the stark white cabin floor. Willis lurched to his feet and cut the ropes from Bones' legs, then set about freeing Corey while Bones worked on reviving Matt.

"What kept you?" Bones called over his shoulder as he tended his crewman's wounded head. "I got so tired of waiting for you I was going to take care of them myself, but then you dragged your tail in at the last minute and played hero."

"Grateful as always, yo," Willis observed. "I had to wait until they split up and weren't paying attention. The guy in the bow made it easy for me. I guess he heard me and thought it was a fish, because he leaned way over the rail. I grabbed him by the collar, put my knife in his throat, and eased him on into the water."

"How did you 'ease' a two-hundred pound man down from the bow while you were still in the water?"

"I'm good," Willis replied firmly. He stared at Bones for a moment, and then rolled his eyes. "Maybe there was a splash, but it wasn't a big one. Got the others the same way."

Bones was impressed. "Divide and conquer. Not bad for a hired hand."

"You didn't warn me this hired hand was going to be a hired gun. My salary demands just skyrocketed."

"Talk to Dane," Bones said. "He's the boss."

After tending to their colleagues, Bones and Willis searched Angelo's body for identification. They were not surprised to find that he was clean. His black jumpsuit was also void of identifying marks. The only personal object he carried was a silver necklace that was tucked into his left pocked. Bones held it aloft.

A silver pendant dangled from the chain. It was a crucifix unlike any he had ever seen. In the place of the cross, the Christ figure, his face staring angrily forward, hung from crossed swords.

"Jesus," Willis whispered.

Bones felt the blood drain from his face. He stared at the object for a moment, then said the one thing that came to his mind.

"Literally."

CHAPTER 14

D ane rapped smartly on the door of the small white cottage. He turned and looked up and down the street. It was a typical pre-World War II neighborhood. The long, narrow thoroughfare was lined with ancient oaks, the roots of some of which were breaking through the sidewalk in places. All of the houses appeared to be in good repair, with neatly trimmed lawns, each bordered by a manicured row of hedge. He should have felt at peace in such surroundings, but he was not. Though he was relieved to have learned that his crew was safe, his senses were on heightened alert. The people who were after them were every bit as dangerous as he had feared. They were well armed, and seemingly had the resources to track their every move.

An elderly woman answered the door. Dane immediately took notice of her sharp, blue eyes. The intensity of her stare was hawk-like, and contrasted with her gently lined face, soft white hair and grandmotherly frock. She regarded them through the screen with an undisguised look of suspicion.

"Mrs. Russell? My name is Dane. This is my friend, Kaylin. Ms. Meyers from the library called you about our visit?"

The woman's face brightened. "Oh, yes. Come in." She pushed the screen door open wide, and motioned them inside. They settled onto an overstuffed love seat. Their host pulled up a rocking chair in front of them. "I understand you're doing some genealogical research?"

"Yes," Kaylin lied. "We've found some drawings in an old family book, and were wondering if you might recognize this house." She held her notebook open for the woman's inspection.

The old woman leaned forward, her nose nearly touching the page. After a moment, she leaned far back and peered down her nose at the picture. She shook her head.

"No, I fear I have never seen that house. I have been the unofficial town historian for fifty-three years. I know most every old house in town. That does not mean, however" she added, noticing Kaylin lower her head in disappointment, "that it was never here. Quite a few old homes were torn down in the forties and fifties." She suddenly cocked her head and stared at the page again. "May I see that notebook?"

Kaylin handed it over, and the historian inspected it carefully.

"These other drawings remind me of the Riverbend Cemetery north of town. There is a stream that runs by it, an old wrought iron fence in the front, and there used to be a giant oak tree on a hill in the center of it. There is a print of it from the nineteenth century that hangs in the funeral home in town."

"Is there a covered bridge?" Kaylin asked, her voice raising an octave. She leaned forward and turned to the next page of the notebook, where she had copied a picture of such a bridge.

"Why, yes there is," Mrs. Russell replied. "I see the gravestone here," she pointed to the sketch. "Is one of your ancestors buried in this cemetery?"

"That's what we're wondering," Dane replied hesitantly. "We heard someone dug up a grave there recently."

"Yes, it was a terrible thing." She pursed her lips and frowned. "An old drunkard from town said some people hired him to do it. What foolishness."

"Was the grave anywhere near the spot where the old oak tree used to stand?" Kaylin asked.

The historian cocked an eyebrow as if this were a very odd question. "I do not know for certain. I have a layout of the cemetery in my records.

It shows the locations of the plots, and who is buried in each. Perhaps I can help you find your ancestor."

She led them through a clean, but cluttered old house jammed with antique furniture and walls lined with paintings in faux-gilded frames to a room in the back of the house. A stout wooden table stood in the center of the room. The walls were nigh-invisible behind bookcases overflowing with books, file folders, and loose papers of various shapes and sizes. The room was the very antithesis of Maxie's meticulously organized library.

Despite the chaos, Mrs. Russell had no difficulty finding what she was looking for. She walked over to one of the shelves and withdrew a cardboard tube, from inside of which she produced a long, rolled paper. She smoothed it out on the table, pinning the corners down with stray books.

The boundaries of the graveyard were marked in bold blue lines. Plots were denoted by faint dotted lines. Each had a name and number written in tiny, precise print. Pathways crisscrossed the entire cemetery.

"Here is where the grave was desecrated." She pointed a knobby, liver-spotted finger at a spot not far from the cemetery entrance on the south end of the graveyard. "A man named Covilha, I believe. A Spaniard, or some such." She moved her hand across the page. "Here is where the oak tree stood." She indicated a point near the center of the graveyard. "And here is the covered bridge." Her finger drew a line to the northwest."

"Do you have a string, or a ruler?" Dane asked, struck by a sudden inspiration.

"Certainly." The old woman exited the room, returning momentarily with an old yardstick which she handed to him.

Dane grinned and smacked it into the palm of his hand. "Just like Mom used to beat me with."

"I whipped my son with that very same ruler," Mrs. Russell replied, a wistful smile on her face. "He still frowns when he sees it."

Dane laid the ruler across the map, angled downward from the top left. He then lined it up so that the edge lay across the center of the drawbridge, as well as the spot where the oak tree had grown.

"Would this line cross the wrought iron fence?" he asked.

"It encircles the graveyard, so yes."

"What would have been up here, outside the cemetery," he indicated the place where the ruler left the page, "back in, say, the mid-eighteen hundreds?"

"I do not know. I suppose I could check." She moved quickly to one of the shelves and began browsing through some oversized books.

"What are you thinking?" Kaylin whispered.

"Just a hunch." He didn't want to tell her until he was fairly sure he was right.

The historian laid an oversized book on the table, opened it, and flipped to an index in the back. After a moment, she turned to the page she was looking for.

"Here we are. This is from 1860." She looked at the cemetery map, then back to her book, did a double-take, then checked each again. "This is a strange coincidence. There was a house here that belonged to Francisco Covilha. I believe that is the same person who..." her voice trailed off.

Dane and Kaylin exchanged excited looks. They were on the right trail. They had to be. Kaylin's eyes narrowed. Dane believed he could read her thoughts. If Dane was correct, and the clues ran in a straight line, they would not lead to Covilha's grave, but possibly to that of another person.

"Let me check something," the historian said. She pulled from the shelf a small clothbound book with a tattered spine, and paged through. "This book was written just before the turn of the century. It has pictures of some of the older buildings that were in the town at that time. I didn't think of it before." She found the page she sought. "May I see your sketch, please?"

Kaylin showed her the drawing of the house.

"This is it." She turned the book around to show them what she was looking at. It was a print of the house in the sketch. At the bottom of the page was a single word: "*Covilha.*"

"Well, that certainly is interesting," Mrs. Russell continued.

"Now, about the ancestor you're looking for; I assume his name was Domenic?" She pointed to the name Kaylin had found in one of Covhila's books.

"Um, that's right," Kaylin said.

"Well, let me see. There is a plot with the name Domenic LaRoche right here." The location she indicated was on the opposite side of the oak tree, in perfect line with the house and covered bridge. "Is that the person you were looking for?" The elderly woman looked at them with a smile that said she was quite pleased with herself.

"That's him," Kaylin said, grinning. She clasped the woman's hand in both of hers. "Mrs. Russell, thank you for your help."

"You are most welcome." The woman smiled kindly.

"There's one other thing," Kaylin began. "If someone were to come asking about me…"

"Ms. Meyers told me about your situation with that terrible man. I'll be happy to keep your confidence."

Dane added his thanks, and they left the house. As they climbed into the car, Dane quietly contemplated what they had learned.

"Do you think that's the answer?" Kaylin asked. "The sword is buried with this Domenic person?"

He turned to face her, his heart racing. "I think we should go to the cemetery, and follow the clues."

CHAPTER 15

They parked on the shoulder of a narrow road that ran between the Burnatches River and a gently sloping hill. Covilha's home had once sat atop that hill overlooking the Riverbend Cemetery. They crossed the old covered bridge, now open only to pedestrian traffic, passing over the river, and arrived at a wrought iron fence.

"It looks just like the drawing in the book," Kaylin said, inspecting the fence.

Dane looked out across the graveyard. It was an old place that carried the evidence of its years in the weather-stained tombstones and eroded statuary. The paint on the fence was chipped. Patches of rust stood out everywhere on its pitted, black surface. Thick patches of clover stood out in the green carpet of grass. There being no gate nearby, he vaulted the fence, and then gave Kaylin a hand over.

They stood in the midst of several old gravestones. Dane knelt down to inspect the nearest one. It was dated 1841. He looked around.

"Where do you want to start?" he asked Kaylin.

She opened her notebook and looked over the images she had recopied onto one page. She had drawn a rough outline of the cemetery, and placed the house, river, bridge, fence, tree, and the name "Domenic" in their proper places. At Dane's suggestion, she had sketched in the compass alongside the house. He pointed out that the objects they had located all were directly southeast of the house; the same direction the compass was pointing.

"Let's orient ourselves with our backs to the house, facing the hill where the oak tree was," Kaylin said. "We'll walk straight ahead, and see if we come across anything that might be represented in these other sketches."

They began their walk, taking care to appear to the causal observer to be a couple on a leisurely stroll to visit the resting place of a family member. Not, Dane noted, that there seemed to be anyone around. He looked carefully at each headstone they passed. The oldest ones were so eroded that he could not make out anything carved into them. One of the stones, however, drew his attention.

"Kay, look at this." He knelt and rubbed a bit of moss from the discolored face of the old marker. As the gray-green moss was scraped away, it revealed the faint outline of a dove carved into the stone. It was weathered, but still easily recognizable.

"Check one more off the list," Kaylin said. She crossed out the picture of the dove at the bottom of the page, and sketched it into its location on her rough map. The ground sloped gently upward as they approached the place where the oak tree had stood many years before. As they rounded a large, above ground vault, she laughed.

"The torch!" She pointed to a statue of a woman that topped the crypt. Dressed in a flowing robe, the figure held a torch aloft in her right hand. We're tied," she said, adding this new find to the map.

They each located one more item. Dane found a headstone with the outline of a cross carved in the top, while Kaylin found a fleur-de-lis. Kaylin added these to the map, leaving only the sketch of a bird unaccounted for. As they topped the rise, they stopped and looked out over the old burial ground. This was the view that Covilha would have had from beneath the oak tree. Might he have stood on this very spot and created his code?

"Maddock, look there." Kaylin indicated a small, worn headstone just down the hill from where they stood. It read, *Domenic LaRoche.* "That's it."

"I don't know," he said. "We're still missing the bird." He scanned the nearby headstones but nothing immediately caught his eye. Where was it?

"The bird," Kaylin said to herself. "What if it was carved onto one of those stones that was so badly eroded that we couldn't make out what was written on is? Or," she held up a finger like a schoolteacher giving a lecture, "the drawing might have represented birds that nested in the oak tree."

"Maybe," Dane agreed, "but let's keep going just to make sure." It was his nature to be thorough. He did not want to miss an important detail because he had made an assumption based on incomplete information or a bad presupposition.

They continued their trek down the hill and across the graveyard. By the time they reached the far boundary, they had seen no bird symbol. Hoping that Kaylin's earlier assessment would prove to be correct, they returned to the grave.

Kaylin knelt in front of the small tombstone. There was a faint inscription beneath the name. She ran her fingers across it gently.

"What does it say?" Dane asked.

"I can't make it out. Hold on." She tore a sheet of paper from her notebook and held it flat against the stone above the inscription. Fishing a pencil from her purse, she made a rubbing of the headstone. When she had finished, she held it up and read aloud. "Domenic LaRoche, Son of Marie-Louise, 1834-1836." She stared at the paper for a moment, then looked back at the small marker. "He was just a baby. That's so sad."

Dane nodded. It was sad, but not unusual for that period in history. Something else was bothering him.

"Don't you think it's strange that only the mother's name is listed?" he asked.

Kaylin pursed her lips thoughtfully. "Maybe he was illegitimate."

"If that's so, I'm surprised he had a proper burial and a headstone. Most mistresses couldn't afford it, and the fathers wouldn't usually spring for it."

"Must have been an unusual circumstance," she mused. A frown creased her brow. She opened her notebook, found the page she was looking for, and grinned broadly.

"Tell me," Dane said.

"The letter you found in the book. You remember, I said it sounded like a letter from Covilha to his mistress? Look at her name." She held the translation up for him to inspect.

"Marie Louise," Dane marveled. "He buried the sword with his son."

"That's why they didn't find anything when they dug up Francisco's grave." Her hands trembled. "It's right here, Maddock! Right here beneath us!" She jumped to her feet and wrapped her arms around his neck.

He hugged her awkwardly and gave her a pat on the back before pulling away gently. Something was not right. He thought about it for a moment, before realizing what was bothering him.

"I'll be right back." He hurried down the hill and over to the fence that encircled the graveyard. A brief inspection of the wrought iron revealed a loose bar: a vertical post topped by a spike. A few twists, and the old solder broke, freeing the rod.

Kaylin greeted him raised eyebrows. "What's that for?"

"You'll see." Choosing a spot in line with the center of the headstone and about three feet out, he pushed the spiked end of the bar into the earth. The ground was fairly soft, and he encountered no large rocks. With only a bit of persuasion, the bar sank slowly into the earth.

"Maddock, don't tell me…" Kaylin covered her face. "You're not going to dig up that little boy's casket, are you?"

"Think about it," Dane said as he continued digging. "Would a regular sword fit into the coffin of a two year-old? We're talking about a sword that was wielded by a nine-foot tall warrior." He stopped as the bar struck something solid. He wiggled it gently, and felt it slip over the side of the object. Ignoring Kaylin's questioning look, he gently drew the bar back up, and continued to probe.

He quickly found the other edge. He guessed the object, the sword, he hoped, was about six or seven inches wide at this point. It was certainly too narrow to be a casket, and it was at a depth of just over two feet. He turned to Kaylin and smiled.

"I think we've got it." They definitely had something. He just hoped it was the right something. What if it wasn't the sword? What if they had come to New York for nothing? He pushed the worries from his mind. Such defeatist thoughts wouldn't get them anywhere, and he'd find out soon enough what lay buried in this child's grave.

Kaylin beamed back at him, confidence gleaming in her eyes.

"Turn around and screen me from the road," he instructed. "Pretend you're writing in your notebook, but keep an eye out."

"No way," she said. "Don't you think we should wait until after dark to do this?"

"And have somebody beat us to it? Those guys have been one step behind, if not a step ahead of us, the whole time. Besides, with Covilha's grave being dug up, they're likely to keep a closer eye on the place at night."

"Right," she said, "because no one in his right mind would rob a grave in broad daylight."

He rolled his eyes and started digging.

Kaylin gave him a mock-frown, then turned and pretended to be writing something in her notebook.

Dane chopped at the ground with increasing vigor. He tore up thick clumps of sod before breaking through to the soft dirt beneath. He wished for a better digging implement, but, as his grandpa used to say, you make do with what you got. He made quite a bit of progress before Kaylin called out a warning.

"Here comes a car!" Her voice was calm, but he could sense tension in her tone.

He tossed the bar behind the little headstone, and knelt down over the trench he was digging, pretending to be reading the inscription. The car passed without the driver taking any apparent notice of them. They were interrupted two more times by passing motorists. Dane had exposed a foot-long by ten-inch wide section of what was obviously an old metal box. The surface was pitted with rust, but still solid.

"Cops!" Kaylin called, this time with a touch of alarm in her voice. "And he's looking this way."

Dane hastily repeated his ruse, tossing away his digging apparatus and kneeling over the hole, which was now starting to resemble a latrine. He hoped the cops didn't take too close a look, as he could not think of any plausible explanation for digging up a grave.

A brown and tan sheriff's department vehicle cruised by, slowing as the deputy in the passenger seat peered at them with undisguised distrust. Kaylin mimicked writing furiously in her notebook, while Dane joined in the charade by pretending to read the inscription aloud to her. The car slowed further, and the deputy rolled down his window. Dane's heart pounded. He was not afraid of going to jail. He feared that if the deputies discovered what they were doing, the authorities would take possession of the sword, or worse, whoever was following them might somehow get hold of it. They had to get the sword now, or face the real possibility of losing it.

Kaylin pretended to have just noticed the patrol car. She smiled and waved. Dane waved as well. They held their breath as the car slowed to a near stop before the deputies nodded to them and accelerated around the bend and out of sight.

Dane let out a breath he didn't realize he'd been holding before returning to his digging. Kaylin looked like she was going to crumple to the ground. Instead, she knelt, found a flat rock that Dane's digging had turned up, and joined in. While she worked, scraping away at the soft loam, she kept an eye on the road.

They attacked the ground with a fury. After a few minutes, the piles of dirt around the forming trench had grown too large to hide. Dane felt his adrenaline surge at the realization that this was it. They had to get the sword out before another vehicle passed by. Droplets of sweat beaded on his forehead and rolled off into the moist dirt in the trench. His shoulders ached from the awkward digging motion necessitated by the wrought iron bar. His hands stung, and blisters were forming on his palms. Beside him, Kaylin panted as she hacked at the soil. He did not know if it was out of fatigue or fear of discovery.

Inch by inch they exposed the box. It looked to be more than five feet long. When the entire top surface was exposed, he used the point of the bar to scrape the dirt from around the sides. He then placed the tip underneath the bottom end of the box, and gently pried it up. Slowly, the box broke free of the soil that had ensnared it for more than a century and-a-half. He soon raised the end of the box high enough to get his fingers underneath. Straining, he lifted it until he could get two hands under it. It was remarkably heavy. Kaylin lent a hand, and the two of them dragged the box free from its grave.

It reminded Dane of a large gift box. The top was slightly wider and longer than the bottom so that it fit neatly over the bottom half. The lid had been welded all the way around at the bottom edge.

"We can't open it," Kaylin complained, her face taut with tension and frustration.

"Not yet," Dane said, "but in any case, we need to fill this hole in before we do anything else."

They hastily kicked dirt and rocks back into the trench they had dug. With the box missing, there was not enough dirt to fill the hole back to ground level. Dane gathered a few stray rocks and sticks, tossing them into the hole, then patched the top with chunks of sod. It would not hide what they had done, but someone would have to be right on top of it before they noticed.

Dane took off his jacket and laid it across the box. Kaylin did the same. Together, they hefted the large metal container. Holding it at waist level, they stumbled down the hill to their car.

When they reached the wrought iron fence, Dane propped his end on the rail and vaulted over. He cautiously dragged it toward him, letting the fence support its weight, and held it while Kaylin clambered over.

As she topped the fence, she looked up the road, her eyes widening and her face pale.

"Maddock, it's the cops again!"

Dane grabbed the box around the middle and lifted it with a grunt of pain. He stumbled to the car and heaved the box down on the ground next to the rear tire. He stood up in time to see the car rounding the bend in the road.

Kaylin calmly walked to the driver's side door, trying to put herself in a position to prevent the deputies from seeing beneath the car. She fished in her pocket for the keys, not realizing they were in Dane's jacket, which lay draped over the box.

The car rolled to a stop. The deputy rolled down the window and leaned as far forward as his wide-brimmed hat would allow.

"Afternoon," he said. His words were friendlier than his expression. His hazel eyes gleamed with suspicion and his narrow face and thin lips were set in a firm manner that said he would brook no foolishness.

"Good afternoon," Kaylin replied, smiling sweetly, leaning forward ever so slightly.

"You folks visiting a loved one?" He smiled as if that were some big joke, eyeing Kaylin with more interest now than suspicion.

Given that the cemetery had met its quota of residents more than a century ago, Dane supposed it qualified as a joke. He smiled and let Kaylin do the talking, as she seemed to have captured the deputy's attention. Dane supposed that sometimes there were definite advantages to being female and attractive.

"We're doing some genealogical work," she said. "We were trying to find the grave of one of my ancestors."

"Any luck?"

"No. We thought we had found it, but we were wrong." She frowned and bit her lower lip as if she were about to cry. "We're so close, too."

"Sorry to hear that," the deputy replied, though the words held little empathy. He looked down and frowned. "What's in the box?"

Dane could have smacked the guy. He told the first lie he could think of.

"Art supplies: an easel, paint, brushes and such." He nodded to Kaylin. "My girlfriend was thinking of painting the cemetery."

"It's quite lovely," Kaylin agreed.

"So I guess you were drawing in that notebook when we drove by a while back?" The deputy acted as if Dane were not there.

Dane didn't care if he was noticed or not. He only prayed that the man would not ask to see Kaylin's sketches.

"Yes, just a few sketches," Kaylin said, beginning to look nervous. "Would you like to see them?"

What was she doing?

"No thanks. I'll warn you folks, though," the deputy said, removing his hat and running his fingers through his short, brown hair. "There've been some strange goings-on around here. If you see anything out of the ordinary, call 911."

"We certainly will," Kaylin agreed, smiling again. "Thank you for letting us know."

The deputy looked them over again, then nodded and told his partner to drive.

They watched until the patrol car disappeared from sight before they loaded the box into the back seat.

"Now what?" Kaylin asked.

"We check out of the hotel," Dane said, "load up the car, and get as far from here as we can. Then," he turned and smiled at her, "we see what's inside this box."

CHAPTER 16

The knife struck the post dead center, its razor tip piercing the soft wood and burying itself a full three inches into its target. Stefan smiled a wicked grin. He never missed. He retrieved the blade with a deft yank and held it up in the afternoon sun, admiring the way the sunlight played off the razor edge. It was a KA-BAR knife, the style used by United States Marines. The weight and feel of it in his hand was perfect.

He flexed his bicep and drew the knife point across the muscle, drawing a faint trickle of blood. He no longer felt pain, and the cutting reminded him of killing. He loved killing with a knife; it was so… *personal.*

Sheathing his knife, he returned to his training. Placing his palms on the ground, he flipped into a handstand, put his heels against the post from which he had taken his knife, and began his regimen of inverted pushups. One-hundred repetitions, and then time for his run.

He was on ninety-seven when his phone vibrated. There was no need to check who was calling. He already knew. He ignored the phone while he finished his exercises, then waited for the next call, which he expected would come in short order. He was not disappointed. The phone buzzed again almost immediately, and he answered on the first ring.

"I have been waiting for your call," he said.

"Stefan, you are needed."

The voice on the other end sought to carry the weight of command, but Stefan could read vocal inflections, and the man was agitated. It pleased him.

"Angelo has failed, as I told you he would." They had been foolish to entrust an important mission to that buffoon. Angelo was good for bullying wayward priests and holding the door for his betters. Nothing more.

There was a long pause on the other end of the line. The man on the other end of the line had already lost whatever advantage he thought he had. They needed Stefan, but Stefan did not need them.

"The operation was not a success."

"Obviously, or you would not be calling me," Stefan said.

"We... should have entrusted this to you at the outset. We need you now. God needs you."

That admission was all Stefan would get. It was enough.

"Give me the details of the operation."

He listened to what the caller told him, asking an occasional direct question. He wrote nothing down. He would remember everything. He was about to hang up the phone when the caller actually surprised him.

"They claim to have found *what?*" Stefan asked, his head abuzz with surprise. He set his jaw and let the information sink in. "This cannot be. It is heresy. You absolutely should have called me first."

He snapped the phone closed and laid it in its place atop the antique rolltop desk. Dropping to the oak floor, he sat cross-legged with his hands in his lap. He gradually slowed his breathing, and willed his heart to slow. He instructed his mind to slow as well, the whirling cacophony of disconnected thoughts and images coalescing into a single ball, which he crushed and discarded. He had one focus: the mission.

He visualized his enemy. He envisioned stalking him, looking him in the eye before killing him. He could not allow this artifact to come to light. The man was obviously a fool, and now he would die for his folly. Stefan would not fail in this quest.

The orphan rescued from the streets of Venice had risen to a unique standing. Important men begged for his services. He named the price and set the terms. His was an uncanny knack for anonymous killing. Many had died by his hand, but suspicion had never fallen upon him. In fact, he did not officially exist. He was a phantom, a product of the organization that had raised and trained him. He owed his life to the order, and his service to it was always free.

He fingered his crucifix, the symbol of his order, feeling the sharp blades that form the cross on which his savior claimed the victory. Anticipation welled up inside of him as he envisioned the hunt. He forced himself to remain calm. This assignment was not for sport; it was a grave responsibility, a holy quest the like of which he had never undertaken. This would be his finest hour. He would recover the relic, kill the heretics, and claim the head of Dane Maddock as a trophy.

CHAPTER 17

D ane greeted Bones with a rough hug and a slap on the back. He then turned and shook hands with Corey, Matt and Willis. It was a relief to see them safe.

""Thanks for waiting for us," Bones said. "I know you're dying to open that box, but we didn't want to miss this." The others added their thanks as well.

"Kaylin didn't want to wait," Dane said. "Truth told, I didn't want to wait either. But you guys deserve to be here. Everything worked out all right?"

"No problem," Bones said. "We recovered the bodies, searched them, stripped them down, took them out to deeper water, and fed 'em to the sharks." He said this as if recounting a trip to the grocery store or a day of chores around the house. "Done deal."

"Did you find anything that will tell us who these guys are?" Dane asked. Why they were being followed was obvious, but the question of exactly who it was that was after them had confounded Dane and his friends.

"Just those weird crucifixes with swords for crosses. Corey took some pictures and e-mailed them to Jimmy. We'll see what turns up." Bones looked around before continuing. "Sorry, I just feel like someone's going to walk up on us any minute. This is not the kind of stuff anyone else needs to hear. We were defending ourselves, but…"

"I understand," Dane said. "This is the most desolate floor of any Naval Academy building I've ever been in. I think it's safe to talk here. Go ahead."

"We burned the clothing, put the ashes, crucifixes and weapons into their speedboat, and blew the whole mess to kingdom come."

"Man, I hated blowing up that boat," Willis said. "That thing was sweet."

"No kidding," Matt said. "Bones wouldn't even let us take a spin in it first."

"Which is why we were able to clean up the mess, get the boat back to its owner, and get the hell out of Dodge before the authorities caught up with us," Bones said.

"Get out of Dodge?" Corey echoed, grinning. "Indians aren't allowed to make cowboy jokes. It's in the rulebook."

"How about we get on with it, gentlemen?" Dane asked, opening the door to the room where Kaylin was waiting, along with Dr. James Sowell. A professor of archaeology and an acquaintance of Dane and Bones, Sowell had arranged for the use of the laboratory, and gained entrance for Dane and his friends.

The room was utilitarian: plain white walls and lots of stainless steel. The metal box, the box holding the sword, Dane hoped, lay on a table in the center of the room beneath a bright fluorescent light. They all circled around, eager to find out what was inside.

"All right, everyone put on your safety glasses," Sowell said. He donned a pair of dark-tinted laboratory goggles, and picked up his saw. The tool consisted of a small handle tipped with a diamond-tipped circular blade. "Watch for sparks and tiny shards of metal," he instructed, then began to cut away the welds that held the lid securely to the box.

The thin, high-pitched whine of the saw rose to a shrill squeal as the blade cut into the ancient bonds.

Dane was so excited that he could scarcely hear it. A tingling sensation ran up his back and down his arms as the moment drew near. He watched as Sowell worked his way down one side, then around the end, and back down the other side. When only one end of the box remained, he felt Kaylin grasp his forearm in both hands and squeeze.

The professor completed the last cut, put down his saw, and knelt to inspect his work. He used a brush and a small vacuum tube to clean away the loose bits of metal from around the cut. Then he probed the cut with a thin bladed knife.

"Should we just come back tomorrow?" Bones asked, a touch of annoyance in his voice. "I mean, if you're gonna' be a while…"

"I was asked to do a job," Sowell replied, not looking up from his work. "It's going to be done properly."

"Sorry," Bones said. "We've been through a lot to get this thing."

Sowell finished his inspection and nodded as if satisfied. He stood up and addressed the group.

"Everyone put on masks and rubber gloves, please." He pointed to a table against the far wall.

"Why?" Willis asked.

"We don't know what's in there. There could be some sort of mold spore that might be harmful if inhaled. And frankly, even if whatever is in there isn't potentially harmful, I don't want you sneezing on it." He turned to Bones. "Since you're so eager, how about you give me a hand with this lid?"

Bones donned a mask and a pair of gloves, and positioned himself at one end of the table. He and Dr. Sowell each took hold of one end of the lid.

"Okay, lift," Sowell instructed. Each lifted his end of the lid. It did not budge.

Bones tried to jiggle the lid, to no avail.

"Don't try to force it," Sowell ordered. He took a small hammer and chisel and began working at the corners of the box, carefully tapping the tool's fine point between the two halves. When he was satisfied, he nodded to Bones, and the two of them pulled up on the lid. With a little persuasion, it came free.

Dane's mouth dropped open in slack-jawed disbelief. The box was filled with moldy burlap. He wanted to curse. Just as quickly as the thought had entered his mind, it fled. The burlap was obviously packing material to protect whatever was inside. He chuckled at his own foolishness. Kaylin glanced at him, a look of curiosity in her eyes. He shook his head.

Sowell carefully lifted the bundle out of the box and laid it on the table. Slowly, delicately, he unrolled the burlap from around the object. Dane held his breath. Around him, the others gasped as the last layer of cloth fell away.

It was a huge broadsword. The pommel was broad, the handle wrapped in dry, aged leather. The scabbard was simple, without ornamentation. When Sowell drew the blade, however, even Dane sucked in his breath with surprise.

The sword was unlike any he had ever seen, and not only in terms of its size. One side of the blade was perfectly straight, and obviously razor sharp. The other side, apparently equally sharp, was oddly shaped, with irregular waves and indentations along the length of the blade, some of them nearly an inch deep.

"It looks like a big key," Bones observed.

Dane was too mesmerized by the magnificence of the sword to comment.

"It's so shiny," Kaylin marveled. "It looks brand new."

"Is it steel?" Dane asked. The sword should not have been in such pristine condition, especially not a three thousand year-old sword.

"No, it isn't," Sowell answered slowly. "It's surprisingly light." He hefted the sword with one hand, and cut a figure eight in the air. "It feels almost like titanium." His puzzled voice was a match for his frown.

"May I hold it?" Kaylin asked.

Sowell nodded, and held it laid out across his upturned palms, as if making a formal presentation. It glistened in the artificial light.

Considering that this was the fulfillment of her father's dream, Dane agreed that a bit of ceremony was not out of order. He laid a hand on her shoulder.

"Congratulations," he said softly.

Bones began clapping. The others quickly joined in, whistling and applauding with enthusiasm. Kaylin turned toward them, and held the sword aloft. The tears streamed down her cheeks, framing her brilliant smile.

"Thank you all," she said, lowering the sword, and gazing at it with a mixture of wonderment and adoration. "You all worked so hard, and put yourself in such danger to help me finish Dad's work. I can't tell you how much…" She broke into sobs.

Everyone surged forward to hug her or pat her on the back. Dane held back. He did not know why, but he felt as if he should not be a part of this moment.

Kaylin quickly regained her composure. She scrubbed her tears away with the back of a sleeve, and smiled anew.

"Who wants to hold it?" she asked, looking around at the others.

"Let Dane hold it first," Bones said. "You guys found it. I mean, all we did was get beat up."

"No, you go ahead," Dane declined, laughing. "This was a team effort, and you guys certainly paid your dues."

Bones took the sword from Kaylin, and held it aloft, letting the light play off the keen edges of the blade. Despite what Sowell had said, his face registered surprise.

"Man, this thing *is* light. And there's not a scratch on it. The edge of the blade is perfect." He gazed at it for a moment before passing it around the circle.

First Corey, then Matt, then Willis took a turn holding the sword. To a man, their faces registered bewilderment at the weight and condition of the ancient blade.

"No way this could be the real thing," Willis said as he passed it to Dane. "I'm sorry to be the stick in the mud, man, but they didn't have metals like this back then."

Dane grasped the hilt of the sword. Light though it might be, it was perfectly balanced.

"You're right, Willis," he said. "They didn't have this kind of metal back then. But there's another problem." He waited to see if anyone was following his train of thought. When no one spoke up, he continued. "But we know that at the very least, this sword is nearly two hundred years old. It's been in the ground almost that long."

"I hear you," Willis said, a sly smile spread across his face.

"I get it," Bones said, pounding his fist into his palm. "Whatever kind of alloy or whatever this is would have been almost as much out of the question in 1825 as it was way back when. It's an anachronism regardless."

"Ms. Maxwell, will you allow me to analyze the blade?" Sowell asked. "I have some tests I can run that will not damage the blade. Perhaps I can shed some light on this puzzle."

"Please," Kaylin said, obviously confused by this revelation. "I thought that finding the sword would be the end of the mystery, but it seems that it's just the beginning."

"Let's assume that Rienzi is correct, and this is truly the sword that belonged to Goliath," Corey said, scratching his head. "How was this thing made?"

"Maybe it was a miracle," Kaylin said. She blushed a little as everyone looked at her. "Why not?" she asked with a touch of defiance in her voice. "David was God's chosen warrior. Maybe when he used the sword to cut Goliath's head off, God *did* something to it."

"Back to reality," Dane muttered. Religion of any sort was not his favorite topic.

"What's the matter Maddock, don't you believe in God?" Kaylin rounded on him, hands on hips and a look of challenge in her eyes. "Don't you?"

Dane did not reply. He focused his attention on the sword, and tried to ignore the heat that was rising up the back of his neck.

"Sure he does," Bones said after an uncomfortable silence. "They're just taking a little time apart right now."

"God doesn't believe in me," Dane growled. How could any of them understand?

"Man, my mama would take a switch to you if she heard you talking like that," Willis said, his arms folded across his chest. He stared disapprovingly at Dane.

"I don't want to talk about it," he said. His voice sounded like winter in his own ears. The others must have heard it in much the same way, because they turned away from him. Only Kaylin was not willing to change the subject.

"How about you, Dr. Sowell?" she asked the scientist. "Do you believe in God?"

The professor cleared his throat and looked down at his feet.

"I'll admit that the universe does show some signs of some sort of, shall we say, intelligent design, but beyond that, I haven't completely decided where I stand."

"Bones?" Kaylin turned to the big man. "How about you? What do you think?"

"I believe in Him, but considering the way I've lived my life, I kind of hope I'm wrong." He chuckled and elbowed Corey. "Ask Star Wars boy here what he thinks."

"I believe the Darwin fish on my car speaks for itself," the computer specialist said.

"How can you be sayin' that?" Willis asked. "You could have been killed when those guys attacked the boat. You should have been killed, but you got out of it. Don't you think someone was looking out for you?"

"Yes," Corey said. "You were looking out for us."

"I shouldn't have been able to do what I did. Everything went my way. And the whole time I was praying, 'Don't let the others hear. Don't let me make a mistake. Don't let my friends get killed.' And they didn't, and I didn't, and you didn't. That's pretty amazing to me."

"So God gave you the power to kill those guys?" Matt asked. "I didn't think that was something Jesus approved of."

"I don't know how it all works," Willis said. "I know that if I didn't believe someone was looking out for me, it never would have happened. I know that everything went our way, even though it probably shouldn't have. And those were bad men, so don't go thinking I feel bad about any of it. I don't!"

Dane did not want to hear any more. He knew for a fact that God did not intervene to help good people, but he was not going to talk about it. Something else had captured his attention.

He held the sword up to the light, and looked closely. Sure enough, there it was. Strange, alien characters were etched into the metal. They seemed to flow together in a regular, but ornate script. Something about them made goosebumps rise on his flesh. The words seemed powerful...and sinister. The others needed to see this.

"If I could interrupt the theological debate," he said, his voice hoarse. He turned the flat of the sword blade out for them to see, "maybe the answer is in the writing etched into the blade."

CHAPTER 18

S o, what have we learned about Goliath?" Bones tossed a folder on the table, pulled up a chair, and produced a can of Diet Coke with lime from the pocket of his leather jacket. He popped it open and took a swig.

"You might know what we've learned if you helped us," Kaylin grumbled, looking askance at him.

"I'm hurt," Bones answered, clutching his chest and twisting his face in mock-anguish.

"Sorry," she said. "I'm just stressed out." She took a sip of coffee and grimaced. "Ugh, who made this?"

"I like it strong," Dane said. He turned to Bones. "What's up with you?"

"I'm celebrating," Bones said. "Ask me why." His eyes twinkled as he spoke.

Dane was still in a bad mood after the religious discussion of the previous day. He knew that he shouldn't be angry at the others. The problem was his own. Nonetheless, he wasn't in the mood to bandy words with his friend.

"Why?" Kaylin asked, her voice tinged with annoyance.

"Because I found a connection between the notes in Rienzi's bible, and the tall man." The brightness of his smile made Dane's headache worse.

Dane waited for Bones to continue, but to no avail. "Bones, if you're going to make us ask you a question after every sentence you utter, this is going to take forever." He tossed the printed e-mails he had been reading onto the table and squeezed his head between his hands. The pressure relieved some of the throbbing.

"Fine, ruin my fun, why don't you?" Bones pulled his feet off of the table, sat up straight, and took another drink before continuing. "I was doing a little research this morning, and came across a website that claims that the story of David and Goliath is a fable inspired by the stars. Specifically, David is the constellation Bootes, the sling is Corona Borealis, and Goliath, drum roll please..." He began drumming on the table with his palms. "...is Orion." He sat back, folded his hands behind his head, and waited for their reply.

"But we know that Goliath is real," Kaylin protested. "So how does that help us?"

"Think about Rienzi's bible," Bones said. "Remember the stick figure drawn in the margin next to the David and Goliath story? Did it remind you of anything?"

"Orion," Dane said. How had he not recognized so familiar a constellation? "You're right. That's what the drawing is. I should have recognized it."

"So Rienzi knew about this idea that the constellations inspired the story," Kaylin said, her voice bland. "I'm sorry, but I still don't see how this is helpful." She paused, waiting for an explanation.

"Think about it this way," Bones said. "Rienzi, at least in his mind, knew that Goliath was a historical figure. After all, he had the sword to prove it. So he must have seen some other connection between Goliath and Orion."

"Like what?" Dane feared this was one of Bones' fancies. "Wait a minute. Maybe I don't want to know." He held up his hands as if warding off an attack.

"Like little green men." Bones rolled his eyes and waggled his fingers as he spoke.

Kaylin buried her head in her arms and groaned.

"Bones, if you had any idea how hard I've worked at doing real research, you would never come to me with this ridiculous idea."

"Why is it ridiculous?" Bones propped his elbows on the table and fixed her with a blank stare.

Dane knew his friend well enough to know that Bones was being serious. At least, as serious as he ever got.

"Come on," Kaylin said, looking up at him. "You expect me to believe that Goliath was a space man?"

"Not a space man," Bones said. "But he was a descendant of an alien race."

Kaylin chuckled and shook her head. She was not accepting the idea at all.

"Let's hear him out," Dane said. He wasn't quite sure why he wanted to hear what Bones had to say. It was, after all, pretty far-fetched. Perhaps it was because he knew it would get under Kaylin's skin. Sort of a petty payback for last night.

"First of all," Bones said. "Remember how Rienzi had marked the passage about the giants being on the earth, and mating with human women?"

"Yes," Kaylin said in a voice that was part tired, part bored. "I remember."

"I did some cross-referencing between my research and Rienzi's notes," Bones continued. "Did you realize he marked every scripture that referred to races of the Nephilim, or the 'giants'. He noted the Emim, who the Hebrews called 'the terrible ones', the Rephaim, and the 'stranglers', the Anakim."

"All right. So the Hebrews came to a new land where some of the native tribes were bigger than they were, so they called them 'giants', and gave them scary names," Kaylin said.

"The Bible says that the Anakim were so big that the Hebrews were 'as grasshoppers in our own sight,' Bones argued. "That's more than just bigger. And remember, these are the descendants of the Nephilim. They've been interbreeding with regular humans for generations."

"Still, Goliath was a big guy," Kaylin said, refusing to give ground, "so it would make sense that Rienzi marked all of the passages that referred to these 'giants'.

"Goliath is generally accepted as being one of the Anakim. By the time the book of Joshua is written, which is well before David, we are told that there are only three places where the Anakim still live. One of those three places is Gath, Goliath's home. Rienzi would have had no reason to note any of the other races unless he was trying to make a connection."

"But why aliens? Why couldn't they just be big people?" Kaylin protested.

"Actually there are several reasons." Bones took a final swig of his coke, draining the can. He belched loudly, crushed the can against his forehead, and dropped it on the table. "The most important of which is that it is the only way to explain that sword." He paused for a moment, and stared at Kaylin, as if challenging her to argue with him.

"That sword is the ultimate anachronism. It's made of some combination of metals we've never seen. It hasn't aged in thousands of years. It has been used in battle but never nicked or scratched. I don't know that it could be duplicated even today."

Dane could see that Kaylin was thinking this over. Suddenly, he had an idea.

"It also explains why Rienzi was threatened with excommunication," he said.

Kaylin looked at him, frowning, while Bones smiled and nodded.

"Now you're getting the idea, Maddock," Bones said.

"Something that's been bothering me is the fact that the church effectively shut Rienzi up about his discovery. You would think that discovering an ancient artifact that proves the truth of a story in the Bible would be a good thing, but in this case, the church didn't want the word to get out." Dane's mind was operating at a fast clip now. "Obviously, Rienzi was making claims about the sword and what it signified that went above and beyond simply claiming that it had belonged to Goliath. Claims that the sword was the creation of a superior alien intelligence, and that Goliath was part alien, would have been objectionable to the church."

"And it would explain why his peers scoffed at his claims," Kaylin said thoughtfully. "I'm still not convinced, but I'm willing to keep listening."

"Fair enough," Bones said. "A million or so years ago, according to anthropologists, homo erectus migrated out of Africa. By thirty thousand years ago, the only hominids around were homo sapiens. Problem is, despite the fact that homo sapiens is a much more highly developed being, there is no fossil record of a progression from homo erectus to homo sapiens. It's as if we just burst onto the scene with our big brains and frail bodies.

"There's also the issue of structure like the pyramids. How did our ancestors build them? There are megalithic structures all over the world made up of giant stones that people did not have the technology to move. Take the walls of Sacsahuaman in Peru. One of the stones was measured at eight and-a-half meters high and weighs over three hundred-sixty tons."

"We can move objects bigger than that," Kaylin argued. "I read about a lighthouse that was moved a while back. It weighed in the thousands of tons."

"You're talking about today, not thousands of years ago," Bones replied. "And then there are the accounts of aliens in the historical record. There are carvings of images that look remarkably like astronauts, rocket ships, even light bulbs. There are also written records. Take the Tulli Papyrus, for example. He opened his folder and selected a single page printout. He held up the page and began to read.

"In the year 22, in the third month of winter, in the sixth hour of the day, the scribes of the House of Life noticed a circle of fire that was coming from the sky... From the mouth it emitted a foul breath. It had no head. Its body was one rod long and one rod wide. It had no voice. And from that the hearts of the scribes became confused and they threw themselves down on their bellies ... then they reported the thing to the Pharaoh ... His Majesty ordered ... has been examined ... and he was meditating on what had happened, that it was recorded in the scrolls of the House of the Life. Now after some days had passed, these things became more and more numerous in the skies. Their splendor exceeded that of the sun and extended to the limits of the four angles of the sky ... High and wide in the sky was the position from

which these fire circles came and went. The army of the Pharaoh looked on with him in their midst. It was after supper. Then these fire circles ascended higher into the sky and they headed toward the south. Fish and birds then fell from the sky. A marvel never before known since the foundation of their land ... And Pharaoh caused incense to be brought to make peace with Earth ... and what happened was ordered to be written in the Annals of the House of Life so that it be remembered for all time forward."

Dane tried to digest what Bones had read to them. It just seemed so far-fetched. He was impressed, though, that Bones had obviously done his research.

"There's also the fact that our ancestors had a great knowledge of astronomy. They knew that the sun, moon, and planets rotate. They also knew the circumference of the earth, and included it in their architecture. Ancient maps have been discovered that showed things that ancient humans shouldn't have known, like the coastline of Antarctica *beneath* the ice."

"Let me see if I've got this," Kaylin said. "You're arguing that aliens not only intervened in human pre-history, but interbred with humans, thus making the aliens the 'missing link'. And that Goliath was closely descended from one of these alien races."

"I'm saying that some people believe that," Bones corrected.

"So we're all aliens?" Kaylin asked, with a sick look on her face. "That's hard to digest."

"I guess so. At least, we're all part alien. The Anakim and the others might have been a remnant of aliens who continued to breed mostly among themselves until so few remained that they had no choice but to mate with humans."

"Did you do all this research, or did you have your friend Jimmy help you?" Kaylin asked.

Bones stuck out his tongue.

"Okay, I think I've heard enough," Dane said. "Without agreeing with you that Goliath was an alien, let's operate on the assumption that Rienzi believed that he had discovered proof of that very idea. The sword, amazing as it is, would not have been sufficient proof, especially two hundred years ago. They would have dismissed it as an undiscovered metal, or perhaps a miracle."

"You're right," Bones said. "There's more that we haven't discovered. Something Rienzi found that supported his claims. We have to find it."

CHAPTER 19

They arrived in Professor Sowell's office to find him seated at his desk, an expression of amused bewilderment on his face. He motioned for them to take seats opposite him.

"We've run tests on the composition of the sword. Frankly, it does not belong."

"It doesn't belong in that time period, you mean?" Dane asked, dropping down into an uncomfortable, straight-back wooden chair.

"I mean it doesn't belong on this planet." The professor paused while this bit of information sank in.

Next to him, Dane heard Bones chuckle.

"What'd I tell you?" He stood behind Dane, and clapped a hand on Dane's shoulder.

Sowell ignored Bones' comment and continued.

"Some of the component elements are terrestrial. Ninety percent of the sword, however, is composed of an unknown element. Whatever that element is, it gives the sword its strength, durability, and lightness. The blade is harder than titanium, lighter, and has an extremely high melting point, though I have only managed a rough estimate. There are other tests I could do, but I do not want to risk damaging it. Not that I have any confidence that I could damage it with anything short of a nuclear explosion."

"You think it's an alien artifact," Bones stated, squeezing Dane's shoulder.

"I can't tell you what it is," Sowell said, "I can only tell you what it is not. And it is not of this earth, at least not of any known element."

"Did you learn anything from the inscription on the blade?" Dane asked, eager to change the subject.

"Yes," Sowell said. "I was able to scan the images and send the information to your friend Jimmy. He just updated me on his findings. The writing resembles hieroglyphics, and will take some time to decipher. That is, if we can decipher it all. He has managed to translate a small portion, and is confident that he is correct."

"Forgive my ignorance, but why are hieroglyphics so hard to translate?" Kaylin asked.

"No frame of reference," Sowell explained. "Decrypting an alphabetic cipher, for example, involves finding patterns such as frequency of occurrence of certain letters, or finding double letters and using them to identify words. Once the code is broken, its child's play. With hieroglyphics, each symbol can represent a word, a sound, a concept, or even a story. That is why Egyptian hieroglyphics were a mystery for so long. Until the Rosetta Stone was discovered, there was no reference from which to translate them."

"How did Jimmy manage to break any of the code, considering the sword may not be of earthly origin?" Dane asked. "It almost sounds too easy."

"Apparently the computer found matches from a variety of sources: Egyptian hieroglyphics, Viking runes, even some Central and South American Indian pictographs. Much of what he has at present are bits and pieces that are meaningless out of context."

"You said he was able to translate a portion of the writing. What does it say?" Dane's curiosity was piqued. Having been the one to first notice the writing on the sword, he was eager to learn what it said.

"Not what, but where," Sowell said, pushing a computer printout of a map across the desk. He turned it around so that the three of them could see it. "The writing pinpoints a location in southwest Jordan." He circled a spot on the map with a ballpoint pen. "A few of the other words he has translated include "rock" and "red". Coupled with these coordinates, we are confident that the writing on the sword is pointing to this location."

"Petra." Kaylin breathed the word more than spoke it. She turned to Dane, her eyes wide with excitement. "Rienzi claimed to have been the first to rediscover Petra. Many of the artifacts he lost on the *Dourado* were discovered at Petra. That must be where he found the sword."

"I take it this is good news?" Sowell asked, smiling a tight, disinterested smile.

"Absolutely," Dane said. Standing, he clasped the professor's hand. "I can't tell you how much I appreciate your help."

"I should thank you," Sowell said, also rising to his feet. "It is the most amazing artifact I've ever seen."

"It certainly seems to.be so. Well, I guess we'll be taking it with us now," said Dane. "Where is it?"

A sudden change came over Sowell. His face seemed to harden. His ears reddened, and his fists clenched.

"The sword?" he asked in a clipped voice.

"What else would I mean?" Dane asked. Warning bells were going off inside his head. He stepped closer to the desk. Out of the corner of his eye, he saw Bones position himself between Sowell and the door.

"Mr. Maddock, the sword requires further study. If we could reproduce this metal, do you have any idea what the implications for industry and defense would be?"

"Give me my sword," Kaylin said in a cold voice that caught Dane by surprise.

"Why do you need it?" Sowell asked. "You completed your father's quest. We will pass all our findings along to you. You have had the satisfaction of finding it. Now let us your country get something out of it as well."

"My father bought that sword with his blood. It belongs to me, and it's not for you to ask why I need it." Her voice remained calm, but her eyes were shining with barely contained rage.

She looked to Dane as if she were about to go over the desk to get at Sowell. If that were to happen, Dane did not know if he would try to stop her.

"Give us the sword, Sowell," Dane said firmly. "You have your test results to study. Don't make this hard on us, and depending on how things unfold, Ms. Maxwell might permit you to study it again at some point in the future."

Sowell's eyes flitted rapidly between Dane, Kaylin, and the door where Bones stood.

"Commander Wrexham deems it in the interest of national security that the Navy takes possession of the sword." He swallowed hard. "He took it this morning."

"You're lying," Dane said flatly. Sowell reached for the bottom drawer of his desk, but before he could get it open, Dane grabbed him by the wrist and yanked, dragging him face down across the desk.

"I'm telling the truth," Sowell sputtered.

"Shut up," Dane ordered. Sowell lay on his desk, head hanging off one side, legs off the other. Dane grasped the hair on the back of his head with one hand. The other held Sowell's arm pinned behind his back. Dane knew just how far the arm would bend before popping out of its socket, and he held it at the threshold.

"You forget that my friend Bones is a Cherokee. Indians have ways of making people talk, don't they Bones?" He looked at Bones, who nodded, smiling wickedly. His white teeth looked like fangs.

"You don't think I believe that voodoo hocus-pocus, do you?" Sowell wheezed. The pressure Dane was putting on the back of his head was forcing his throat down against the edge of the desk. His face was turning purple from lack of oxygen.

Bones knelt down in front of the man. "We Indians do have our ways," he crooned. He reached into his jacket pocket and pulled out his Swiss Army knife. "But they aren't mysterious, spiritual ways. They're just plain nasty." He opened the corkscrew and held it up to Sowell's eye.

The professor squirmed and kicked, but Dane held him firmly in place. The man had to be running out of air by now. After a moment, the struggling ceased, and Dane felt the man relax.

"It's in the safe," he said, his voice a faint whisper.

Dane decreased the pressure on Sowell's neck enough for the man to draw a breath and tell them the combination to the safe, which was, predictably, hidden behind a framed Ansel Adams print. While Dane continued to hold the professor, Bones opened the safe and retrieved the sword which, along with its scabbard, was now protected by a layer of bubble wrap, which seemed odd considering what they knew about the sword's durability. He supposed it was a good idea to protect the aging scabbard.

"The commander was going to pick it up tomorrow," Sowell said, as Dane let him stand. A miniscule flick of his eyes toward the clock on the wall was enough to give lie to his statement.

"Tell him we knocked you out and stole the sword," Dane said, and drove the heel of his palm into Sowell's temple. As the professor crumpled to the floor, Dane doubled up his fists and struck the man a two-handed blow to the base of the skull. He turned to the others.

"Sowell was lying about Wrexham picking it up tomorrow. We've got to get off this campus now. He's probably going to be here any second."

The three of them scrambled out of the basement office and hurried to the elevator. Dane looked at the numeric display. The elevator had stopped on the first floor, and was now descending to the basement.

"Come on!" he shouted, dragging Kaylin down the hall. Behind him, the bell rang and he heard the elevator doors begin to open. They were not going to make it to the end of the hall in time. Their options exhausted, he darted through an open door, with Kaylin and Bones right behind him.

It was another office, much like Sowell's. Fortunately, the occupant was out as was the light. There was no way to shut the door without drawing attention to whoever might get out of the elevator. They stood just inside the office door. Dane strained to listen, but did not hear anything. For a moment he thought he had overreacted, that the elevator had been empty, but then he heard footsteps. Someone knocked on a door.

"Sowell?" a voice boomed down the tiled hallway. "Open up!" The person knocked again. A pause, then the sound of a doorknob turning. Dane heard the sound of the commander entering Sowell's office. "Sowell, what in the…" He heard thumps as if someone were shoving furniture aside. Wrexham had found the professor. Perhaps there was a chance.

"Go," Dane mouthed to Kaylin, and bobbed his head toward the door. To his surprise, she neither questioned him nor protested.

Hastily removing her shoes, Kaylin hurried to the door, glanced toward Sowell's office, then sprinted in the opposite direction. Dane watched her disappear around the corner, and then moved to the door himself, with Bones behind him. Just then, he heard the sound of the commander coming back out of the office.

After a moment, footsteps again echoed down the hall, followed by an insistent tapping sound, which Dane took to be Wrexham pressing the elevator button. The metallic ring of the elevator bell a moment later confirmed his instinct. He heard the doors open, then close seconds later.

Dane placed his hand on Bone's chest. They needed to make certain that the commander was really gone. He silently counted to twenty, all the while listening for the sound of footsteps that would indicate that they were not alone in the basement of the building.

Twenty seconds.

Nothing.

He nodded to Bones, then peered around the door.

Still nothing.

He moved silently on the balls of his feet out into the empty hallway. He had taken no more than five steps down the hallway when a firm voice rang out from behind him.

"Stop right there."

CHAPTER 20

A short, stocky, balding man with pale skin and a neatly-trimmed gray moustache stepped out of the next office. He held a Beretta pointed at Bones, who clutched the sword against his chest. Dane was tempted to leap at the commander, but the distance between them was too great. Besides, if Wrexham were any kind of soldier, his reflexes would be too quick.

"Commander Wrexham, what a pleasant surprise," Dane said, filling the words with as much sarcasm as he could generate.

"Spare me the small talk," Wrexham said. "I want the sword. Give it to me"

"No can do," Bones said, keeping his eyes trained on Wrexham's pistol.

"You can and you will," Wrexham snapped. "When the M.P.'s find out how you attacked Dr. Sowell and stole Navy property, I think you'll be all too happy to surrender the sword."

"The sword is not Navy property. It's belongs to Kaylin Maxwell, the daughter of…"

"I know all about Maxwell," the officer said. "He was acting on behalf of the United States Navy. It is a matter of national security. The Navy is grateful for your assistance in recovering the sword. Hand it over, and I'll let you leave unharmed."

"Don't think for one minute I believe you're going to let us out of here," Dane said. Over Wrexham's shoulder, at the far end of the hall, something caught his attention. Kaylin had circled around, and was coming up from behind. She held her father's .380 trained on Wrexham's back. Dane could not believe she had smuggled that thing onto the campus of the academy. She was too far away at the moment to be of any help. Dane needed to keep Wrexham talking. Careful not to let his eyes betray their only hope, he continued talking.

"We're the only ones who know about this," Dane said. "You are acting on your own. If this were a Navy operation, Sowell would have immediately turned the sword over to his superiors, but you had him hold on to it for you."

Wrexham turned his pistol toward Dane. "Maybe I should shoot you both right now. You talk too much."

"What about me?" Bones asked, apparently trying to help Dane's stalling tactic. "I haven't been talking. That's not fair!"

"I don't like your face." Wrexham smirked.

Kaylin, still in her stocking feet, was about halfway down the hall, about even with Sowell's office door. Close, but not close enough.

"Wait a minute," Dane said thoughtfully. "You aren't going to shoot us."

"You are sadly mistaken my friend," Wrexham said, adjusting his grip on his pistol.

"You can't shoot us. If you try and use this story of us stealing Navy property, you're going to have to turn the sword over to them. You want it for yourself. I don't know who you're working for, or what your angle is, but I'm willing to bet that you've already negotiated a fat bonus for yourself."

Kaylin was creeping closer, narrowing the gap between herself and the commander.

"Who is it?" Dane asked, watching for the officer to make a mistake. "A private corporation, or another country?"

Wrexham's eyes twitched at the mention of a private corporation, but otherwise did not react.

"I'll bet it's the French!" Bones shouted.

"Excuse me?" Wrexham said, raising an eyebrow.

Dane was grateful that Wrexham had not recognized their stalling tactics, and had allowed himself to be distracted by the absurdity of Bone's exclamation.

"The French, they're always pissing Americans off." Bones looked at Dane, feigning earnestness. "Wouldn't it piss you off if they had the sword?"

Dane shot Bones a withering glance and shook his head.

"Well, wouldn't it?" Bones acted as if all was normal. "I mean, everybody hates the French."

"The only person who is pissing me off right now is you," Wrexham said. "Drop the sword or die."

"Drop the gun!" Kaylin had finally crept up behind Wrexham and now held her pistol pressed against his temple.

Wrexham slowly turned his gun hand sideways, the back of his hand facing upward, and began to spread his fingers. He knelt with equal care, Kaylin's gun remaining pressed to his temple.

It happened suddenly. Wrexham dropped to the ground, spinning to his left. He drove his left elbow into Kaylin's side. He simultaneously fired off a wild shot. Bones fell back with a grunt. Kaylin, apparently not expecting resistance, stumbled awkwardly, nearly losing her grip on her pistol.

Dane, having expected Wrexham to try something, leapt forward the moment the naval officer moved. He grasped Wrexham's right wrist in his left hand, and banged the man's gun hand hard against the ground twice. The gun clattered to the floor. With his right hand, he pressed down on the commander's windpipe. The man struggled in Dane's grasp, but could not get loose.

Kaylin appeared at Dane's side. She had recovered her pistol, and held it trained on Wrexham's forehead. At the same time, Bones stepped up and delivered a vicious kick to the officer's temple. The man ceased his struggles.

"I thought he shot you," Dane said to his friend as the two of them stripped off Wrexham's jacket and bound his arms behind his back.

"I think it bounced off the sword," Bones replied, his eyes wide in amazement. "I heard the ping."

There was no time to discuss it further. They dragged Wrexham into Sowell's office and dumped him behind the desk alongside the still-unconscious professor.

"Let's move," Dane ordered. "Someone is bound to have heard those shots. I don't want to be here when they come around to investigate."

They dashed down the hall and around the corner. Dane heard the elevator bell ring again. He was growing to hate that sound. At the far end of the hall, where it made another right turn, was a door marked *Stairs*. Dane threw it open, and they sprinted up, taking the stairs two at a time. When they reached the first floor, Bones grabbed for the stairwell door.

"No!" Dane shouted, and continued running up the stairs. Bones and Kaylin followed. "If anyone did hear the shots, they're probably watching the stairwells as well as the elevators."

"We have to leave sometime," Kaylin huffed. "What do you want us to do?"

"I've got an idea," Dane said. Below them, he heard the first floor stairwell door open. He halted and motioned for the others to stop as well. They stood silently, listening as the clatter of footsteps echoed from below. The noise diminished, then, with the sound of a closing door, faded away.

Dane led them to the fifth floor. He pressed his ear against the metal door, but heard nothing. Cautiously, he opened the door and led the others into the corridor. He led them quickly down the hall, and breathed a sigh of relief when they came to a glass door labeled, *Admiral Franklin J. Meriwether, Professor Emeritus*. Suddenly wondering if this was such a good idea after all, he took a deep breath, turned the handle, and stepped inside.

An attractive woman, probably in her late thirties, sat behind a small desk. She had short, blonde hair, green eyes, and fair skin. The nameplate on her desk read, *Jill Trenard*. A civilian, Dane noted.

"May I help you?" Her smile was polite but perfunctory. Her eyes took in Dane's sweaty brow and disheveled appearance, and her brow creased. Here eyes widened when she caught sight of Bones.

"Yes," Dane said. "Dane Maddock to see Admiral Meriwether, please."

The woman consulted her computer screen. "Do you have an appointment?" She knew perfectly well he did not, but she was a military secretary, and she had to go through the motions of asking.

"He's expecting us sometime today," Dane said. "We weren't certain what time we would be getting here."

Ms. Trenard was apparently too professional to point out that the Admiral had said nothing to her of their expected arrival. She gave him a long, sour look.

"Just a moment," she finally said. She tapped a button on her telephone console, and spoke softly into the hands-free mouthpiece.

Dane stepped away from the desk, so as not to appear as if he were eavesdropping on her conversation. He pretended to take an interest in the photographs of World War II era naval vessels. All the while, he kept watch on the hallway outside. After a moment, Ms. Trenard spoke to him.

"Admiral Meriwether will see you now, Mr. Maddock." Her surprise was evident in her voice and her expression.

Dane smiled and thanked her, then followed her into a small office, Bones and Kaylin following behind.

Admiral Franklin Meriwether, a broad, white-haired man, sat behind a massive mahogany desk. A laptop computer, telephone, and a ship in a bottle were the only items on the dark, wooden surface. Spread across the wall behind him were framed degrees, certificates of achievement, and photographs of Meriwether with various comrades which told the story of his naval career. One of the photographs, a framed color print, showed Meriwether with his arm around the shoulders of his former underling, Dane Maddock.

"Maddock," the Admiral greeted him in a surly tone. "When am I ever going to have to stop pulling your chestnuts out of the fire?" He stood and reached across the desk, clasping Dane's hand in a firm shake.

"Come on, now. Why would you say that, Admiral?" Dane feigned innocence, knowing that he was not fooling his old commanding officer for one moment.

"I'm not sure. Either it's because you show up in my office unannounced after my not having heard from you in two years, or because you had the audacity to lie about my expecting you." Meriwether sat down, an angry look in his eyes.

"I'm sorry I haven't kept in touch," Dane said, truthfully. "After Melissa…" He halted. If he said no more he could still retain his composure. Even after two years, it still hurt more than he could stand.

"I know, son," Meriwether said, his voice softening. "It was a shock to us all."

From the corner of his eye, Dane saw Kaylin cock her head and fix him with a questioning glance. Bones tapped her on the shoulder and shook his head.

"Besides," Meriwether said, "the phone lines work both ways. I have not been in touch, either. Sit down, all of you." He gestured to a large leather sofa that sat against the wall opposite him beneath a framed oil painting of a three-mast sailing ship battling a vicious storm.

The three of them seated themselves, then Dane introduced his companions.

"Admiral, this is my friend Uriah Bonebrake." Bones stood and shook hands with the retired admiral, who fixed him with an appraising look.

"A SEAL," he said, nodding at Bones, "if I don't miss my mark. And I rarely do."

"Yes, I was," Bones said, looking surprised. "Do we know one another?"

"No, I can just tell sometimes," Meriwether said. "I've had a few years of experience with your lot." He turned his attention from Bones to Kaylin.

"And may I present," Dane said, "Miss Kaylin Maxwell. Her father was…"

"I remember your father," Meriwether interrupted. "A fine officer, Maxwell was. Damn fine."

"Thank you," Kaylin said, her head bowed a little. Dane suddenly remembered he was not the only one grieving a loved one. "That's kind of you to say."

"How is he doing?" Meriwether asked. "Haven't heard from him in more years than I've heard from Maddock here. Hope he's enjoying his retirement."

Kaylin's face turned red and her eyes glistened. She looked away, unable to reply.

"I'm sorry to tell you," Dane answered quickly, "Maxie died last month."

"Oh, I didn't hear," the Admiral said. An odd look crossed his face. "You have my sympathy. I wish I could have been there to pay my respects."

"We kept the memorial service very small," Kaylin said quietly. Apparently being around Navy men was bringing back painful memories.

"Now, tell me why you're here," Meriwether said. "I assume it's important, so you'd better fill me in."

Dane quickly recounted their tale, beginning with Maxie's search for the *Dourado*, and finishing with the details of Sowell and Wrexham's treachery.

When Dane had finished his story, Meriwether sat quietly, rubbing his chin. He turned around and stared at the pictures behind his desk for some time. Finally, he spoke.

"How did you come to choose Professor Sowell to examine the sword?"

"I know him mostly by reputation," Dane admitted. "Bones and I have used him as a resource on a few projects. We've mostly exchanged e-mails." He folded his arms across his chest and stared at the ship-in-the-bottle, thinking how foolish he had been to trust a relative stranger. "I figured whoever was following us couldn't infiltrate the academy. I didn't count on an entirely new adversary."

"Sit there for a minute. Let me check something out," Meriwether said in his abrupt manner. He picked up the phone and dialed an extension. He asked the person on the other end a few pointed questions about Sowell and Wrexham, punctuated by disapproving grunts. Finally, seeming satisfied with the answers he received, he hung up the phone and returned his attention to Dane and his friends.

"Neither Sowell nor Wrexham have reported anything about this sword to their superiors," Meriwether said, clearly annoyed. "They are definitely acting on their own. That alone is probably enough to keep the three of you out of hot water."

"Thank you," Bones and Kaylin said in unison.

"Not so fast." The Admiral held up a beefy hand to silence them. "Maddock beat up a Naval Academy professor. Then you," he turned to Bones, "knocked out an officer, tied him up, and left him in the basement.

"I believe I could let those things slide, considering that the two of them were dishonest at best, traitors at worst. What concerns me is that this sword might actually be of some benefit to our armed forces. If this metal has the qualities that you say it does, I think the military needs to know about it." He turned and fixed Dane with an intense gaze. "It's quite a conundrum, isn't it?"

"Admiral Meriwether," Kaylin spoke up, "my father lost his life in pursuit of this sword. We have to finish what we started. There's a mystery that must be solved."

"Why do you need to solve the mystery?" Meriwether boomed., slamming his palms on his desk. "You've found the sword. You've done what Maxwell set out to do."

"My father was killed because of this sword. We have almost been killed as well. We have no idea who is after us, or who killed him. Perhaps if we can solve the mystery, we can find out who these people are."

Meriwether stared at Kaylin. His face betrayed nothing.

"It's also possible," Bones said, "that even if we were to turn the sword over to you, those people could still be after us for what we know, either to get the information or to suppress it. The only way to end this is to solve the puzzle."

The Admiral nodded thoughtfully, cupping his chin in his hand and staring at the portrait behind them.

Dane saw an opening, and took it.

"Admiral, the Navy has all of Sowell's findings to work with until this is over. Let us finish what we started, and I promise you that when this is over, we will do our best to see to it that you have the opportunity to study it." He looked at Kaylin, hoping she would not contradict him. She looked back at him angrily, but nodded in agreement.

Meriwether exhaled long and loud. With a shake of his head, he returned his gaze to Dane and the others.

"Well then," Meriwether said, clapping his hand, "I'll make a deal with you."

CHAPTER 21

D ane rubbed his eyes and fought to stay awake as the tour guide droned on. The guide was an American, and appeared to be in his early retirement years. A fringe of white hair showed at the back of his head beneath his tan pith helmet. The sun was apparently not agreeing with the man, as his burned, red face attested, but he did seem knowledgeable, if a bit dry.

"Petra was the stronghold and treasure city of an ancient Arabic people who were called the Nabateans. It was situated near the points of intersection of great caravan routes from Gaza on the Mediterranean Sea, Damascus, Elath on the Red Sea, and the Persian Gulf. From the fourth century BC until the second century AD, Petra was the capital of the Nabataean Kingdom. The Romans conquered it at the beginning of the second century AD, and made it part of the Roman province of Arabia Petraea. The city continued to thrive in the second and third centuries, but later, when the rival city of Palmyra took away most of Petra's trade, its importance declined. It was conquered by the Muslims in the seventh century and captured by the Crusaders in the twelfth century. Afterward, it gradually it fell into ruins."

Dane looked at Kaylin, who was seated next to him. She was studiously making notes in a small journal book, despite the fact that they both already knew these things.

"The site of the ancient city was rediscovered in 1812 by the Swiss explorer Johann Burckhardt," the guide continued.

Dane was tempted to ask him who was the first to excavate the city, but knew that he should not risk drawing that sort of attention to himself. He shifted in his seat, and exhaled loudly. Kaylin frowned at him and kept writing.

"Petra is known both for its natural beauty and for its magnificent monuments. You will see, when you approach the city, that it may be entered only through a chasm which is, in some places, no more than twelve feet wide. Along the ravine are the ancient structures carved out of the walls of solid rock, the most famous of which include the Khaznet Firaoun, a temple also known as the Treasury of the Pharaohs, and a semicircular theater capable of seating about three thousand persons. All along the rock face are rows of tombs hewn out of the solid stone. The remains of Petra bear witness to its former power, wealth, and prestige."

Dane looked around. About twenty yards away, Bones sat in the midst of a different tour group, probably getting the same boring spiel. He wore a ridiculous looking wide-brimmed straw hat, wraparound shades, and an orange and yellow Hawaiian print shirt. He appeared to be amusing himself by constantly raising his hand and asking questions. Dane could not hear what his friend was asking, but judging by the look on the tour guide's face and the snickers of the group's other members, Bones was up to his usual foolishness. Next to Bones, looking annoyed, sat Admiral Meriwether.

Meriwether's "deal" had been to make all of the arrangements for this trip to Petra, including false identities for the four of them and inspection-free transportation on a Navy plane, in exchange for Dane and the others allowing him to take part in the "adventure", as he called it. Dane wondered if his old commanding officer were regretting his decision right about now.

The four of them were registered in separate tour groups for today. Beginning the next morning, they would be volunteering for one of the archaeological digs that was taking place within the ancient city. Dane hoped that they could slip away in time to find whatever lay at the coordinates the writing on the sword had pinpointed.

"If there are no questions, we'll head down to Petra," the guide said. He removed his hat and ran his fingers through the fringe of short, white hair. The look on his face indicated that he was not eager to field questions. Hearing none, he motioned for the group to follow him.

The track wound down the hill from the small village of Wady Musa, with its neatly terraced gardens and vineyards looking more like a model than reality. Upon entering the valley, Dane had his first impression of the strangeness of the place. Rocks weathered by time into rounded masses like domed towers stood above them. As they continued on, the facade of an occasional tomb showed in a side valley or recess. Everything was so different from what they had just left behind that Dane had the sensation of having wandered into another world. It felt nightmarishly surreal, like he was walking through the abode of the dead.

The valley narrowed. A sheer cliff in front seemed to offer little promise of further progress. Rounding a corner, a great dam built of carefully dressed blocks of stone filled the valley from side to side and confirmed the impression, but the guide led them through a narrow cleft in the cliff face just by the wall.

"So this is the road to Petra," Dane said to himself. "A handful of men could hold it against an army."

Kaylin nodded in agreement.

The path ran along a dry torrent bed, the sheer cliffs on either side rising higher and higher as they penetrated deeper into the heart of the mountains. Here it seemed to be perpetual twilight, with an occasional glint of sun on the cliff face high above. The pathway widened and narrowed intermittently. Dane looked above him and saw that in places, the cliff tops nearly touched. There was little sound beyond the shuffling of feet and the occasional rustle of shrubbery in the faint breeze.

"This road is called the Siq," the guide announced. "As you can see, on this side is a channel cut in the rock, which originally carried water to the inhabitants of Petra from the springs at Wady Musa."

The road twisted and turned. At this point, Dane could only see a few yards ahead. The way became interminably slow, one featureless stretch giving way to another, then another. He was beginning to feel antsy when suddenly, startlingly, the end of the chasm appeared.

Framed in the cleft before them was the facade of a great tomb, dazzlingly bright in the sunlight. The sudden change from the gloom of the Siq was so sudden that, for a moment, Dane felt dazed and bewildered. He glanced at Kaylin, who was squinting and shading her eyes.

Gradually their consciousness began to absorb the glowing beauty and perfect proportions of the sculpture, the subtle coloring of the rock, and the soft green foreground of oleanders.

"This tomb is called the Khazneh or Treasury, and the urn at the top carries the marks of many bullets which have been fired at it in the hope of shattering it and releasing the treasure which local tradition says is hidden there. The rock face in which it is carved is sheltered from winds and rain, and the Khazneh is in consequence the best preserved of all the monuments. Most others are badly weathered, for the soft sandstone quickly submits to the battering of wind-driven sand and rain, and the sharp lines of the sculpture are reduced to a vague outline. Even here the bases of the columns, where it is a softer strata of stone, have weathered somewhat." The guide quickly led them through the open area.

Dane looked at his wrist, checking the GPS monitor that was made to look like an oversized watch. Meriwether had made certain that all four of them had one. They were not far from their target location.

Beyond this clearing, the gorge narrowed again, with great tombs on either side. A little further on was a theatre cut out of the living rock. Apparently, in the course of cutting this theatre, many tombs were sliced in half, and their inner chambers now gaped open to the sunlight.

Soon they came to a place where the hills fell back on either side, leaving an open space about a mile long and three- quarters of a mile wide.

"Here, on the slopes," the guide said, "was the actual city, its temples, palaces, baths and private houses, with a fine paved street following the line of the stream, and bridges reaching across at intervals. This was the great capital of the Nabataeans, from which, at the height of their power, they ruled the country as far north as Damascus. There was an earlier Edomite town on the site, but of that, practically no traces now remain. The city was extensively occupied from about the fifth century B.C. to the fifth century A. D., and was at its heyday during that time.

"All the monuments and buildings now visible belong, however, to the Nabataean and Roman periods. The extreme softness of the sandstone prevented any finely detailed work being done, and the sculptors had to devise a style to suit their material. This they did very effectively, and it is a tribute to their skill in design that none of the tombs, however small, seems dwarfed by the great cliffs which tower above them. They all fit perfectly into the general picture, and do not in any way detract from the natural beauties of the site.

Dane looked around. From the open space of the town site, valleys went off in all directions. Thank goodness for the GPS units. Otherwise, they could spend hours wandering up and down these narrow ravines. The ravines appeared to be lined on both sides with houses and tombs, of infinite variety and size. Occasional flights of steps wound their way up the sides of the mountains. They were not straight channels, but winding courses, their depths hidden by twists and turns.

"Many of the tombs are occupied by Arabs. During the day, you will hear them herding their flocks of goats. After sunset, you will likely see their campfires, and perhaps hear occasional snatches of song."

Dane was surprised at this bit of information. He had always been under the impression that the entirety of Petra was abandoned, like the cliff dwellings of Mesa Verde. At least the throngs of tourists and the many natives would make their searching around less noticeable.

The guide paused and motioned for everyone to circle around. He began describing some of the larger tombs, which were found in the northeast area of the city. Dane gradually worked his way to the back of the crowd. When he was out of sight of the tour guide, he consulted his GPS again, and then looked around to get his bearings. If his estimation was accurate, the location indicated in the writing on the sword lay to the northeast of where they stood. Looking in that direction, he saw that two narrow defiles snaked out of the canyon. Either could be the right one. Kaylin squeezed through the crush of the crowd, and sidled up next to him.

"Well, boyfriend," she said the word with intentional irony, "what do you want to do first?" She had a pretty smile. More than pretty. Why hadn't he noticed it before?

Dane ignored the boyfriend comment. Meriwether had suggested that the two of them pose as husband and wife. Dane had refused, but Kaylin took it in stride, though she seemed disappointed.

"The tour ends in an hour" he said, pushing away thoughts of her smile. "We don't have to report for the dig until after lunch. Let's see if we can 'accidentally' wander away from the group."

She nodded her agreement, and reached out to take his hand. They walked slowly around the ring of tourists, pretending to take in the scenery. When they were certain that their guide's attention was diverted, they strolled quickly but casually away from their group.

About fifty yards away, they blended into the fringes of another tour group. Bones and the Admiral were in this group, but the two pairs made a point to pretend that they did not know one another. Dane and Kaylin casually skirted these people in the same fashion that they had moved around their old group. When opportunity arose, they wandered away.

They were now very close to the two ravines that Dane had identified as likely candidates. Still pretending to gawk at the scenery, though in truth the gawking came easily in this magnificent setting, Dane pulled out his cell phone and called up Bone's number. He felt a bit foolish calling someone who stood less than a hundred yards away, but it was the only way he could communicate with his friends without anyone seeing them talk to one another.

It took what seemed an interminably long time for the connection to be made, which was fine with Dane. Not that he believed anyone would realize that the two of them were talking to one another, but the delay did not hurt their ruse.

"*Yep*," Bones answered.

"We're headed northeast," Dane said.

"*East northeast,*" Bones corrected, "*I saw you pass by.*"

"I can't tell for certain where exactly the GPS is going to place us. We'll take the ravine on the right. Let us get out of sight, then you and Meriwether take the defile on the left. I'm assuming the cliffs will block cell phone reception, so let's get back into the open in one hour and call each other."

"*Do you really want us coming out of the clefts at the same time?*" Bones asked.

"Negative. We'll head out in fifty."

"*If I don't hear from you, I'm coming after you,*" his friend said.

"Same here," Dane replied.

"*Yes, Kemosabe,*" Bones joked, and ended the connection.

Dane and Kaylin entered the narrow cut in the rock façade. Dane half expected to hear someone calling for them to rejoin the tour group, but apparently no one had noticed their departure. They came to a sharp bend in the rock, and behind them, the tour groups disappeared from sight.

The shade was even deeper in this constricted space. Faint sunlight bounded down the walls, casting a dull pink glow on the hard, sandy loam at their feet. Dane consulted his GPS. Fortunately, the unit was still receiving a strong signal. They were coming closer to their destination. He picked up the pace.

They made two more turns, eventually ending up at a blank rock face. Dane scanned the rocky ledges above, letting his sight gradually trail down the walls to the ground below. He saw nothing. He felt Kaylin tugging at his arm.

"I see something up there." She pointed up and to the left, high up in the rocks.

Dane looked in the direction she indicated. Behind a small outcropping of scrub lay what appeared to be a small cave. In the half-light of the gorge, his eyes had passed right over it.

"How do we get there?" she asked. "Did they have hand trails like the Anasazi?"

The ancient settlers of the American southwest had built their cities in rock overhangs high in cliffs not entirely unlike these. The dwellings were accessible by hand and foot trails, which were little more than depressions chiseled in the wall.

"I don't know," Dane said. "But I believe the hand trails usually ran from the top of the cliff down to the overhang. Looks like we'll have to free climb."

Kaylin consulted her wrist unit.

"It's in the right direction," she said. "Ready for a climb, monkey man?"

"Sure," Dane said, laughing, "send the scuba diver clambering up the precarious rock face."

"Forgive me," she said, grinning, "but doesn't SEAL stand for 'sea, air, land'?"

"No," Dane replied with a straight face. "It stands for 'seduce every attractive lady'."

"I guess I should be offended then," Kaylin said. "You certainly haven't tried to seduce me. "What's the matter? Am I not pretty enough for you?"

Her tone was playful, but there was a questioning look in her eyes. Why did women always have to twist everything you say into a criticism of their physical appearance?

"I'm retired, remember?" Dane said, trying to lighten her mood a bit.

"Sorry, but you're not using that line one me. Once a SEAL, always a SEAL. Now let's check out that cave."

Dane scanned the rock face from the ground up to the opening of the cave. He studied it carefully, selecting the cracks and outcroppings that would provide the best handholds. When he had planned his route, he set to climbing.

He made his way up the face of the rock at a steady pace. He looked neither up nor down, but kept his eyes just ahead of his hands, picking out the next hold. He trusted the route he had selected and allowed himself no second-guessing. Foot by foot, he sacaled the wall. It was a strenuous climb, but not a particularly challenging one. The route he had chosen avoided sections in which the rock wall leaned out over the chasm. Without proper equipment, he would not have attempted to scale any of the more dangerous outcroppings.

After what felt like an hour, but was probably more like six or seven minutes, he hauled himself up onto the narrow ledge in front of the small cave. He turned and offered his hand to Kaylin, who shook her head and pulled herself up.

Dane felt a pang of disappointment when he looked at the cave. It was small: no more than five feet high, and about the same width. It ended in a blank wall about twelve feet back.

"Sorry," Kaylin said, clearly disappointed. "All of that climbing for nothing."

Dane checked his GPS and found that they were very close to the targeted spot. In fact, their targeted location was to the west of where they stood: either atop the plateau between the two ravines, or inside the mass of rock. He took a few steps into the cave, hunching so as not to hit his head on the ceiling. He could have sworn that he felt a gentle breeze on his face. Fishing his mini Mag Lite out of his pocket, he flicked it on and played the beam across the back wall.

"Kay, look at this!"

The cave did not end in a blank wall, but took a sharp turn to the left. Kaylin, her enthusiasm apparently renewed by this bit of good fortune, hurried to his side, her own flashlight in hand.

They turned the corner and found themselves in an even tighter passage. They could still walk side by side, but barely so. The ceiling gently rose to a height of over six feet, allowing Dane to stand up straight, though he still instinctively felt that he ought to duck down. About twenty paces in, he noticed goose bumps rising on his arms. The air had grown markedly cooler, and he could still feel the faint breeze on his face.

The tunnel snaked back to the right. The path began to slope gently downward, and was slightly moist. Dane put his hand out against the wall, and was surprised to feel that it was smooth to the touch. He halted and shone his light along the wall.

"Pictographs," Kaylin whispered in awe.

There was no one around to hear their voices, but it somehow seemed appropriate to speak softly.

"Do you have your notebook with you?" Dan asked in an equally quiet tone.

"I've got my digital camera," Kaylin replied. She produced a small camera from her fanny pack, and began snapping pictures of the carvings.

The pictographs ran horizontally from left-to-right, just above Dane's eye level, along the left wall in a single row for a distance of about eight feet. Below them was a row of characters that resembled writing. Dane could not decide if they looked more like runes or alphabetic figures. There was something vaguely familiar about them, but he was no scholar. He checked the opposite wall, and confirmed that it was bereft of any carving.

"Got them," Kaylin said. She checked the display on the back of her camera, using the zoom feature to insure that she had gotten a clear picture of every part of the carving. Apparently satisfied with her work, she led them deeper down the tunnel.

Dane estimated that they had traveled about seventy yards, including the jog to the left. Measuring from the outside wall, he guessed they were about fifty yards deep into the massive stone plateau. Though he knew it was a futile attempt, he checked his wrist unit. Sure enough, the rock walls precluded any signal from reaching them.

As they progressed down the tunnel, Dane caught a faint whisper of sound, like wind rustling through tree branches. As the sound grew louder, he realized that he was hearing the sound of running water. Somewhere far beneath them was an underground stream. Was there a passage leading down?

The tunnel veered to the right and they came to an abrupt halt. A narrow crevice, no more than six inches wide, cut across the tunnel. A few feet beyond the crack, a massive rock fall blocked the tunnel. Most likely, some sort of seismic activity had caused both the fissure and the tunnel collapse. Dane stepped across the gap, and carefully inspected the pile of rocks and debris. There was not sign of any opening. He shone his light all over the pile, looking for a sign of empty space behind the wall, but he could see nothing. Even if he had believed that it might be possible to clear away some of the debris, he dared not risk another collapse. Based on his inspection, though, he was satisfied that the tunnel in front of them was impassable.

"There's no way through?" Kaylin asked, her voice tinged with disappointment.

Dane shook his head as he turned. He knelt and shone his light down into the crevice. Kaylin added her brighter beam, and they peered into the depths of the ancient stone. The cut was incredibly deep. Dan thought he could make out a slight twinkle of light reflected on water, but he could not be certain. The sound of the underground stream was audible, and the cool breeze, though faint, was decidedly refreshing. They sat there for a moment, silently peering into the thin defile. Dane finally broke the silence.

"I guess we'd better head back. Bones will be looking for us if he can't reach us by phone."

Kaylin nodded, her face twisted in a disappointed frown. She said nothing, but Dane believed he could read her thoughts.

"We're close," he said, laying a hand on her shoulder. "I can feel it."

CHAPTER 22

Bones muttered a curse under his breath and adjusted Goliath's sword, which hung strapped across his back inside a long, leather, camera tripod case. Neither he nor the others of his crew had come up with a good idea of how to safely store the sword while they were out and about. They all had also agreed, perhaps irrationally, that the sword should remain with them at all times. Consequently, the camera equipment bag had been the best idea they had devised. Bones had concealed the sword inside a black cover made of the same material as the camera bag, and kept it inside along with a camera and an actual tripod. He had maintained the ruse by setting up the apparatus and taking several very bad pictures. He had not actually developed the film, but he knew what his talents were, and photography was not one of them.

The dig had quickly grown boring. At Dane's instruction, he and Meriwether, or 'Franklin' as the Admiral insisted on being called, had explored this same ravine the previous day, and found nothing but an occasional tomb or shallow cave. Nothing like the passageway that Dane and Kaylin had discovered. According to the GPS readouts, their target area lay somewhere in the center of the giant mass of rock directly between the gorges.

"This blows," he said aloud to no one in particular. "Some vacation."

"Come now Uri," Meriwether said, hefting a bucket of parched earth, "archaeology is fun."

"Tell you what, *Frankie*, you call me Uri one more time and I'll scalp you with my *tripod*."

The broad-shouldered man chuckled and returned to his task of putting buckets of dirt through a mesh sifter.

So far, they had uncovered some fascinating rocks, and something that Bones believed was a fossilized goat turd. Muttering a curse, Bones took off his straw hat and fanned his face. Archaeology required a meticulous nature. That was why it was a perfect pastime to an officer, and a total drag to an impulsive, eccentric treasure hunter like himself.

"Mister Uriah, would you come here please?" The dig foreman called.

Bones, unaccustomed to being called by his Christian name, did not respond at first. The man called his name again. Bones had quickly earned the reputation of being a bit surly. The foreman, a wisp of a man who looked to Bones more like a missionary than an archaeologist, seemed more than a bit intimidated by the tall, muscular Cherokee with the long ponytail and perpetual scowl. Bones had not helped matters by constantly playing with his hunting knife.

"Mister Uriah, a word please?" the man said petulantly. He stood with his hands folded across his chest, his chapped lips pursed in a pouty scowl.

Bones stood and slowly turned and faced the man. He bared his straight, white teeth in a predatory grin, and narrowed his eyes wickedly.

"You want something Mr. Jonas?" he asked. Behind him, Meriwether whispered something disapproving. Bones ignored him. He was hot, bored, and anxious to do some exploring.

"Uh, yes," Jonas said, drastically altering his tone of voice. "I was wondering, since you don't seem to be, shall we say, enjoying yourself, if you might like to take some photographs of the dig?"

Bones inwardly cringed. The last thing he wanted to do was to take more pictures of these pasty skinned, middle aged, Indiana Jones wannabe's in their fresh off the rack safari clothes, and their John Lennon-style shades that he supposed were supposed to make them look professorial. Framed by sunburned faces and perched atop zinc oxide coated noses, they looked silly at best. He took a deep breath, looked up at the sky, and tried to think of a good lie.

As he stared up at the crest of the ridge, inspiration struck. His cold smile melted into one of warmth and sincerity.

"I'd love to," he said. He was amused at the look of surprise on Jonas' face at this sudden bout of agreeability. "Tell you what. I'd like to get some overhead shots. I'm going to climb this ridge over here," he pointed behind them, "and take a few pictures from up above. Shouldn't take to long."

Before the dig supervisor could protest, Bones turned and strode down the defile, leaving the thin man standing open-mouthed behind him.

A few quick twists of the gorge, and he had reached the spot where yesterday he had observed the remains of an ancient staircase running down from the top of the cliff. Time and weather had worn away the bottom portion of the stairs, and they ended about halfway down the stone face. There had been neither time nor opportunity to explore the cliff top on the previous day. He wanted to get up top and take a GPS reading, to see if there was anything suspicious-looking up above. He positioned the sword comfortably on his back, tightened the straps of the camera case, and began his climb.

The rocky face was irregular, with lots of protrusions upon which to find footholds. An experienced climber, he quickly made his way up the face until the rock wall smoothed out about ten feet below the foot of the ancient staircase.

Bones inspected the stone above him, and noticed a thin crack running upward from left to right at about a thirty-five degree angle. The crack appeared to be just wide enough to fit his fingers inside. Taking a deep breath, he let go of the rock with his left hand and reached over and upward for the crevice. He could not quite reach. He drew his hand back, carefully centered his right foot on the outcropping on which he stood, and slightly loosened his grip on the wall with his right hand, allowing his fingertips to slip back until they had only a small purchase on the rock. *Sometimes, it's a matter of inches,* he thought. He refrained from mentally turning the thought into a crude innuendo, and instead focused on the task at hand.

Biting his lower lip, he raised his left foot and stretched out to his left, reaching again for the crack in the wall. His stomach fluttered, and for a brief instant, he felt certain that he was going to fall. Then, he felt his fingers grasp the lip of the crevice. Pressing his body against the rock, he worked his fingers deeper into the fissure until they were in up to the second knuckle. Certain now of his grip, he scrabbled with his left foot until he found what amounted to little more than a rough edge against which to brace the bottom of his foot. He exhaled slowly, took another breath, and pushed up hard off his right foot, at the same time pulling up with his left hand.

His right hand caught the edge of the crevice, and he hung suspended on the cliff face.

"Why in God's name am I doing this?" he asked aloud. No one answered, so he decided to keep climbing.

He pulled up as much as he could with his left hand, allowing his weight to swing to that side. He then scooted his right hand farther up the crevice, gripped tight, and shifted his weight to the right. Repeating this process, he worked his way up the wall. It was slow going. Twice he had to stop to catch his breath. The muscles of his shoulders and neck were knotted and his fingers screamed in agony. He felt with the bottom of his foot and found a tiny indentation in which he could fit the tip of his boot. It was a small relief, but it took some of the burden of his body weight from his fingers.

A strange tickling sensation ran across the back of his right hand, and slowly down his arm. He looked up.

"You have got to be kidding me!" he shouted.

He had read about the black scorpion, but had never seen one in person. It was monstrous, nearly four inches long. Rather than black, its color was a dark reddish-brown. Its stinger, thick and menacing, curled up above its body like a snake poised to strike.

Bones froze, irrationally hoping that the deadly arachnid would turn around and creep away. No such luck. The scorpion paused, then proceeded further along his arm. Bones tried blowing at the creature, but to no avail. It held fast to his arm, and continued to make its way ever closer to his head. Up close, its pincers looked like crab claws. Bones flexed and relaxed the muscles of his arm, blew another hard puff of air, and then another, but could not dislodge the scorpion.

He groaned. As he saw it, there were two choices. Climb to the top and hope that the scorpion did not sting him before he could get it off him, or let go with his left hand and try to dislodge the scorpion without falling or being stung. Figuring his odds were better if he reached the top before dealing with the nasty creature, he made up his mind to continue his climb. His plans changed when the scorpion, for no apparent reason, but on a burst of speed and shot over his shoulder and onto his neck.

Instinctively, he grabbed for it with his right hand. His stomach lurched as he swung to his left, holding on with one hand. Without thinking, he grabbed the scorpion and flung it away in one quick motion. He exhaled slowly, unable to believe what he had done, and even more surprised that he had not been stung. His adrenaline pumping full-force now, he hauled himself the last few feet up to the ancient stairway.

He reached the top of the steps and took a moment to catch his breath and gather himself. After a moment, he stood and surveyed the wide plateau. It was a featureless landscape, save a few stray boulders and some sparse patches of dry grass. At least it would be an easy walk. Bones consulted his GPS, and found that his target location lay to the southeast. He quickly made his way to the site, keeping an eye out for more scorpions. When the GPS display told him that he had hit his spot, he stopped, looked down, and swore.

He saw nothing. The ground beneath his feet was flat, clear of any debris. Whatever the sword was pointing to must be underground somewhere. After a visual inspection revealed nothing out of the ordinary, he set about inspecting the area around the target location.

Keeping his eyes on the ground, he began by walking around the spot in a square pattern: four paces, turn left, four paces, turn left, and so on. With each complete circuit, he stepped out two paces, and enlarged his square. Eventually, he had covered most of the plateau, and found nothing.

He supposed he had better snap a few pictures before the folks at the dig started wondering what had happened to him. He unslung the long case that held his camera equipment and the sword, and removed his camera and tripod. Making his way to the ledge directly above the dig, he wondered if perhaps the blocked tunnel Dane had found might be the passageway they sought. From what his friend had said, that would be a hard row to hoe.

The faint sound of shouting caught his attention. It seemed to be coming from beneath him. He laid the camera down, knelt and looked down over the edge. The dig was deserted, but at the base of the cliff, he could see several people milling around and talking loudly. They appeared to be looking at something in the face of the rock. He called down to them, but they seemed to be unable to hear him above the sound of their own conversation.

His cell phone rang. Dane was calling him.

"Yeah?"

"Bones, you've got to get down here right away," Maddock's voice, though tense, sounded excited.

"Sure. Where are you?"

"Look down."

Bones peered back over the edge and saw Dane standing on the outer fringes of the crowd. Neither of them ventured to gesture to one another, maintaining the fiction that they were complete strangers.

"What are you doing with my dig group?" Bones asked. "Mr. Jonas will smack you with his pocketbook if he catches you."

"Just get back down here. You'll see when you get here."

The connection went dead. Bones cursed, and debated dropping a rock down on Maddock's head. Just a very small pebble, something that would sting a bit. He thought the better of it, though. He was eager to find out what exactly was going on down below.

The climb down was much easier than the climb up had been. A few minutes later, he trotted up beside Dane who was standing at the edge of the crowd. He fixed his friend with a questioning look. The blond man merely nodded toward the wall. Bones turned toward the wall and gasped.

Someone had apparently uncovered a false wall in one of the broad recesses in the rock. The wall had been knocked down and the rubble hastily cleared away. *Real archaeologists will have a fit at the impulsiveness,* Bones thought, *but they won't scream too much once they see what these amateurs have uncovered.*

Beyond where the wall had been, was a deep alcove. In the foreground was what appeared to be a well, but it was the back wall that drew everyone's attention.

Carved into the back of the alcove was an incredibly well preserved relief sculpture depicting five giant men engaged in battle with a throng of much smaller warriors. The two giants on either side were displayed in profile, laying about themselves with heavy broadswords. Dead soldiers lay strewn about their feet, graphically depicted in various states of dismemberment.

In contrast, the warrior in the center was rendered from the front, facing directly toward them. Bones was fascinated by the detail. The towering warrior was outfitted in typical Bronze Age armor and a small helm, from which flowed a wild mane of hair. His face was framed by a thick beard, and his eyes seemed to bore into Bones with evil intent. He held his giant sword upraised, and his small, round, shield in the center of his body.

Dane turned to Bones, smiled broadly, and whispered on word. "Goliath."

CHAPTER 23

Dane, Bones, Kaylin, and Meriwether crept along the pathway that led down into Petra. The full moon cast odd shadows among the tombs and dark recesses in the walls. In the places where the pathway narrowed significantly, the darkness was almost complete.

"What do you think we're going to find?" Bones whispered, looking around.

"Hopefully, a doorway of some sort," Dane answered in a hushed voice. He was not certain what they would discover, but he had a strong suspicion. "The carving in the center," he began.

"The one you believe represents Goliath?" Kaylin asked.

"Right. You notice he's facing forward, but the others are all facing sideways. Well, there's another difference." He paused, waiting to see if anyone was thinking along the same lines. "His shield is different, as well. It's much smaller, perfectly round, and held at the very center of his body."

"You're right," Bones said after a moment. "I didn't really think about it at the time, but it does look...wrong."

Dane held up a hand to silence everyone as they approached the dig site. Though the discovery had initially caused a bit of a stir, it had quickly become business as usual in an area rife with history. Only one person, an archaeology student from Tel Aviv, minded the site. The term "minded" was used loosely, Dane thought, as the young man was apparently asleep in his tent, a good fifty yards away.

They crept closer to the site, moving cautiously so as not to disturb the sleeping scientist. They cautiously made their way around the ceremonial well, gaping black in the darkness, and walked to the center of the wall.

Dane knelt in front of the center figure of the carving, produced a small flashlight, and shone its tight beam on the carved shield. After a brief inspection, he put the flashlight between his teeth, stood, and grasped the shield with both hands. Meriwether and Kaylin added their flashlight beams to his. His heart pounded. He hoped this would work.

He gave the shield a great twist to the right, grunting with the effort. Nothing happened. He took a breath and tried again, with the same result.

"What do you think?" Bones whispered.

Dane did not answer. He was thankful that the darkness kept the others from seeing the redness in his face. He had been so certain. What if…

He grasped the shield again, and this time twisted counterclockwise. The stone held fast. He threw every ounce of his strength into the effort, until he could feel the veins in his head bulging. He was about to give up when he felt the stone give. Slowly, inch by inch, the shield rotated. It spun a full quarter turn to the left before grinding to a firm halt. Dane let out the breath he had held, and then pulled. The shield came free in his hands. His eyes widened with excitement when he saw what lay in the center of the carving.

Where the shield had hung in the middle of the warrior's chest was what could only be described as a giant keyhole. It was a large, iron circle, with a vertical slot slicing through the center. It appeared to Dane to be rust-free, and in good condition, protected by the dry climate. The others pushed forward to examine it more closely.

"How do we open it?" Kaylin whispered, running a long, slender finger around the edge.

Dane paused, taking a moment to gently lay the stone shield on the ground. Perhaps he should be nervous, but having been correct about the shield, he was even more confident in his hypothesis. He reached back over his left shoulder and slid the sword free of its scabbard.

"Ahh," Bones intoned, understanding now evident in his voice. Dane shone his light along the length of the blade, examining it carefully. He then turned the light onto the keyhole and inspected it. Satisfied, he took the sword's hilt in both hands, and leveled it at the keyhole. He rotated it so that the serrated edge faced up, and before doubts could arise, he thrust it forward.

The sword slid home with a scarcely audible hiss. Kaylin gasped as the blade disappeared into the slot. Dane pushed it in until it stopped about ten inches short of the hilt. He let go of the hilt and grasped either side of the cross guard. He first tried turning it counterclockwise, as he had done the shield, but the sword held fast. He then twisted it clockwise. Nothing. He gave it another twist, and felt something give. Slowly, the sword turned in the keyhole, rotating a half-turn. It halted with a metallic clank, followed by the sound of something behind the wall snapping into place. In the silence of the night, the noise sounded like a thunderclap. All four of them jerked their heads toward the darkened tent, but saw no evidence of anyone stirring. Suddenly, Dane felt the sword being pulled from his grip.

He turned to see the carving of Goliath recede into the wall, revealing inky blackness on either side. Instinctively, he had tightened his grip on the sword when he first felt the tug, and he was pulled off-balance, stumbling toward the dark opening. He loosed his grip on the cross-guard, and felt someone grab his belt, steadying him.

"That was graceful," Dane said, looking back at Bones, who had caught him. "Are we ready to go in?" he asked the group. They all nodded in affirmation. In the dim flashlight glow, he could see that each of them wore the same look: a mix of wonder and excitement.

"You do the honors," Bones said, motioning for Dane to lead them into the inky blackness behind the wall.

He stepped through the narrow space between the receded carving and the wall. He played his light around in front of him, involuntarily sucking in his breath at what he saw.

"What is it?" Bones whispered, concern in his voice. "Are you all right?"

"Get in here," Dane said. The others were quickly at his side, shining their lights in front of them.

The cavern was enormous. From the wall behind them, the ceiling swept upward at a sharp angle, peaking about fifty feet above their head. Dane played his light down the wall, revealing a stone well, the twin of the one outside, and five huge, lidless stone coffins fanned out along the wall behind the well. He took a step forward, and then remembered the sword. He turned to see that Bones had already removed it from the keyhole. Accepting the blade from his friend, he returned it to the scabbard.

Meriwether scrutinized the back of the door.

"It's actually a very simple mechanism," he said with surprise. "It's counterweighted and set in a track. Whoever forged the sword didn't make this." He sounded disappointed and more than a bit puzzled.

Kaylin moved ahead of the others to inspect the well. She shone her flashlight down into the blackness. Dane joined her, and peered down into the depths of the hole. Far below, he could see the glint of their beams on water. He heard a faint gurgle.

"An underground river," Kaylin whispered, "and look!" She focused her light at water level. Dane could barely make out an archway on either side of the well shaft. "It's more than just a ceremonial well. There's something down there. A tunnel?" she mused.

"I don't know," Dane said. "But this must be how Rienzi got into the tomb without having the sword to unlock it."

"How did he climb up?" Kaylin asked, frowning.

Bones stepped up to the opposite side of the well and squinted down.

"Ha! I thought so. Turn off your flashlights." Dane, Kaylin, and Meriwether extinguished their lights, leaving the depths of the well illuminated only by the light of Bone's flashlight, which he held above his shoulder, pointing down at an odd angle.

"If you look at it in just the right way," he explained, "you can see handholds carved up one side. I'll bet the well outside is the same."

Dane tilted his head and moved to his right until, as if by magic, a series of small, oval shadows appeared on the wall. "So whoever made this place sealed it up, and climbed out through the wells."

"But what's beyond here?" Kaylin asked.

"Why do you think there's anything else to see?" Meriwether asked, placing his meaty hands on the rim of the well and leaning forward. "Perhaps this is all there is."

"The tunnel goes both directions," Kaylin explained. "I think if we were to climb down and follow the river, we'd find more."

"Why don't we take a look at what's in here, first?" Dane suggested, turning to face the coffins. He walked to the coffin on the right, and shone his light down inside.

The coffin contained a large, humanlike skeleton. The man must have been nine feet tall, with a broad chest and shoulders. The bones were intact, but appeared to Dane to be brittle. Behind Dane, Bones whistled softly. The man had been buried in full Bronze Age armor. His arms were crossed over his chest, and his sword lay behind him. Though all that remained of him was a hollow shell, he seemed to exude power.

"This one in the center has no head," Meriwether said.

Dane and the others hurried to the Admiral's side. The skeleton was the twin of the one they had just inspected, *or at least from the shoulders down*, he thought.

"I guess we've found our friend Goliath," Dane said. He gripped the edge of the open stone coffin and silently gazed upon the remains of the legendary warrior. He realized, after a few moments, that he was holding his breath. *Goliath!* Even when they had recovered the sword, he had not truly believed that it was Goliath's weapon. It was a remarkable and mysterious artifact, to be sure, but to be proof that a biblical tale was factual? The idea had been hard for him to swallow.

He had never been a religious man. After Melissa died, he gave up on any notion of a loving god looking down on creation. But now, looking down upon the remains of the unfortunate half of the children's Bible story, he wondered what it all meant.

Beside him, Kaylin fell to her knees and crossed herself, like a good Catholic. Bones and Meriwether knelt down on either side of her, the full impact of what they were seeing evident in their faces.

"It's true," Kaylin whispered, tears running freely down her cheeks. "We did it. I wish Dad could be here."

"He's here," Meriwether whispered, putting his arm around Kaylin's shoulder, and giving her a grandfatherly hug. She laid her head against him and continued to gaze in disbelief at Goliath.

Dane did not say anything. They had proved that Goliath was a historical figure, but that was all. It did not prove anything about God, or life after death, or anything else. He was not selfish enough to say so, not when Kaylin needed to believe it. He stood in silence, and tried not to imagine that Melissa was looking over his shoulder.

"It's not enough," Bones suddenly said, raising his head to look at the others.

"What?" Meriwether asked, fixing him with a quizzical glance.

"This doesn't answer everything. There's got to be more somewhere."

Dane nodded. He understood exactly what Bones was saying. He was feeling the same lack of...*completeness* was the only word he could think of to describe it.

"We know that this is Goliath's sword," Dane said. "We know how Rienzi got it. But it doesn't explain the sword itself: how it was made, what the writing signifies."

"Not to mention," Bones added, "why the writing on it pointed to this location."

"Because Goliath and his brothers are buried here," Kaylin said, a look of bewilderment painted upon her face.

"No," Dane said. He turned the conundrum over in his mind as he spoke. "According to the Bible, David took Goliath's sword after he slew him. The priests kept it for a while, and then David took it for himself when he needed a sword. Obviously, the Philistines recovered it some time later. Which means..."

"Which means that either the writing was etched into the sword long after Goliath was dead," Meriwether interrupted, his face aglow with understanding, "which is unlikely, considering none of our tools could do a thing to it, or it was etched into the blade when the sword was forged."

"Meaning that the coordinates for this location point to something else," Dane said. By the time he had finished saying it, he was certain. There was more to be discovered.

"You're right," Kaylin said. "Why would you put directions to a gravesite on the sword, and then bury the sword *in that same grave?*" She stood and put her hands on her hips, looking around. "So what now?"

"I don't know about you three, but right now, I'd like to find a way out of here," Bones said. "We've got company," Bones whispered.

CHAPTER 24

D ane turned and peered through the opening in the rock face, back in the direction from which they had come. Shadows moved stealthily across the moonlit sand. He caught glimpse of pale light glinting off the barrel of a gun. He could not tell what type, but the length of the barrel told him all that he needed to know.

"How many?" he whispered to Bones.

"At least eight," Bones said. "Probably more. Either way, they've got much more firepower than we do. "

"Should we turn out our flashlights?" Kaylin asked.

"No, then they'll know we've spotted them," Dane said." Let them believe they're taking us by surprise, and maybe they'll be less cautious." Dane hoped his voice carried more optimism than he felt.

"Who do you think they are?" Meriwether whispered, drawing his pistol, an old, Swiss-made SIG P-210 from his fanny pack.

Dane shrugged. "Probably the same guys who've been after us all along. Either that, or Wrexham's got friends."

"How would they find us?" Meriwether protested. "We've been so careful in every detail." His words sounded like a statement, not a question.

"Right now, I don't think that's as important as how we're going to get out of here," Bones said, "because there's no way we'll be able to get back out the way we came."

Dane knew that his friend was right. He scanned the room one last time, seeing no sign of a secondary egress. He knew what they had to do.

"Down the well," he said, "and make it quick. Bones first, Kay next, then Meriwether."

Bones clamped his small flashlight between his teeth, tucked his Beretta into his belt, and swung over the side into the well. The others complied without protest, although Kaylin appeared quite displeased. Cautiously, they climbed over the edge. Finding their footholds, they slowly disappeared from sight.

Dane knelt behind the well, positioned so that he could see outside. His Walther he held trained on the opening. In his left hand, he played the flashlight back and forth across the far wall of the cavern, trying to create the illusion that they were still inside looking around.

He stole a quick glance down into the well. The others had not yet reached the bottom, their flashlights bobbing far below where he stood. His heart pounded. How much longer could he wait? He wanted to cover their descent, but if one of their stalkers appeared in the doorway, Dane would have no choice but to shoot him. After that, the odds of him making it safely down to the bottom would be slim indeed.

He strained to listen for the sound of approaching footsteps. He heard nothing. Whoever these people were, they were good. They had to be close by now. He looked down the well again and thought he saw the reflection of light on the water. The others were close to the bottom. He could start his climb down.

He laid his flashlight on the ground with its beam pointed toward the coffin farthest to the right. Perhaps the intruder's attention would be temporarily diverted from the well when they first entered the room. Tucking the Walther into his waistband at the center of his back, he climbed onto the edge of the well, all the while certain that, at any moment, an armed man was going to appear in the doorway while Dane was at his most vulnerable.

He hung his left foot over the edge, and felt for a toehold, but there was none to be found. He moved his foot in a circle against the smooth stone, seeking to gain purchase in the darkness. *I should have spotted out my path before I put the pistol down,* he thought. Frustration welled up inside of him. Finally, he found a niche in the well. Gripping the edge with both hands, he swung the other foot over and quickly found another hold. Cursing the darkness, he began a slow descent.

He had descended no more than twenty feet when he heard a shuffling above him. Someone had entered the burial chamber. The sword bounced off the back of his thigh as he went. He paused, hastily adjusted it, and then quickened his pace, wondering absently how deep the water down below was, in case he should miss a step.

The hand and footholds were set at regular intervals, and he soon fell into a rhythm. He stole a glance upward, and saw that he had covered a good fifty feet. He guessed that he was about halfway down.

He heard a clattering sound, and the faint glow above him seemed to waver. He guessed someone had kicked the flashlight. The followers had obviously proceeded with caution, thoroughly searching the cavern before declaring it empty. He wondered how long it would be before they looked into the well.

He had has answer sooner than he would have liked. A shadowed form appeared in the faint circle of light up above. Now grateful for the darkness, Dane scrambled down the wall at a pace that bordered on incaution. The figure up above moved away. Dane kept his eye on the circle that seemed to grow no smaller no matter how quickly he moved down the wall. *They couldn't be giving up, could they?*

As soon as the thought entered his mind, two faces appeared above him. A gleam of dark metal, and then the sound of automatic weapons fire shattered the cloak of silence. Dane froze as the bullets ricocheted off the wall behind him and down the shaft below. Holding on tight with his left hand, he freed his Walther as a second burst of gunfire ripped along the wall, this time farther below him.

Taking aim, Dane squeezed off two shots. He heard a scream, and one of the shadows disappeared from sight. The second man, however, ripped off a long, steady stream of bullets that tore into the wall only a few feet above him. Sharp, stinging pain danced across the top of his skull as fragments of ancient stone cut into his scalp. *Idiot!* he cursed himself. *You gave them a target!* Hoping that the others were clear of the shaft, he let go, and plunged toward the river below.

As he fell, he pulled his knees to his chest, tucked his chin, and drew his hands up to his face. He had only a moment for the fear of being hit by ricocheting bullets to do battle with that of too-shallow water, before the tickling sensation of falling was replaced by the icy impact of his body striking the surface of the underground river.

He kicked downward, and fanned his arms out, trying to keep himself from plunging too deeply. The dark, cold water enveloped him, and then his feet struck bottom. The impact sent waves of pain coursing up his legs, through his groin, and up his spine. He felt his body crumple. A coppery taste filled his mouth. For a brief, panicked moment he thought, *I'm paralyzed.* Then his legs seemed to find a life of their own. Reflexively, they kicked out, and he felt himself rising toward the surface, even as a hard current swept him down the tunnel and away from the deadly gunfire.

He broke the surface in total darkness. He blew a mixture of water and blood from his sinuses, and took a wet gulp of air. Coughing and spitting, he struggled to keep his head above water. He was surprised to find that his arms worked as well as his legs. The cold water dulled the pain in his back, knees, and ankles, but it was there.

His head struck something hard. A loud sound burst through his ears. He felt a brief flash of pain, and then fading…

"Hey, baby. Thought you'd be home by now."
"Sorry, I had to make a stop. I've got a surprise for you!"
"I hate surprises. What is it?"
"Dane! You are no fun at all."
"I know. Now, what's my surprise?"
"I'm not telling."
"Come on. You know I'm going to get it out of you."
"Fine, just be that way…Daddy."
"What did you say?"
"You're going to be a…AAAAAH!"
Scream. Tires screech. Crash. Glass shatters.
Silence.

"Melissa! Melissa, speak to me! Melissa!"
Silence.
"Melissa?"
Call ended… 0:59

A scream of primordial rage filled his throat, and he rent the veil of unconsciousness. His head was still above water. He must have only been out for a few seconds. Suppressing an angry sob, he focused on staying afloat, and pushed the memories back into the recesses of his mind.

The tunnel was about seven feet wide, and he quickly paddled to one side. He tried to find something to grab onto, but the arched walls were smooth and slick. He kept kicking and paddling, already concerned that hypothermia might set in if he did not get out of the frigid stream sometime soon. He wished that he still had his flashlight. What if he passed by a side passage and could not see it in the darkness?

He banged into the side of tunnel as the current swept him around a bend, and then silver light exploded around him. Blinded after so long in the semi-darkness of the burial chamber, and the underground waterway, he squeezed his eyes shut. He felt something tighten across his throat. Then several hands were on him, pulling him free of the water. He opened his eyes to see Bones, Kaylin, and Meriwether leaning over him.

"Good thing you had the sword on," Bones said, grinning. "I missed you, but I caught hold of the scabbard."

"Are you all right?" Kaylin asked, looking frightened. "You aren't hurt, are you?"

"Oh yeah," he groaned. "I feel great."

Accepting a hand up from Bones, he climbed to his feet. His ankles screamed in hot pain, but he did not think they were broken. Likewise, his knees and back.

"We heard shots," Meriwether said.

"They almost got me," Dane said hoarsely. He paused to hack up the last of the water in his lungs. "I don't know if they'll try to follow us, or not. We'd…" He paused as he took a good look at his companions. "Why aren't you wet?" They all laughed.

"Three tunnels branch off of the shaft of the well just above water level," Bones explained. "They were pretty well concealed, so we couldn't see them from above. Lucky for you we picked the one that came out downstream."

Dane looked around. The room was wide, about one hundred feet square. The walls were incredibly smooth, seemingly cut with laser precision from the native rock. Ornate, ivy-wrapped columns were carved into each corner. The underground river flowed through a cut channel nearly twenty feet wide, dividing the room evenly in two. Where the channel met the wall on either end, the water ran beneath a decorated archway. Above each was carved two angels dueling with swords.

Each half of the room was twin to the other. At the center of each of the two walls that ran parallel to the river, broad stone steps led up to high, arching doorways, each opening into a dark tunnel beyond. Above the arch on either side was the carved figure of an angel in flight. Its wings, rendered in painstaking detail, swept downward around either side of the doorway. Each angel, its face an implacable mask of fury, held aloft a fiery sword in its right hand.

High above, at each compass point, a small window-like opening was cut in the center of every wall, about ten feet down from the ceiling. Dane craned his neck to look at them. He could not make out anything in the darkened recesses behind the windows, but he could tell that there was open space beyond them.

A random thought broadsided him without warning, and he looked at the other three in confusion.

"Wait a minute," he said. "Where do you think all of this light is coming from?"

"From these." Kaylin pointed to a diamond-shaped stone protruding from the wall nearby. It was about the size of Dane's hand, and glowed an opalescent white. A row of them ran at regular intervals around the room about a third of the way up from the floor. Another row circled the room about two-thirds of the way up, and more were set in a grid-like pattern in the ceiling. *How had he failed to notice them?*

"Watch what happens," Meriwether said, his voice an excited whisper. He shone his flashlight on one of the stones. When the beam hit the diamond-shaped object, the surface seemed to swirl and flash in an array of colors like mother-of-pearl. The glow that emanated from the stone grew in intensity, and as the light that it generated touched the lights on either side of it, they too shone more brightly. "It absorbs the light and amplifies it." Meriwether sounded entranced.

"What is this place?" Dane marveled. Before anyone could answer, footsteps sounded from the other side of the room.

Dane whirled and drew his pistol, hoping that the water had not treated it too roughly. He had allowed himself to be mesmerized by the magnificence of what he was seeing, and now their pursuers had caught up to them. Four men in dark clothing, armed with automatic rifles burst through the doorway on the far side of the room. They looked around in confusion for a moment, and then caught sight of Dane's party.

"Get up the stairs!" Dane yelled. Bones shouted back, but his words were lost in a raging torrent of gunfire.

CHAPTER 25

D ane dropped to one knee, bringing the Walther to bear on the four armed men, all the while expecting to feel hot lead ripping through his flesh. But the roar that filled the room was not the staccato rattle of automatic weaponry, but the sharp report of large caliber rifles. Across the room, two men crumpled to the ground. The remaining pair fired wildly into the air as they backed up, seeking shelter in the passageway from which they had come. The rifle fire continued unabated.

Dane, now retreating toward the safety of the doorway on his side of the room, looked up to see men leaning out of the upper windows, sending a steady stream of bullets toward their pursuers. *What is going on?* Not waiting to find out, he turned and ran as fast as his injured legs would allow. Bones waited at the top of the stairs, covering his retreat. The big Indian grabbed Dane's upper arm and helped him into the dark hallway where Kaylin and Meriwether waited.

"Who are those guys?" Meriwether asked.

"Which ones?" Bones replied, still watching the room behind them.

Dane looked back. The two fallen black clad men still lay at the foot of the stairs on the far side of the room. The others had disappeared, and the gunfire had ceased.

"I don't know who any of them are," he said. "Let's stick together and try to find a way out of here. Do you remember which direction you came from?" Meriwether nodded, and led the way.

All four had their weapons drawn, and they moved together down the hallway. Bones kept an eye out behind them. About fifty feet down, the passageway ended in a cross-hall. Meriwether paused, and peered around the corner, checking in both directions. He turned back to Dane and the others, and tilted his head to their left. "That way?" he asked softly.

Bones and Kaylin nodded in agreement. Meriwether nodded, turned, and stepped around the corner.

A blistering peal of gunfire rent the quiet of the hall. The old Navy man was spun half around as bullets ripped into him. Instinctively, Dane leapt forward, hitting the ground and rolling, his gun held out in front of him. Another of their dark clothed pursuers, rifle in hand, and sprinted toward him. The man had obviously been watching at head-level for someone to round the corner. His brown eyes widened in surprise as he looked down at Dane, and he swung his rifle forward, but too late. Dane opened fire, catching him full in the chest and knocking him flat on his back. Dane sprang to his feet and looked up and down the hall for more attackers. Seeing no one, he turned to check on Meriwether.

Kaylin and Bones knelt over the Admiral, who held both hands clamped over his stomach. Blood soaked his shirt, and his face was ghastly pale. Dane moved behind Kaylin and placed a hand on her shoulder. He looked down at his old friend, a mixture of fear and anger roiling inside.

"We've got to get you out of here Meri," he said hoarsely, though his words rang false in his ears. They all knew that Meriwether was not going to make it out of here.

"Leave me here," Meriwether whispered, grimacing with the pain of speaking. Kaylin started to protest, but he shook his head vigorously. "Sit me up," he gasped. Dane and Bones grasped him under each arm, gingerly brought him up to a sitting position, and propped him against the wall. Meriwether's face twisted as they moved him, but otherwise he made no sound. He was still as tough as old leather, Dane thought. He could not believe the old sailor might die.

"I am going to be fine," Meriwether said softly, his face placid. "Don't you worry about me."

"You're not going to be fine unless we get you out of here and to a doctor," Kaylin said. Her fair skin was flushed, and unshed tears glistened in her emerald eyes. "We'll find a way. We will."

"That's not what I mean," Meriwether grunted. "You see, I have cancer." He paused to take a raspy breath. "They give me six months, a year if I'm lucky."

The words hit Dane like a sledgehammer. His blood seemed to turn to ice.

"I don't know what to say," Dane said after a long pause. Bones and Kaylin were silent.

"It's all right," Meriwether said. "When I first found out about it, I was scared. I realized I was afraid to die. I had too many unanswered questions. But after what I've seen tonight, I don't have any more questions." He closed his eyes. For a moment, Dane thought the man might have expired, but then Meriwether opened his eyes again. "So, like I said, I'll be all right."

"I wish there was something I could do for you," Dane said. A feeling of helplessness swelled up inside of him, all thoughts of their pursuers were forgotten in his pain and frustration. First his parents, then Melissa, and now Meriwether. What good was he? He had not been able to do anything for any of them.

"You've already given me a gift that I couldn't repay if I lived forever. You've given me hope." He coughed, a loud, rasping song that was painful to hear. He winced, and then extended his hand, first to Bones, who shook it regretfully. He next took Kaylin's hand. She took his in both of hers, and kissed him gently on the forehead.

Finally, Meriwether reached out and clasped Dane's hand.

"Good luck, Swabbie," he said hoarsely.

"You too," Dane replied. After a moment, he let go of the older man's hand, but Meriwether held on.

"You need to have hope, son," he whispered. His eyes had gained a sudden clarity. "It's nobody's fault." The intensity of his expression took Dane aback.

"What isn't?" Dane asked.

Meriwether did not reply. He closed his eyes and let his head rock back against the wall. He sighed deeply. Dane leaned closer, and could hear the man's shallow breathing. He gave his old friend's shoulder a squeeze, and then stood.

"We need to go," Bones said. "I hate to leave him as much as you do. We're too vulnerable here."

Dane knew that his friend was right. Someone could come upon them from any of three directions. He stood and addressed the other two.

"All right, let's get our directions straight. We'll call the direction from which the river enters the main hall 'north'." He pointed down the hallway away from the dead attacker. "Left is west, right is east, behind us is south. Got it?" Bones and Kaylin nodded. "Now, can you tell me how you got here?"

"Go 'south', as you called it, to the end of this hall," Kaylin said. "Then two rights and we'll hit the passage to the well."

Dane turned wordlessly and led the way south down the passage. Over his left shoulder, he could hear the faint rushing of the river through the main hall. Approaching the end of the hall, he paused to relieve their attacker of his rifle. It was an older model NATO CETME. At .51mm, it carried serious stopping power. He tucked the Walther into his belt and stood, rifle at the ready.

Bones knelt down over the attacker. Reaching under the man's collar, he grasped something. With a curse, he gave the object a forceful yank. He held up his hand, displaying a silver chain with a familiar pendant.

"The sword crucifix." Kaylin's voice was scarcely a whisper.

"The same guys who came after us before," Bones said bitterly. He stood and gave Meriwether's assailant a vicious kick in the ribs.

Dane gritted his teeth. He would find out who these people were, and he would make them pay. He stalked angrily to the end of the hallway. He peered around the corner to the right, and saw another short hallway, twin to the one in which he stood. To his left, a spiral stone staircase wound upward. He heard a faint sound coming from the stairwell, and held up a warning hand to Bones and Kaylin.

Moving to the inside wall, he knelt down, and waited. Bones squatted behind him, gripping his Beretta. The faint sound came again. Someone was coming down the stairs. A brief glimpse of black clothing was all the motivation Dane needed to open fire, cutting his target down. Bones hastily appropriated the man's rifle and pointed back down the hallway.

Dane led them along the featureless passage. The corridor was dimly lit by the same diamond-shaped rocks that illuminated the main hall. They made a sharp right at the end of the hall. Far ahead of them, he could see the pathway leading to the tunnel. He made a mental note that they were now moving north, parallel to the inside hall where Meriwether lay, and to the river.

He paused where the passageway intersected a hall on the right. A careful look revealed no pursuers, but in the faint light he could just make out a spiral staircase at the far end. Kaylin came up beside him, her gaze following his. "Do you think…"

"It's a big old circle," Bones said, pausing between them. "Or a square, I mean. I guarantee you, you go down there and hang a right, you'll be in the hall where we left Meriwether."

Bitterness and frustration welled up inside of Dane as he thought again about leaving the Admiral behind. The rational part of him knew there was nothing they could do. Meriwether was probably already gone.

Kaylin seemed to read his thoughts. She squeezed his arm, and then pulled him forward. "Come on. Let's get out of here." They hurried across the hall and into the tunnel that led back toward the well and, hopefully, safety.

This tunnel differed from the one they just left. There were none of the glowing stones on the wall, and they had to use their flashlights to find their way. Also, this passage gradually curved back to the right.

"Smell that?" Bones asked, raising his head and inhaling deeply. A smile spread across his dark face.

"What?" Dane asked.

"Water. We're almost there." Bones claimed to have heightened senses due to his ancestry, but Dane suspected that his friend was usually blowing smoke. This time, he hoped Bones was right.

Behind them, shots rang out again. They were muted, sounding far away. First one barrage, then another reverberated down the hall. The sound was unexpectedly drowned by a deep rumbling that seemed to come from within the bowels of the earth.

"Tremor!" Dane shouted, dropping to the ground. The hallway shook as if some giant hand had grasped it and given it a jiggle. Chunks of rock fell around him. The vibrating lasted several seconds. As the force dissipated, he heard a loud crashing from down the tunnel ahead of them, and a cloud of dust filled the air.

"No way," Bones said flatly, his voice filled with resignation.

Dane did not say anything. He stood and trotted down the hall. Just around the next bend, the ceiling had collapsed, blocking their exit. He and Bones climbed onto the pile of rubble, and attempted to dislodge some of the top stones, but to no avail.

"The tremors are getting worse," Kaylin said, a worried look on her face.

"Maybe they feel bigger because we're underground," Bones said. "What do you think, Maddock?"

Dane took a deep breath and exhaled slowly. "I think we need to find another way out, and soon."

CHAPTER 26

C oming back out of the tunnel, Dane led the group to the left,
moving back toward the main room.

"So, we're headed, *east?*" Bones asked.

Dane nodded and guided them down the hall. When they reached
the end, where the passage terminated at the spiral staircase, they looked
down the hall to the right. Meriwether lay where they had left him,
obviously dead. Nearby, another body lay on the ground.

"He got him one," Bones said. "Good for him."

They walked over to where their friend lay. Dane knelt and checked
Meriwether's pulse, confirming that their comrade was, indeed, deceased.
A lump in his throat, he opened the top button of the Admiral's shirt,
and removed his dog tags. "I'll take care of these," he whispered, tucking
them into his pocket. Then, he reached down and picked up the SIG P-
210, and handed it to Kaylin.

The blonde looked sadly down at their fallen friend. She brushed at
her eyes with the back of a sleeve, and turned away from Dane and
Bones. Regaining her composure, she cleared her throat and turned back
to face them. "You were right, Bones," she said. "We've just looped
around."

"That means the only way is up," Bones said. "Where the bad guys
are."

"What about the bad guy over here?" Dane asked. He walked a few steps to inspect the man whom Meriwether had shot. He was surprised to see that this man was not clad in black, like the others. Instead, he was garbed in bulky, loose-fitting brown pants, and a pullover, white cotton shirt. The shirt was of an odd cut, with no collar and blousy sleeves. The man's features were obviously middle-eastern, but Dane could tell no more.

"The guys who were shooting from upstairs, I presume" Bones said. "We've got to get up there and somehow get past them."

"Can't we get across the water?" Kaylin asked.

"Too wide," Dane said, shaking his head, "and the current's too strong for us to swim across. We'll have to chance it upstairs." He led them back up the hall to the stairwell. "Let's re-orient ourselves," he said, turning back to face them. "We're on the northwest corner of the main room. Got it?" Both nodded, and he turned and led them upward.

Silently, they crept up the stairs, listening for the sound of approaching footsteps. The turn was so tight that they would be right on top of anyone coming in their direction before seeing them. The narrow staircase, hewn out of the rock, curled up and to the left. The walls were smooth, like those of the lower halls, broken up only by the occasional glowing stone high on the outside wall. Dane winced as he took each step. The climb made him feel every pain in his feet, knees, and back, in a way that level ground did not. He gritted his teeth and focused on his anger, allowing his bitterness at the loss of Meriwether to overcome his pain. Slowly, he continued the seemingly interminable upward trek.

When they reached the top of the stairs, Dane peered out cautiously. They were at a corner of the upper hallway. He looked too his left. The hall ran the approximate length of the main chamber, turning left at the end. Halfway down the hall, an arched window was cut in the inside wall at chest level. This must have been one of the windows from which the snipers had fired down upon their pursuers. Directly across from the window was a high, arching door set in the outside wall. Dane could not see into the darkness beyond. Looking around the other corner, he could see that this upper hall definitely formed a hollow, walled balcony that wrapped around the big chamber below. This hallway also had a window at the center of the inside wall, and a doorway on the outside. He turned and motioned for Bones and Kaylin to follow him.

Stepping out of the stairwell, Bones surveyed the area, just as Dane had. "Another square," he whispered. "But where are the bad guys?"

Dane shrugged, and led them down the hallway to the left, moving south. Reaching the window at the hall's midpoint, he glanced through, surveying the courtyard below. The black-clad bodies of their pursuers still lay at the top of the steps on the far side of the room. Nothing moved, save the water flowing through the canal in the center. He turned to see Bones peering into the dimly-lit room on the opposite side of the hall. Bones nodded and tilted his head toward the doorway. Rifle at the ready, Dane hurried inside, with Bones behind him.

The crystals in this room emitted only the faintest light, but it was enough to see that they were standing in what looked like a quarter of a sphere hewn into the rock with laser-like precision... Carved into the rounded ceiling above, he thought he could just make out familiar constellations.

A whisper of warning from Bones brought Dane's head down in time to see that he was staring down into a well like the ones in front of and behind the Goliath carving outside. *Outside.* The place in which he and his friends now found themselves was so surreal as to make it strange to think that somewhere up above, the world was going about its business. Kaylin hurried up, and shone her flashlight down into the well. Unlike the other wells they had seen, this one was only a few feet deep.

"What's back there?" Bones asked, pointing into the gloom. Kaylin redirected the light to reveal a lidded, stone coffin. It was every bit as large as those of Goliath and his brothers. They moved forward to examine it. Kaylin shone her light across the lid. Something was carved in the surface, the deep shadows cast by the flashlight's beam distorting the image. Dane pulled out his own flashlight, held it up above his head, and pointed the beam directly down onto the image. Kaylin gasped.

The being carved into the coffin lid was like no other Dane had seen. It was tall, much like Goliath, but impossibly slender. Its arms were disproportionately long for its body, and ended in large hands with long, wormlike fingers. The odd appearance did not end there. Its head was too big by a third. Garbed in a simple robe, the odd being had large, round eyes and a serene face. Just looking at it gave Dane a strange sense of inner calm, as if this were the gentlest of beings.

"Little green men," Bones whispered. "Well, big green men in this case."

He placed a bronze hand on the lid and pushed. With a soft, scraping sound, it gave way, exposing a sliver of darkness where the lid shifted from the lip of the coffin. "It's not beveled," Bones whispered in surprise. He pulled his own small flashlight from his pocket and shone it down into the coffin. Dane and Kaylin hurried over to look inside, but Bones turned the light out before they could reach his side. He looked up, the disappointment evident on his face even in the semi-darkness. "Empty," he said.

The crystals on the wall had absorbed enough stray light to cast a dusk-like glow around the room. Aside from the well and coffin, the room was obviously empty. Nonetheless, they made a quick search, looking for any sort of hidden egress, but they found nothing.

Leaving the room, Dane led them to the right. They moved counterclockwise around the second story hall, turning left at each corner. They found that each hallway was exactly like the one before: courtyard window at the center of the inside wall, doorway to an empty burial chamber on the outside wall. At each inside corner, a spiral staircase wound down to the first floor.

The differences between the crypts, as Kaylin called them, were few. The rooms on the north and south sides of the main chamber lay directly above the underground river. The wells in these rooms emptied down into the water. The biggest differences lay in the images carved on lids of each empty sarcophagus. In the second room, they found the image of a squat, simian-looking hominid with a prominent brow and short, thickly-muscled legs. Its face was angry, and exuded violence. In the third room, they found a representation of a small creature, no more than four feet tall. In terms of proportion, the body was very much like that of a human child. The features of its narrow face were those of an adult, though its eyes were vaguely impish.

They stood now in the room that lay upstream of the main chamber. The carving on this sarcophagus was that of an angel, but unlike any angel Dane had ever seen. No trumpet-bearing herald or Valentine cherub, this creature was fully ten feet tall, with broad, powerful shoulders, a narrow waist, and muscular legs. It wide forehead shaded narrow, slightly upturned eyes. Wrapped around its shoulders and cloaking its body were huge wings, rendered in such fine detail that Kaylin reached out and stroked the feathers.

"They're all empty," Bones said. "I don't get this place. All of these halls are just alike. I guarantee you that downstairs on the other side of the river is nothing but a mirror image of the side we were on. Just an empty, square tunnel."

Something clicked in Dane's mind. "It's a deathtrap," he said, suddenly quite certain of himself. Anyone who finds this place just runs around in circles while whoever is defending the place picks you off one-by-one."

"Why haven't they gotten us yet?" Bones asked. He paced to the open doorway as he spoke, looking into the hallway.

"Maybe they're so busy slugging it out with the other guys that they haven't really paid us much attention," Dane said, shrugging. The answer was not satisfactory, but he had no other at the moment. "That, and we've been lucky."

"Why did they ever build this place?" Bones said, turning back to face Dane. "If it's a killing ground, then it has to exist to protect something else." A faint tremor shook the room.

"Don't know, don't care," Kaylin interrupted, putting a slender hand on the sarcophagus as if to balance herself. "I'm sure I'll wonder about it later, but all I want right now is to get out of here." As if to punctuate the point, a quick burst of gunfire, the first they had heard since reaching the second level, echoed down the corridor.

"Where do we go?" Bones asked. "The tunnel's blocked."

Something in what Bones had said earlier gnawed at Dane's consciousness. The thought broke through with a sudden and surprising clarity. "I've got it!" he said. "If the two halves of the first level are mirror images of one another, then there should be…"

"A tunnel leading back to the well!" Kaylin said, completing his thought. "There was more than one tunnel leading off of the well. The guys who came shot at us in the main room must have come in that way."

"But won't they be guarding the exit?" Bones asked.

"They weren't guarding the other one," Dane said. If the battle between the two yet-unidentified groups continued, perhaps the three of them could slip through the net. "You take the lead. I'll bring up the rear. With my legs the way they are right now, I can't keep up with you anyway."

"We're not going to leave you," Bones said.

"No matter what happens, you are to get Kaylin out of here. I'll take care of myself," he gave Bones what he hoped was his most commanding stare.

Bones stared back for a moment before shrugging. "Let's try it," Bones said. He led the way out of the room. Turning left, they ran to the end of the hall, where it turned to the right. Like the other three corners, a stone staircase spiraled down from the inside corner. They mounted the steps, and moved cautiously, listening for any sounds of approaching enemies. They were on the northeast corner of the big room, Dane thought to himself, thus putting them as close as possible to where the exit tunnel should be. As they wound their way down to the bottom, he thought he heard distant shouts coming up from below. He bit his lower lip and steeled himself for another firefight.

They hit the bottom of the stairs at a trot. Bones looked around quickly and shouted, "Run!" He sprinted out the door, spraying bullets down the hall to the right.

"I'll cover you!" Dane called to Kaylin. Taking his Walther in his left hand, he reached around the doorway and blindly fired three shots down the hall. Then, giving Kaylin a push, he leapt out in front of her, opening up with his rifle.

Bones had taken out one man. He lay limp on the ground, his rifle near him. Two others, wearing the same style white shirt and brown pants as the man Meriwether had killed, charged down the hall, firing erratically. Dane fired another burst, then turned and ran around the corner. Ahead of him, Kaylin reached the end of the hall and disappeared to the left. He had been right. There was a tunnel there!

Behind him, another shot rang out, and a voice shouted in English for him to stop. *Is this guy kidding me?* Dane thought. He dodged right, then left, thankful that the pursuers did not have automatic weapons. He was within twenty feet of the tunnel when another tremor shook the ground. This one was the strongest yet. He fell hard, his Walther clattering from his grip. He still held on to the rifle, and turned and fired another burst at his pursuers, who had fallen to the ground. Both had lost their weapons, and Dane, still oozing with cold anger over Meriwether's death, took them out without compunction. He hopped to his feet and turned around. What he saw made him curse. The mouth of the tunnel had collapsed.

CHAPTER 27

Before Dane had time to contemplate being cut off from his friends, shouts and footsteps reverberated down the corridor to his right. Not waiting to see who was coming, he turned and sprinted back the way he had come. How was he going to get out of here?

He reached the corner and the stairs they had just descended. More voices came from his left. Cut off from either avenue on the first floor, he dashed back up the stairs. As he climbed, he considered his options. They were few. He supposed he could try to work his way back up the river, but the current was so strong, he would likely be swept away. It might be worth a try. He could always try going down one of the sacrificial wells. He had not seen any handholds or tunnels coming off them when he had examined them before, but he could have easily missed them in his haste.

He reached the top of the stairs to hear even more voices and footsteps that seemed to come from all around. Whoever these men were, they were converging on his position. His luck had run out. Taking a chance, he dashed to the north room, the one with the angel on the sarcophagus. Just as he ducked through the doorway, he caught a glimpse of several brown and white clad men rounding the corner. Their attention was on a black clad man whom they held at gunpoint.

Dane hurried to the edge of the well. Knowing that he did not have much time, he scanned the interior for handholds. Seeing none, he took one long look at the faint glimmer of the water far below. It was much too far to jump.

The voices were closer now. He turned and looked at the giant stone coffin. He had no other choice. Giving the lid a hard shove, he slid the end to the side, creating just enough room to squeeze through. He clambered in headfirst. Flipping over onto his back, awkward with the sword still strapped over his shoulder, he reached up and scooted the lid back into place.

The voices drew near. Dane realized, to his chagrin, that the men were coming into the room where he was hiding. He strained to hear what they were saying. Someone was speaking in Arabic.

"I don't speak your language, primitive," a deep voice, brimming with arrogance, replied.

"Very well," a strange, almost musical voice said. "Tell us, please, who you are and why you come armed into the temple."

"I won't answer any of your questions." A heavy grunt told Dane that the man had been punched in the stomach.

"Answer my questions truthfully, and you will be released." The odd voice spoke again. "I caution you: God will tell me if you lie, and it will go badly with you."

"*We* are the agents of God," the deep voice snapped, "the Order of the Blades has been sent to stamp out the heresy of the sword."

"The sword has been gone from this place for many years. In any case, there is no heresy in this place, only a celebration of God's creation."

The prisoner laughed, a sharp, nasal sound. "Don't you know? Someone has brought the sword into this very place. That is why we are here: to stop them and take the sword."

"Are you certain?" The speaker did not try to hide his surprise. "How do you know this thing?"

"A man confessed to his priest that he had found the key to finding the sword."

Maxwell, Dane thought.

"Knowing the damage it could do if the sword came to light, the church neutralized the man, but he had passed the clues along to his daughter. We tracked her to this place."

"You have done an evil thing."

"Protecting the faith from this alien relic is not evil," the man said. "Rienzi spouted his heresies about God being a spaceman, and alien creatures populating the earth. Had he been able to support his claims, the church might have been destroyed."

The man with the lilting voice laughed long and hard. "The sword is not an alien relic. True, its origins are not of this earth, but neither are they detrimental to the truth of God."

"The church believes that they are," the man hissed.

"Where does your loyalty lie: To your God, or to your church? They are not necessarily one and the same."

"Heretic!" the man shouted. Dane heard sounds of a struggle. "What are you doing? You said you'd release me!" the man cried, his voice strident.

"The well will be your release, my son. You will be released from the bondage in which your church holds you. Make your peace with God, whatever the name by which you know him."

The prisoner's angry cries were suddenly squelched by a gurgling sound. Dane had heard that sound before: a knife across the throat. They had killed the man and dropped him into the well. He had to get away.

He waited, listening, as the men conversed in Arabic. A few forceful words from the man with the strange voice, and then footsteps running from the room. He waited. What if they were not all gone? What if they came back? He started to count backward from three hundred, struggling to count slowly. A new thought came to him. How much air was in this coffin? He had noticed cracks around the edge of the lid, and hoped that some of them were allowing air inside.

He completed his countdown, five minutes, as close as he could guess, and took a deep breath. He had not heard a sound since the men left the room. He could not remain here forever. He had to take a chance. Pushing the lid aside as gently as possible, he squeezed out. As his feet hit the ground, he heard a voice behind him.

"Welcome."

Dane whirled about, rifle at the ready. The man who stood before him was old-very old. He wore a loose-fitting brown robe, cinched around the waist with a thick length of rope, over off-white, homespun pants and shirt. Short, snowy hair peeked out from under a brown head cloth. He had a closely-cropped white beard and mustache. Shining against his leathery face, heavily lined with age, his alert, gray eyes looked past Dane, his gaze settling on the hilt of the sword.

"You *did* return the sword," he said in amazement. Dane recognized the musical voice instantly. This was the apparent leader of the group-the one who had ordered a man sacrificed. "It seemed too much to hope."

"Who are you?" Dane barked. The man was not physically imposing, but Dane kept the rifle trained on him.

"I am *Atiq Yomin*. In your language, the "Ancient of Days.""

"You're God?" Dane asked, trying to convey in his voice all of the scorn that he felt.

"No," the man laughed, "it is but a title. You may call me Atiq."

"All right, Atiq," Dane said. "Are you planning on calling your cronies back?"

"Very rude. You have not yet identified yourself," the strange man said. "In any case, as you are an intruder in my domain, you should permit me to ask the questions. But to answer your question, no, I do not expect my men to return to this place anytime soon. They are scouring the temple."

Dane knew that he had few cards to play, and Atiq was likely his only way out of here. "The name's Dane Maddock."

"Do you plan to shoot me, Mr. Maddock?"

Dane was caught off guard, not only by the directness of the question, but also by the calm way in which the question was asked. "I guess that depends on how things go," he said.

"You are an honest man. May I know why you are returning the sword, Mr. Maddock?"

Dane wanted to lie to the man, but something about Atiq compelled him to tell the truth. The man had a hypnotic air about him, almost holy. "An old friend of mine learned that the sword had been found and then lost almost two hundred years ago by a man named Rienzi. My friend was killed for what he knew. We found the sword, which led us here."

Even as he spoke, he could not believe that he was telling this man his story.

Atiq turned and paced back and forth. He looked up at the ceiling. Each time he passed the stone sarcophagus, he let his fingertips trail across the edge of the stone lid. "So many came to Petra," he whispered, "that we did not know who had taken the sword. We were inattentive to our duties." He stopped pacing, shook his head, and then turned to face Dane. "On behalf of the Protectors, I must thank you for returning the sword, and alleviating our shame."

"Well," Dane said, "we weren't trying to return the sword. We just wanted some answers."

"We?" Atiq appeared calm, but his eyes retained their intense stare.

"The daughter of the man who was killed came with us, along with two of my friends. They got away. At least, two of them did." Inside, Dane still seethed when he thought of Meriwether.

"And have you found the answers you seek?" Atiq sounded as if he were toying with Dane.

"Not all of them," Dane admitted. "Obviously, it was this 'Order of the Blades' that was following us. They killed my friends. But..."

"But you have other questions yet to be answered."

"Yeah, like who built this place? What is it? What does it have to do with Goliath?" All the confusion he had felt, further clouded by adrenalin and grief came spilling over. "This place isn't anything! It's like you made it just to trap people and kill them. But what are you protecting here?"

"To answer your first question, God built this place," Atiq said, matter-of-factly.

"God," Dane replied flatly.

"Yahweh, Allah, Jehovah, whatever you wish to call the supreme deity," Atiq said. "But I can tell by your tone of voice that you will not accept that answer. Consequently, I cannot answer your other questions, as you will not believe those answers either."

"There is no God," Dane muttered. He looked Atiq directly in the eye. "If there's a God who loves us out there, why do people die?"

"We all die, Mr. Maddock," the old man said with casual indifference. "That is a reality of our mortal existence."

"I'm not talking about ninety year-olds who die in their beds. I mean young people who have their whole lives ahead of them. A God who loves us wouldn't let that happen." He had no idea why he was unloading years of pent-up anger on this strange old man. Atiq, for his part, took it calmly.

"You are obviously a military man. Odd that a man who has been trained to kill has such high expectations for his God in terms of saving lives. When you shoot a man, do you expect your loving God to come down and heal him, so that you may shoot him again and again?"

Dane did not answer. The man was talking nonsense.

"Do your parents love you, Mr. Maddock?" Atiq asked, folding his arms across his chest and sitting down upon the stone coffin.

"My parents were killed in an auto accident. So was my wife," Dane said bitterly. "But yes, my parents loved me."

"I am sorry for your loss," Atiq said simply. For some reason, Dane actually believed that the old man meant it. There was an air of simple sincerity about him that suggested he did not say things he did not mean. "Did these loving parents approve of your choice to take up arms for your nation?"

Dane nodded. "My Dad was career Navy. So, yeah, they were proud of me." What was the old man getting at?

"But surely, loving parents would not permit their child to do something dangerous. Does a loving parent permit his child to go to school, where the child could contract illness, or possibly be harmed by another child, or even an adult?"

Dane stared at the ground. He did not have an answer for the old man.

"Free will, Mr. Maddock. Your loved ones exercised their free will to operate a motor vehicle, statistically a dangerous undertaking. Just as you made a choice to enlist in the armed forces. Just as you have, no doubt, exercised your free will to take a life, or perhaps more than one in your time.

"Sometimes we use our free will in ways that harm others. That is regrettable. But without free will we are little more than robots."

"But what about babies who die? What about cancer? Natural disasters?" Dane pressed. "Why is everything so arbitrary?"

Atiq chuckled. His eyes took on a faraway stare. "I once had a discussion with a friend of mine from China." The man caught the surprised look in Dane's eye. "I do live in the world. Being a Protector is my calling, but I live and love just as you do." He paused as this sank in. "At any rate, my friend and I were discussing the ending of a Chinese movie. The character did something that flew in the face of all reason. Even with my friend's attempts at explanation, I could find neither practical nor symbolic meaning in that character's choice. He finally grew frustrated, threw up his hands, and said, 'You simply do not understand the Eastern mind.'" He turned and looked at Dane. "It occurs to me that if I cannot understand the mind of my fellow human being, how can I ever presume to know the mind of God?"

Dane stood in silent contemplation of the old man's argument. In his bitterness over losing Melissa, he had been so confident in his belief that there was no God. What Atiq said was far from satisfying, but perhaps it could be true.

"God is real," Atiq said, standing and moving to stand face-to-face with Dane. "This place is the proof. If you have the courage to return the sword to its resting place, you will see that for yourself." As the old man spoke, another tremor shook the room. Dane staggered back before regaining his balance.

"There were three tunnels coming off of that well shaft. Two of them are blocked. Show me where the third one is before this place comes down on our heads."

Atiq stared at the gun, his face void of all emotion. "Do you think I am afraid to die?" he asked. "For I am not." He fixed Dane with an appraising look. "Here are my conditions: put down your weapons, and return the sword to its proper place. Only then will I show you the way out."

"I don't have time for this," Dane said. "These tremors are getting stronger. Take me out of here." The last, he said slowly, pronouncing each syllable.

"This place has seen worse," the old man replied. "You have heard my conditions."

"Why do I have to leave my weapons?" Dane asked, suddenly suspicious. "Your goons waiting outside for me?"

"As long as you are in my company, no harm will come to you. You need to understand faith, Mr. Maddock. Leaving your defenses behind will be the first step."

Dane looked long and hard at the old man, and read the resolve in his face. He considered shooting the man down on the spot, but quickly dismissed the idea. Atiq had not threatened him. Furthermore, he was the key to getting out of this place. Slowly, he laid the automatic rifle on the floor at his feet. Next, he drew the Walther, popped the magazine out, and removed the unspent bullets. "I've had this for a long time," he explained, holding the pistol up. "I can't leave it behind."

Atiq nodded his acceptance, and silently led the way out of the chamber.

CHAPTER 28

D ane followed Atiq down the stairs and into the main chamber, which the old man called the "Temple". Walking to the stream that bisected the room, they followed it down to where it emptied under the wall. The man turned to face him.

"There are metal rungs in the ceiling of this tunnel. You must climb hand-over-hand for about ten meters. Where the rungs end, let go." Before Dane could ask what he would be dropping down onto, the old man reached into the tunnel, grabbed a handhold, and swung into the darkness.

Dane swallowed a curse. He reached into the tunnel with his right hand and felt along the curved ceiling, cool and slightly damp. His hand found cold iron, and he grabbed hold and swung forward. The faint glow from the temple did little to illumine the blackness of the passageway. He brought his left hand forward, and was surprised to find the next rung right where he needed it to be. *Just like the monkey bars,* he thought. He found his rhythm with ease born of harsh SEAL training. He moved along so effortlessly that he forgot that the handholds ended, and when after a short distance, his left hand grasped only air, he nearly lost his grip on the last rung.

"Atiq?" he called, feeling rather foolish as he hung by one arm. There was no answer. *Had the old man somehow tricked him?* "Hey!" He paused, waiting for an answer, but none was forthcoming. He listened to the sound of water rushing beneath him. No other sound met his ears. "Must be one of those *faith* things," he growled. He took a deep breath and steeled himself for a drop into the cold water below. Eyes closed, he let go.

He scarcely had time to feel the sensation of falling before his feet struck solid ground. With a grunt, he dropped to all fours, feeling every jolt and bruise his body had received from his earlier fall down the well.

"You are correct." From the nearness of his voice, Atiq stood only a few feet away. "I told you that you needed to learn about faith. Follow me."

Dane stood and followed the faint sounds of the old man's footsteps into the darkness. He moved at a tentative pace, uncertain what lay before him. The floor beneath him was solid. The rustling of water all around suggested that he might be on some sort of walkway in the middle of the channel.

The faintest glimmer of light appeared in the distance. He could just make out Atiq's form about twenty feet ahead. He picked up his pace, moving to catch up with the strange old man, who did not acknowledge him, but stared resolutely ahead.

The passageway grew brighter as they walked on. Soon, there was enough light for Dane to confirm that they were, indeed, on a pathway in the middle of the underground river. The tunnel made a sharp bend to the right. Dane turned the corner and gasped.

Stefan peered out through the arched doorway that led into the large central room. He watched with interest as first the old man, then Maddock, disappeared into the tunnel where the river flowed out of the room. Apparently, there were handholds of some sort in the tunnel roof. He smiled. They were leading him directly to whatever it was that this empty stone warren protected.

He stepped into the room, and was disappointed to see that someone had removed the bodies of Peter and Michael, along with their rifles. Stefan had long since emptied and discarded his own weapon. No matter, he still had his knife, and the other weapon. He resisted the urge to pat his midriff, just to make certain it was still there.

He hurried toward the tunnel where his quarry had vanished, all the while feeling vulnerable to the snipers that had dogged them throughout this debacle of an operation. Reaching the archway, he paused for a moment to feel for a handhold of some kind. His hand closed around some sort of metal rung, and he smiled again.

He would kill Maddock first, and recover the sword. Next, he would wring the old man's secrets out of him before taking care of him. Finally, when he had learned all that he could, he would blow this pagan abomination back to the hell from which it was conceived.

Dane stared in amazement at the wondrous sight that lay before him. About fifty yards ahead, the tunnel opened into a broad, circular cavern, at least two hundred feet across. The river spilled over the edge and into the depths, but the pathway upon which they trod extended out over the chasm. Where it ended, hanging out over the abyss, was a sight unlike any he had ever beheld.

It was a giant cage, spherical, and about thirty feet across. It appeared to be constructed of the same material as the glowing crystals that illumined the temple and hallways. The thick, finely wrought bars, spaced vertically about a foot apart all the way around, gave it the appearance of being both delicate and sturdy at the same time. A doorway set in the near side stood open, revealing a bright, white object of indeterminate shape inside. Dane could see no sign of bolts or hinges. Rather, it appeared to be one single piece. The entire object shone with the incandescence of a full moon, casting a faint glow around the cavern. Pearlescent light swirled and danced on the water as it tumbled into the darkness below.

"Your answer, Mr. Maddock," Atiq said.

Dane could not begin to comprehend what he was seeing. Memories crowded in one after another in the span of a heartbeat: the fight in the slave market, diving for the *Dourado*, digging up the sword, Sowell's betrayal, and the battle in these very halls. All had led him to this moment, and he *had no idea* what stood before him. He only knew that it was breathtakingly magnificent. He stared in silence.

"God created many wonderful creatures, nearly all of which are long gone," Atiq said, as if beginning a lecture. "The greatest of these, though few, were those we call the angels. They were beautiful, powerful beings, and they were God's favorite. But they were vain creatures, and they lorded their superiority over human beings, taking their pleasure with human women, producing the races of giants, the Anakim."

"What about the other creatures we saw carved in the sarcophagi?" Dane asked.

"Two of them died out long ago," Atiq said, "but their legacy lives on in our fables." He paused, waiting for Dane to catch on. After a moment, he continued. "Little people? Ancient alien visitors?"

"Ah," Dane said, not certain what to think of this revelation. "And the ape-man? The missing link?"

Atiq chuckled. "Not precisely. All of the beings depicted in the carvings symbolize many beings of a similar nature. But yes, the simian-looking creature generally represents hominids."

"If all of these creatures lived, why is there no fossil record?" Dane asked.

"I don't have all the answers," Atiq said. "These beings were historical before history existed. There were few." He shrugged. "Perhaps God removed their remains from the earth for some reason known only to Him? But there is one.

"One angel grew in wisdom and power, even a limited power to create. He formed the crystals that illumine the pathways, and he created the sword." He stared over Dane's shoulder at the hilt of Goliath's sword. "Already an arrogant creature, when he learned to create, he was convinced that he was a god in his own right. He tempted the vainest of his race with promises of might and glory, and he led a rebellion against God himself."

Dane felt cold. He took a step back, his heart racing. The sword seemed to hang heavy on his shoulder. *It could not be!*

"God crushed their rebellion. The bodies of the traitorous angels were cast into the depths of the earth. Their leader was locked away in a prison wrought from the stone of his own making, to contemplate the error of his ways. Angels take a long time to die." Atiq turned and dramatically swept his arm out toward the glowing cage and yawning chasm. "Welcome to the bottomless pit."

Stefan crouched in the shadows, seething at what he heard. This was an even greater heresy than he had been told! He freed his knife from its sheath, and absently tested the edge against his thumb. Anger roiled inside of him. He had intended to slip up behind Maddock and kill him quietly. Now he wanted to hurt the man, to make him pay. Stefan wanted the man to know who was killing him and why. He wanted the man to feel fear. To know the power of the order. With a cry of rage, he leapt forward.

Dane whirled and pivoted to his right as the shape hurtled out of the darkness and directly at him. He saw a glint of steel, and he struck out with his open left palm, turning the blade past his body. Ignoring the pain as the knife sliced into his hand, he drove his right palm into the attacker's face.

The man was quick, though, and turned his head, catching the brunt of Dan's blow on the side of his head, just behind the right eye. He swung the knife backhanded in a vicious arc, scarcely missing Dane's throat.

Leaning back to avoid the deadly knife stroke, Dane delivered a roundhouse kick to the man's stomach, but to little effect. The guy's abs were like iron! The man struck again with his knife, low and hard. Dane turned the thrust again, this time receiving a deep cut across the back of his left forearm. He stepped in close to his assailant and drove his elbow into the man's left cheekbone. He grunted and stabbed at Dane again, this time a sloppy, overhand stroke. Dane caught the man's wrist in his left hand, but immediately felt the man's arm slipping free of his bloody palm. Fingers clawed at his eyes, and Dane grabbed the man's left hand in his right.

They struggled, nose-to-nose, strength against strength. If only Dane could get some distance between himself and the attacker, enough to give him time to draw the sword. He squeezed tighter with his left hand, and pain shot down his arm from the gashes his opponent's knife had opened. Still hurting from the fall down the well, he felt himself gradually being forced back. As they came into the light, he could see the man more clearly.

The attacker had short, dark hair, and eyes to match. His olive skin and dark clothing made him appear a shadow in the darkness of the tunnel. He was an inch or two taller than Dane, and solidly muscled. In the dim light, only his white teeth stood out as he fixed Dane with a toxic smile.

"My name is Stefan," he said in a voice trembling with exertion and rage. "I am of the Blood Order. I wanted you to know who is killing you."

Dane felt his right heel slip over the edge of the path. If he went into the water, the current would sweep him over the edge in a matter of seconds. "You've got bad breath, pal," Dane muttered. He yanked his head forward, driving his forehead into Stefan's nose. Letting go with his right hand, he grabbed the man by the hair, and yanked his head forward butting him in the face again. He felt blood on his face, and knew that it was not his own. A fierce tremor rattled the ground beneath them, and Dane felt Stefan's footing give. Another blow, and now Stefan was pushing away from him. Dane gave the man a shove, reaching back for the sword as his assailant stumbled backward.

Stefan recovered himself quickly. The man's face was a mask of blood, and he fixed Dane with a crazed, broken-toothed grin as he leapt forward, knife at the ready.

Dane brought the sword free, swinging it in a sharp, downward arc. He heard Stefan scream as the sword parted hand from wrist. The dark-clad man reeled, staggering blindly toward the edge of the pathway. Dane sprung toward him, delivering a vicious kick to the small of Stefan's back, and sending him crashing into the water. Dane watched as the current swept him away. He turned to find Atiq waiting for him, hands folded across his chest.

"Thanks for the help," Dane muttered, letting the sword hang down by his side.

"You were doing fine on your own," Atiq said. He turned and walked toward the glowing object. "Come."

Dane followed, his eyes fixed on the apparition before him. As the light touched him, his cares seemed to drain away. All thoughts of the fight with Stefan, his concerns about escaping the underground temple, all evaporated as he marveled at the sight before him.

The light that radiated from the white sphere touched him as if it had substance. His pace slowed. He felt as if he were swimming through a sparkling stream of mother-of-pearl light. Overcome with wonder, he shuffled along the path. He scarcely noticed that he was now trailing the tip of the sword along the stone walk.

"It is all right, Mr. Maddock," Atiq said calmly, "come inside." The old man stood at the door, beckoning to him. Dane took another slow step forward.

Stefan clutched the huge stone with all of his remaining strength, straining against the force of the current that threatened to drag him to his death. The tremor had jarred loose a sizable portion of the tunnel roof, blocking his descent over the falls and into the pit below. He lay motionless as first the old man, then Maddock passed only meters away. The rock lay between them, and the half-light in this portion of the tunnel rendered him nigh invisible. When the two men moved out onto the walkway that extended above the yawing abyss, he knew that he was safe.

Holding on tight with his left hand, he kicked hard, struggling to pull himself up. He gained an inch, then another. Soon, he was able to hook his right arm over the rock. The cold water had slowed his heartbeat, but blood continued to flow from the stump where his right hand had been. He pulled with both arms now, and felt the jagged stone tear through the fabric of his clothing and cut into his exposed flesh. He struggled forward, inching closer to the path in the middle of the passageway.

He felt no pain, only rage. For the first time, he had failed. His team had been picked apart by the old man's henchmen. The sword was beyond his reach now. He could not hope to recover it unarmed and in his present condition. His all-consuming goal now was to live long enough to obliterate the unholy sphere, Maddock and the sword along with it. He would cleanse this pagan sanctuary with holy fire.

CHAPTER 29

D ane walked slowly into the glowing sphere, scarcely noticing the bars that seemed to envelop him like a porcelain web. In the center lay a rectangular slab of the opalescent stone. But it was what lay atop the block that drew his attention.

A huge skeleton lay in full repose. Its form was vaguely human, but with a broader chest and a tiny waist. Sturdy arm and leg bones spoke of powerful muscles. Its skull was like that of a human, but with a higher forehead. The face was like an inverted triangle, ending in a narrow chin. Spread out on either side of the body, curving up above the head and sweeping down below knee level was a lacework of delicate bones.

"He has wings," Dane whispered. Even in death, the creature was both beautiful and terrible. He felt strangely serene in its presence. He stood silently for a moment.

"So, the Devil is dead?" he finally asked.

Atiq laughed, and placed a hand on Dane's shoulder. "A common misconception. Lucifer was a sinner like the rest of us." The old man paused, scratching his bearded chin. "Well, not like the rest of us, but a sinful creature still. Over time, his story became intertwined with theology, resulting in the Satan story that many people believe in today."

"How did Goliath come by the sword?" Dane asked. It was all so confusing. "Did Rienzi know about...*this?*" He could not tear his eyes from the amazing creature before him.

"Tradition holds that Goliath found this place. Claiming descent from the Nephilim, he believed that it was his destiny to wield the sword. He and his brothers built their tombs in the rock above, in imitation of the upper chambers. The false wall, with the carvings of the Philistine giants, was built to conceal their resting place, with the sword as the key. Some time after the death of King David, the sword was recovered, and buried with Goliath. "

"Behold, I saw a star fall from heaven to earth, and he was given the key of the shaft of the bottomless pit," Dane whispered. He did not know how he managed to recall that bit of scripture, but in this situation it seemed to fit.

Atiq nodded and continued. "Centuries later, the Nabateans rediscovered the temple. The sword was returned to this place, Goliath's cavern walled up, and the Protectors formed to guard the wonders of the temple. Sadly, as Petra's importance diminished, so did the diligence of the Protectors. When word of Rienzi's claims reached the Protectors, they verified the loss of the sword. They reconstructed the exterior wall, which Rienzi had broken through, and reaffirmed their commitment to protecting the temple. My grandfather's great-grandfather was one of those Protectors."

Dane drew his gaze away from the dead angel, and stepped to the edge of the sphere. He looked down into the blackness beneath. The walls of the cavern plunged straight down, vanishing into the depths. The river that poured over the edge fell silently in a sparkling curtain of droplets. He could certainly understand why they called this the bottomless pit. Wherever the bottom was, it was a long way down. "So that isn't hell, down there?" He turned back to see Atiq shaking his head. "Why did you want me to see this?"

"I sense in you a need to believe in something." The elderly man paused, as if expecting Dane to say something. When no answer was forthcoming, he continued. "I do not expect to change your life in one moment, Mr. Maddock. I do have a question, though. Do you now believe that God is real?"

Dane gritted his teeth. He looked back at the skeletal remains of the angel, *of Lucifer*, and then back to Atiq. "I don't know what I believe," he admitted, speaking slowly in order to choose his words carefully. His mind was still struggling to come to grips with all that he had seen and experienced. "But I'm more inclined to believe now than I was an hour ago." He looked again at the mythical seraph, and then stepped over to where the body lay. Raising the sword, he took one long, last look and laid it gently, respectfully on the surface of the stone. It was home.

Atiq nodded sagely. His brown eyes narrowed, and he raised his chin and fixed Dane with an appraising look. "I wonder, when you leave this place, will you tell of what you have seen?"

Dane thought for a minute, and then shook his head. He could not put words to it, but the very thought of sharing this place with the world felt wrong. The experience was too… intimate was the only word that came to mind.

"I believe you," Atiq said softly. "I should have you killed for what you have seen, but I cannot do that to the man who returned the sword. Come, I will show you the way out."

Dane saw the man turn, then stiffen as if frozen.

Stefan stood in the doorway, his olive skin pallid from immersion in the icy water. His right arm hung limply at his side, blood oozing from the stump and pooling on the stone by his right foot. His shredded pants revealed scraped and bleeding flesh. His black shirt was rent. What Dane saw beneath it made his eyes bulge. A wide, gray swath of neoprene was wrapped around Stefan's abdomen, holding in place a device that was obviously a bomb.

"I told you," Stefan whispered, his voice slurring from cold and loss of blood, "I wanted you to know who it was that was killing you. I have come to complete the task." His left hand moved sluggishly toward the bomb strapped to his body. "Behold", he said, his eyes glassy and his speech deliberate, "I open the scroll and break the seal."

"You will *not!*" Atiq screamed. Springing forward at a speed Dane would not have thought the old man capable of, he was on Stefan before the injured assassin could react, forcing him out of the doorway and back onto the walk.

Dane watched as the two men, as if in slow motion, tumbled over the edge, and into the emptiness below. He opened his mouth to call out, but Atiq was gone.

Stefan's mind was playing tricks on him. He seemed to be floating in darkness. A gentle breeze blew his hair. *Where was he? What had he been doing?* He thought for a long moment, and then remembered. His numb fingers sought the number pad on the side of the bomb. *The Bringer of Holy Fire*, as he now thought of it. He found it difficult to concentrate. The floating sensation was growing uncomfortable, and he was feeling dizzy. Deliberately, he punched in the five-digit code, then pressed the hot button.

The walkway beneath Dane trembled, and the sphere rocked sickeningly from one side to the other. *Another tremor,* he thought. Then he saw, far below him, a faint orange glow appear in the depths of the pit, glowing brighter. He turned and dashed back up the walkway toward the underground tunnel. He felt the bridge that connected Lucifer's prison to the path in the river begin to give. He stumbled and fell down on all fours. He scrambled to his feet, then felt his footing slip as the stone rampart slowly fell away from the rock wall. He leapt forward, extending his arms as far as he could reach, and grunted as his fingers caught the edge of the stone path where the walkway had broken free. He felt the stone collapse beneath him. Clinging by his fingertips, he looked back to watch as the final resting place of the rebellious angel dropped noiselessly into the bottomless pit. Lucifer had finally joined his comrades in arms.

The entire pit shook harder, and a wave of hot, dry air swept up the shaft, engulfing him. A hollow rumble rolled up on its heels. The river rushed angrily by on both sides. He felt the froth on his face. The cool spray seemed to give him a renewed surge of energy. Dane's feet scrabbled against the rocky surface of the cavern, seeking a toehold. He gained a footing and pushed up, getting first his arms over the edge, then his chest. Finally, he lay sprawled face down on the cold stone. He was spent, but knew he had to run.

As he regained his feet, a wave of heat coursed through the tunnel, searing his back. An intense, golden glow illuminated the passageway. The tunnel shook. He dodged to the left as a large block of stone dislodged from the ceiling and came crashing down alongside of him. He staggered forward, feeling the rock beneath his feet shift. The pathway was breaking up!

The rumbling grew louder as the ground heaved and the river flowed over the broken ground. Icy waves crashed over the undulating pathway, nearly sweeping his feet from under him. He reeled forward, the glow from the flames scarcely evident this far down the passage. He gasped for breath. The fire was sucking the oxygen out of the tunnel. Only a frantic, desperate desire to live kept him on his feet as the stone crumbled beneath him.

The ground gave way beneath his left foot, and he dropped to one knee, cold water lapping over his leg. He staggered to his feet again, only to feel the path below him fall way. As he fell, a strong hand grasped him by the back of his collar.

He dangled in midair, the front of the shirt cutting off his wind. Whoever had hold of him was not strong enough to pull him up; at least not with one hand. Dane reached up and felt for a handhold. His fingertips found a rung like the ones he had used to climb into the tunnel. He grabbed hold and pulled up with all of his remaining strength. The added lift of his rescuer was enough to vault him up and into a dark passage.

"That's twice I've fished you out of the river," Bones voice sounded in the darkness. "Come on."

Dazed and unable to believe how close he had come to death, and how fortunate he was to be alive, Dane let himself be hauled to his feet by the back of his belt. Someone slid beneath his right shoulder and wrapped a slender arm around his waist. Kaylin! His two companions half-carried, half-dragged him down the passageway. The rumbling continued unabated, the tunnel shaking all the while. Apparently, Stefan's bomb had exacerbated the seismic activity in the area.

They rounded a bend, and the tunnel glowed faintly in the light of a single glowing stone set high in the wall. Through the dust raised by the tremors, Dane could barely see Bones' face.

"We came back up the third tunnel," Bones explained, pausing often to gasp for breath. "It branches off in several places, and we had to try them all. Kaylin thinks that one of them leads to the blocked passage you two found yesterday. Anyway, it isn't too much farther to the well."

"It better not be," Dane gasped. "I don't have much left." The earth trembled again, and Dane staggered to his right. He heard Kaylin grunt as she slammed into the side wall.

"I'm fine," she said. "Keep moving."

They turned another corner, and Dane could see that the tunnel ended up ahead. He felt the damp cool of the well shaft, and smelled the moist air. Both were welcome to his senses.

Reaching the end of the tunnel, Bones pointed to the handholds in the wall of the well. "You first," he said. "Don't argue with me, Maddock!" he shouted as Dane opened his mouth to protest.

Dane saw there was no point in arguing. He found two handholds and a foothold and began his ascent. He did not bother to look up. The memory of his fall down the well was fresh in his mind, and he knew how deep it was. Tired as he felt, if he were to actually *see* how far he had to climb, he would be tempted to give up and let himself fall back into the cool, inviting arms of the river.

One handhold at a time, one foot at a time, he scaled the cold, slick stone wall. Twice, he nearly lost his grip as the well shaft undulated with the tremors. Both times, Kaylin's voice spoke from beneath him.

"If you fall, I fall too," she said in a matter-of-fact tone. "No pressure."

Dane climbed higher. Pieces of the well shaft broke away as the underground complex continued its collapse. Chunks of rock struck him on the head and arms, but he no longer felt pain. He wanted to live.

He was surprised when he finally reached for a handhold and found only air. He was so taken aback, in fact, that he nearly lost his remaining hand grip. Clutching the edge of the well, he drew himself up and over the side, and fell heavily to the floor. With the last of his strength, he stood and offered a helping hand first to Kaylin, then to Bones. Arms linked, the three of them ran from Goliath's tomb.

The bright morning sun was a shock to Dane's eyes as he stumbled out into daylight. The dry, dusty air burned his nostrils. A number of diggers were gathered outside the tomb, and they stared in astonishment as the friends appeared from within the heaving bowels of the earth. The shock wore off quickly, and several of them rushed forward to lead Dane and his friends away from the collapsing tomb.

A safe distance away, Dane turned and fell heavily to the ground. He sat and watched as a cloud of dust poured forth from within the stone sepulchre. With a final heave, the entire plateau fell in upon itself.

He stared in numb disbelief. The sword was gone. Meriwether was gone as well, with naught to mark his passing but a pile of rock. There was no tomb, no temple. It was as if none of it had ever been there. As far as Dane was concerned, that was the case.

EPILOGUE

T he sun shone bright across the green expanse of Arlington cemetery. The white headstones, arrayed with military precision, gleamed like polished buttons on a uniform. Many considered it an honor to be buried here. Bones, of course, thought it was bland and lacking the individuality that he so valued. He had already planned his own memorial, and intended his cremated remains to be sprinkled into ashtrays at his favorite Vegas casinos and adult entertainment establishments.

Dane had warned Bones that he had better produce offspring, because Dane was not about to carry out those final wishes. The picture of himself at eighty years old, tottering through a strip club with a bag of ashes in one hand and a cane in the other nearly made him smile.

Returning his thoughts to the present, he watched in silence as the honor guard folded the flag and presented it to Melinda Wells, Meriwether's granddaughter and only living relative. She accepted it with a firm nod of thanks.

She's got her grandfather's spirit, Dane thought. As the uniformed men and women marched away, his gaze fell to the small mound of earth where they had interred Meriwether's dog tags, along with an urn containing the ashes of Rienzi's Bible.

The minister, a short, stocky young fellow with a voice much too big for his body, said a few words, none of which came close to doing justice to so fine a man. He closed with the Lord's Prayer.

When the mourners were dismissed, Dane turned to leave. Bones caught his eye long enough to indicate that he planned to stay with Melinda for a while longer. Dane nodded, and turned to find Kaylin waiting for him. She stood with her hands on her hips and a slight, upturned smile on her face, tempered only by the solemnity of the occasion.

"What?" Dane asked.

"I saw you back there," she said, a mysterious look in her eyes. "You were praying, weren't you?"

"I thought you weren't supposed to open your eyes when you pray," he kidded. "Come on, I'll buy you lunch." He offered his hand, and she clasped it in both of hers. Together, they strolled through the manicured green grass.

"You know," Kaylin said, "you still haven't told me what happened after we got separated back in the temple."

Dane looked up at the azure sky, and took a deep breath. Somehow, what he had experienced was too personal to share, even with Kaylin. Exhaling, her turned to her and shrugged.

"It's all so… I don't know what to say about it. I'm still trying to figure it out. It could take a while."

He could tell that she was dissatisfied with the answer, but she did not push. "I've got time. How long do you think it might take?"

"I don't know," Dane said. "Maybe a lifetime."

Turn the page for a preview of the forthcoming
second Dane Maddock adventure!

Cibola Preview

J ade tapped on the divelight strapped to her head. The beam flickered again, and then shone at full strength. *Shoddy university equipment,* she thought. Drifting back to the wall, careful not to disturb the fine layer of silt that coated the floor of the subterranean cavern, she again ran her fingers across the striations in the rock. They were definitely man-made. Much too straight to be natural, and this part of the wall appeared smooth and level underneath the coating of plant life and debris that had accumulated over a half-millennia. She scrubbed her gloved fingertips harder against the rock, instinctively turning her head away from the cloud of matter that engulfed her.

Turning again to inspect the spot she had cleared, she waited with heart-pounding anticipation for the sluggish, almost non-existent current to clear her line of sight. With painstaking slowness, the haze cleared away, and her eyes widened. It was a joint, where precisely-hewn stones fitted precisely together. She could see the vertical lines where the blocks met end-to end. She scrubbed away another patch, and revealed more worked stone.

Raising her head, she let her eyes follow the beam of light as it climbed the wall. About six feet above her head, the regular pattern of the ancient stones gave way to a rough jumble of broken rock and tangled roots. It was a collapsed well, just as she had believed she would find. Remarkably, the thick roots and larger rocks had wedged in the shaft, preserving this bottom section almost intact. She made a circuit around the base, inspecting the rocks. They appeared to be solid. No danger of further collapse. Nonetheless, she grew increasingly aware of the mass of stone directly above her. It had obviously been in place for hundreds of years, but the thought of loose stone filling the shaft of a well made her feel distinctly vulnerable.

She checked her dive watch and was disappointed to see that she had exhausted her allotted time. She had carefully planned her exploration so that she would have time to return, plus two minutes, giving her as much time as possible to seek out the well.

Reorienting herself toward the upstream channel, she kicked out and felt resistance, like something tugging at her from behind. Cautiously she again tried to swim forward, and again she felt something pull her back. She was an experienced diver, and knew that she needed to move slowly and remain calm. A sudden movement could tangle her further, or worse, tear a hose loose. She turned her head back and forth, seeking out the obstruction, but to no avail. Whatever she had snagged was directly behind her. Reaching back behind her, she felt for the obstruction, but found nothing. A moment's irrational fear rose up inside of her, but she quelled it almost immediately. She had to approach this rationally.

Reaching back behind her head she ran her hands along the surface of her breathing apparatus, and soon found the obstruction. A root was wedged between her twin tanks. What were the odds? She tried moving backward, then from side-to-side, but to no avail. She freed her dive knife and tried to saw at the obtrusion, but it proved ineffective against the gnarled root. Besides, it was nigh impossible to accomplish anything while reaching blindly behind her back. She would have to unstrap her tanks and work them free of the obstruction. The thought frightened her a little, but she had practiced the maneuver as part of her training. And then she looked at her watch. She was well past time to be done.

Her heart thundered and her pulse surged. Stay calm, Jade, she reminded herself. Panic led to unnecessarily heavy breathing, which led to faster oxygen consumption which led to... Stop it! None of it mattered right now. She would work the tank free, and then she would make up the lost time on the return swim. Yes, that would work.

Taking two calming breaths, she methodically unbuckled the straps holding her tanks, and slipped free. With a last breath of sweet air, she took her mouth from the mouthpiece. Holding her breath, and keeping a firm grip on the tanks, she turned about in the tight space. A few deft tugs and it was free. Putting the gear back on was awkward in the dark, confined space, but she managed nicely, and was soon breathing the blessed air again. No time to pat herself on the back, though.

She set out at a rapid clip up the dark, narrow channel, wimming against the current, and what had seemed like a lethargic flow of water now seemed to be putting up serious resistance. Bits vegetation and silt particles flew past her face as she shot recklessly up the channel. She passed through a twisting section a little too carelessly, and she banged her shoulder against the edge. She felt her neoprene suit tear, but under the present circumstances that was no great concern.

She wondered if Saul knew that something was amiss. Did he even know how long she had been gone, or when she should have returned? Probably not. He was not a diver. Great. No one to send in the posse. When I get out of here, I'm finding a dive partner.

The ceiling was low at this point, and her tank banged against a low-hanging rock. She kept going, certain that the distance had not been so great on the way in. What if I've missed the way out? What if I've gone too far? Panic again battled for control, but she forced it down. She remembered this low spot: it was about the halfway mark. Halfway! Down to the dregs of her tank, and she was only halfway.

Her legs thrust like pistons, her cupped hands pulled at the water as if she were dragging herself through sand. She tried holding her breath for longer periods, but quickly gave up the idea Her body needed the oxygen that was no longer there. Her muscles burned, and the rushing of blood in her veins was now an audible roar. She tasted copper in her mouth, and her lungs strained against invisible bonds. Shadows appeared around the perimeter of her vision, and slowly crept inward. She was going to die.

Still biting down on her mouthpiece, she screamed in mute frustration. She tried to fight, but her desperate flailing and kicking quickly subsided as darkness consumed her. She released her bite on her useless air supply, and surrendered.   As consciousness faded, she saw a light coming toward her.

What do you know? All the stories are true. She watched with detached awareness as the light grew brighter. She was drifting up to heaven... or wherever. The glare grew intensely bright, and then she could have sworn she felt arms around her. An angel has come to take me to heaven... A sudden tightness encircled her middle, pinning her arms to her sides, and before she knew what was happening, something was being forced into her mouth. She opened her mouth to protest, and cool, sweet air poured into her lungs. A coughing fit immediately ensued. She had taken more than a bit of water into her mouth, and now it felt like all of it was in her lungs. She tried to twist free, but whatever it was held her tight.

Instinct took over, and she gradually regained control of her lungs, and spat the water free. With the fresh flow of oxygen came a renewed sense of calm and awareness. Someone had come to her rescue after all. He was holding her tight so that she would not, in her panic, drown both of them. She took few long, calming breaths from the pony tank she saw he was holding in his right hand. At least, she hoped those thickly muscled forearms belonged to a he. Making a point to keep her body as relaxed as possible, she slipped her right arm down, and tapped him twice on the thigh. His grip relaxed a touch, and she raised her hand and she circled her thumb and forefinger to make the "OK" sign. He slid the mini-tank into her hand, and let go of her.

Turning to face her rescuer, she saw that it was indeed a he, but other than his blond hair, she could not tell anything about him. Giving him a nod and a quick wave of thanks, she led the way back up the channel. She could not believe how close she had come to dying. What's more, she could not believe someone had rescued her.

Relief gave way to embarrassment and anger as she neared safety. She couldn't believe how her own bad judgment had almost killed her. Stupid! She was a professional, not some weekend scuba diver. This guy, whoever he was, probably thought she was one of the dozen grad school bimbos working the dig aboveground. She was going to beat herself up over this for a long time.

The glow of sunlight flickered in the distance, and soon she was up the shaft, and breaking the surface. Strong hands grabbed her under the arms and lifted her free of the water. Her feet touched ground, and she dropped down hard on her backside.

Saul rounded on her, his square face marred by concern. "Why were you down for so long? What happened in there? Are you trying to kill yourself?" He shook a big, meaty fist in her face. "Because you nearly killed me from worry. Do I need to take up diving so I can keep an eye on you."

Shrugging off her tanks, she laughed. "I'm fine, Saul. Really I am." She ran her hand through his short, neatly coiffed brown hair. "Thank you for sending someone for me. I was wondering if you had even noticed." She didn't catch his reply. Her attention was focused on her rescuer, who was clambering out of the water.

He wasn't the tallest fellow, not quite six feet even with the spiky blond hair, which was already sticking up as it dried in the hot Argentinean sun. He pulled off his dive mask to reveal a lightly tanned face, a friendly smile, and intense blue-gray eyes. Jade smiled back, taking a moment to admire the thickly muscled legs. The guy wasn't the type she usually went for, but he was definitely cute. He took a step toward her, and she hauled herself to her feet to greet him, but Saul was quicker.

"Thank you again for helping us." Saul stepped between them, clasping the man's hand in both of his. "She had been down for so long, and I always tell her she takes too many unnecessary risks. Thinks she's immortal, she does." He suddenly seemed to realize that he was still shaking hands with the fellow, and let go.

"It's quite all right." She liked his voice. It was cheerful yet firm, and had a rich timbre, like one of those guys who reads audiobooks. What was she thinking about? She hadn't even spoken to the guy and already she was mentally babbling. "I'm just glad I was nearby. It was a close thing getting her out of there."

Saul opened his mouth but Jade pushed him to the side and offered her hand. "Thank you so much for your help, Mr..."

"Maddock," he replied, looking her directly in the eye. "Dane Maddock. And you're welcome."

"I'm just so embarrassed that I let myself run out of air like that. I'm really an experienced diver. I just pushed it a little too far." She stopped, realizing she was babbling. He was still looking her in the eye, though, which scored him a few points in her book. Most guys would have let their eyes wander by now.

"You know what they say," he replied, waggling his finger like a grade school teacher. "One third of your air going in, one third going back out..." He was grinning ear-to-ear.

"...and one third in reserve in case of an emergency, one of which I did arise. I'm well aware of the rule of thirds, Mr. Maddock. I just..." she felt her face warm. "I just didn't follow them this time." She wanted to be annoyed at his condescension, but the goofy grin on his face said that he was toying with her.

"Understood." He folded his hands across his chest. There went the eyes. Just for a second, but he was definitely checking her out. Typical guy. "I would tell you to call me Dane, but I still don't even know your name."

"Oh, I'm sorry." What was it about him that made her feel like a complete idiot? She was a professional. "I'm Jade Ihara."

"A beautiful name." He sounded like he even meant it. "You don't have a Japanese accent."

"My father was Japanese," she said. "My mother is Hawaiian. I was raised on Oahu."

"Well, that explains it." He cupped his chin and looked thoughtfully into her eyes. "I was trying to figure it out, but I couldn't place it."

"Explains what, may I ask?" She resisted the urge to squirm like a schoolgirl under his cool gaze.

"You have the traditional Japanese beauty, with just a touch of the robust splendor of Polynesia. Japanese women tend to be a little too skinny. They look peaked. You, on the other hand are quite stunning."

"I don't know whether to be flattered or totally creeped out." He had her laughing again. "Where did you get that line about 'robust splendor of Polynesia' anyway?"

"From a coffee commercial," he said, hanging his head in mock shame. "Forgive me?"

Saul cleared his throat loudly, reminding them of his presence. He stood with hands on hips, tapping his foot. His mouth was twisted in a sour frown. Jade sometimes found his jealousy amusing, but this was not one of those times.

"Saul, if you will please pack up my equipment, I'll be with you in a moment." She cut off his protest with a raised hand. "Thank you, Saul. I'll join you shortly." She met his stare with a level gaze until he turned away, muttering something under his breath. He snatched up her dive gear and stamped off through the tangled growth. "I'm sorry," she said, turning back to Dane. "Saul is very protective of me. He means well."

"Not your boyfriend then?" Dane's grin was wolfish. He already knew the answer. "Lucky for me, then."

"No, he's definitely not my boyfriend. He's my assistant." That was technically true, she supposed. "And how do you figure that's lucky for you?" She couldn't wait to hear his reply. The guy must really like himself.

"Didn't your mother ever teach you about the old Hawaiian tradition? When someone saves your life, you have to have dinner on his boat that evening." He made a show of checking the time on his dive watch. "At exactly 18:00 hours. Give or take a few minutes, of course."

"Is that so?" She really didn't have time to socialize with this, or any guy. But he had saved her life. Besides, an idea was forming in the back of her mind. "This Hawaiian tradition my mother forgot, it doesn't come with any other expectations, does it?"

"I guess it could," Dane replied, his teasing smile replaced with a look of pure innocence. "I'm open to suggestion. What, exactly do you have in mind?"

Jade shook her head and waved a hand at him in exasperation. "You're incorrigible." She couldn't believe she was doing this. "Six o'clock it is. I'll need directions to this boat of yours." His goofy grin was back. "And Dane? Dinner had better be spectacular."

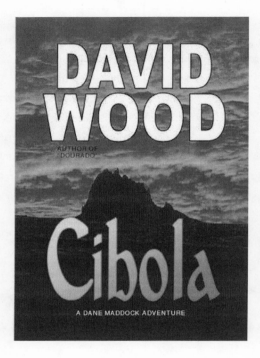

Symbols on a Spanish artifact that could point the way to fabled cities of gold…

A secret hidden for generations in the Utah desert, that could re-write the Bible. One side will kill to reveal it. The other will kill to keep it hidden.

Join Dane Maddock and "Bones" Bonebrake in a gripping adventure that carries them to legendary sites across the American southwest as they search for the Seven Cities of **Cibola**.

813357